THE BUDAPEST CONNECTION

THE BUDAPEST CONNECTION

by

Elizabeth J. Jung

ISBN: 1-58721-069-X

This book is printed on acid free paper.

1stBooks - rev. 12/22/00

About The Book

Jean Martin finds herself all alone in the big family house after her parents' death. Jason, her only brother, is countries away. He is assigned to the American Embassy in Budapest, Hungary.

In the early morning hours and before leaving on a short vacation, Jason telephones Jean to tell her of his vacation plans to visit Greece. He promises to do shopping for her and to keep in touch. Within days of their conversation, Jean receives notification that Jason has been killed in Romania.

Suddenly, her world is turned upside down. The CIA, Jason's employer, dispatches a man to help Jean through the funeral and with all the necessary arrangements. However, the CIA fails to answer all the questions Jean has concerning the accident. Their evasiveness only adds to Jean's confusion.

With the assistance of Jason's best friend, Jean finds herself enroute to Europe. Eventually, they both arrive at Jason's apartment in Budapest.

Determined to find the truth, Jean finds herself in the middle of a modern day spy network. The plot penetrates through the back streets and tourist sights of Hungary and Romania. Speeding cars, flying bullets and nothing being as it seemed only adds mystery, intrigue and suspense.

CHAPTER ONE

"Jean? Jean, is that you?" The low masculine voice questioned as his words snapped and cracked through the still winter air.

Jean Martin held the phone away from her ear, until the noise stopped, then rested the receiver on the pillow beside her head. Her voice was barely above a whisper. She said, "Yes, speaking."

Her eyes were still closed and she couldn't help yawning. With her left elbow, she pulled her long slender body closer to the edge of the bed. She punched her pillow, shifted and rested her head against the cold black receiver.

"It's Jason," the man said, speaking loud and distinct.

Jean jerked, frowned and blinked several times. She knew the name but couldn't recognize the voice. Still uncertain, she squinted and stared at the frost on the bedroom window. "Who's this?" she asked.

"Me, dummy. Jason. Your loving older brother." The telephone reception suddenly became abnormally clear and his words were completely free of static.

Jean smiled. She raised her eyebrows and her dark brown eyes widen. A sigh fell from her lips. "Jason, is this really you?"

"Yes." He chuckled. "Who else would you expect to be calling at this time of day?"

"I suppose I should have known," she answered quickly. Her tone crisp but filled with that special tenderness only she and her only brother shared. She brushed at her messy long brown hair, pushing it away from her eyes.

With her free hand, she tried straightening the blankets and her flannel pajamas. In doing so, her left arm became entwined in the telephone cord. Turning her head and shoulder, she struggled and tried balancing the phone between her chin and ear.

Suddenly, the moon broke through the heavy clouds sending light rays through the frosted glass and against the white bedroom wall. A loud crunching sound came from outside filling the quiet winter night air.

It sounded as if it were directly below her bedroom window. Startled, Jean jerked her arm and the telephone went flying off the nightstand.

"Oh," she cried, grabbing the phone and catching it in midair. Struggling to get herself back in the bed, she gasped aloud when she saw a dark moving shadow reflecting against her bedroom ceiling.

"Are you all right?" Jason asked. "What's wrong? You sound weird."

Jean shivered and took several deep breaths. Holding the mouthpiece tight against her mouth, she nodded too scared to speak. Her neck and shoulder muscle tightening. Without moving her head, she turned her eyes slowly back toward the window. Goose bumps covered her entire body.

Finally, she stopped shivering and spoke barely above a whisper, using her empty hand to rub her cold, chilled arms. "Jason, I think someone is walking around outside in my yard."

She took a deep breath and stared at the huge scary shadow slowly moving across her ceiling. Turning her head slightly, she caught her reflection in the large mirror across the room. Her eyes rolled upward.

She glanced back at the ceiling. The shadow was gone. Exhaling, she let her muscles relax. She looked around the room and shivered as she turned her head back toward the window. Everything was quiet.

Now, she felt foolish but relieved. "I guess it was nothing," she finally sighed, snuggling back under the warm blankets.

"It was probably a cat," Jason said. He paused for a moment and asked, "Do you hear anything now?"

"No, everything is fine," Jean answered cheerfully after regaining her confidence. "You're right. It was probably Collins' dog or cat. You know how they like to prowl the neighborhood all night long."

Jason chuckled. "I sure do. They kept me awake many nights when I was home," he said. "Well, it's noon here in

Hungary and I'm getting ready to leave for Greece. I wanted to touch base with you before I left town."

Jean pressed the cold instrument tighter against her ear, reached for the clock and pulled herself back to an upright position. The hands of the clock pointed to four.

She glanced back at the window. It was pitch black again. The moon was back under the clouds. Her mind registered, it was four in the morning.

"Did I hear you say you're going to Greece?"

"I sure hope to," Jason answered. "I'm standing here all dressed for my trip and have my airplane tickets on the desk in front of me."

"I'm jealous. I'm stuck here in Iowa. It's January and colder than all get out. Even Clear Lake is frozen solid. What's the temperature like in Budapest? No, better yet, what's it like in Greece this time of year?"

"Hope it's warmer there. It's been cold here in Hungary," Jason said. "But, to be honest, it really doesn't matter what the weather is going to be in Greece, it's time for a vacation and I need it. Time out of the office will be great. I've been under a lot of pressure lately and I need some time to unwind and take my mind off of work." He paused for a few moments and then added, "How are you? Any different love interest or is it still that same one? I can't seem to remember his name."

Jean chuckled, she could feel her face getting warm from her brother's special way of teasing. She knew perfectly well Jason knew her fiance's name. "Jason, you know his name is Paul Barkley. I don't know why you always have to tease me about him. I get the impression you don't really like him."

"Oh, he's all right," Jason answered quickly. "I just like to bug you about him."

"Well, he's fine, thank you," Jean said.

Jason's laugh echoed across the line. Jean held the phone away from her ear and shook her head. She could picture Jason leaning back in his chair and enjoying the moment.

"That's great," Jason said. "You will let me know when it gets really serious, won't you? After all, how long have you been engaged now, is it going on two or three years?"

"It's only been two years and one of these days we'll set a date, but don't rent your tux just yet." She glanced at the clock. "Thanks for calling. Be sure and have a great time in Greece." She thought for a moment and added, "Say, I'd like a Flokati rug if you happen to have the time to shop."

"Sis, I always have time to shop for you. Any special size?"

"Something large enough to place in front of the fireplace," she said. She thought for a moment and added. "But, I'll take any size."

Jason gave an exaggerated gasp. "Typical woman. Not planning on using it for something I wouldn't approve of, are you?"

"Hardly," Jean said, not even wanting to know what her older brother might have been imagining.

"I'll see what I can do. I can probably have it shipped through the Embassy in Athens since I won't have my car. It'll get to you a lot faster than if I brought it all the way back on the plane with me."

"Whatever you can do is fine with me. Let me know when you get back to Budapest. Oh, don't forget, I'm still planning on visiting you in Hungary this summer."

There was a long silence. Jean could hear loud static and wondered if Jason had heard her remind him of her visit. She opened her mouth to repeat it when Jason spoke.

"Let me know when you get a fixed date," he said. "I want to be sure that I have time off while you're here. Need to show you the sights and maybe we can spend a weekend in Vienna."

Jean's proposed summer schedule flashed through her mind. "That sounds great. For now, I only know my vacation's scheduled for late summer or early fall. It all depends on the work load. But, I already have my passport." She paused, sensing there might be a problem with her pending visit. "It's still all right with you if I come to Budapest, isn't it?"

Without hesitation, Jason answered, "Sure, that time frame sounds fine."

Jean heard a loud clicking sound. She sensed someone had just picked up the extension phone. Her heart raced. She glanced around her bedroom and her eyes froze on her open bedroom doorway.

Holding her breath, she stared at the faint light which crept across the open space. The dark was beginning to spook her, now she imagined that someone was in her house and creeping up the stairs toward her.

Her hand shook as she pressed the phone tighter to her ear. She could hear voices. Jason was talking to someone in his office.

The clicking was on Jason's line, she thought. Now, she knew Jason was calling from his office in the American Embassy rather than from his apartment in the castle area.

"Listen, Jean, I have to go," Jason said. "I just wanted to hear your voice and tell you that I love you and miss you. Take care. I'll call when I get back to Budapest. Forgive me for waking you."

Before she could answer, his voice faded. There was a click, then another one, and the connection went dead.

Jean sat in bed and stared into the darkness. She reached for Jason's picture on her nightstand. Tears filled her eyes as she began tracing the image of his face. "Have a safe trip," she whispered.

Her mind flashed to the events of the past couple months. She began sobbing. The pressure of her parents' deaths, their unexplained car crash, Jason's trip home for the funeral and the problems at the bank became too much for her.

Suddenly, cold fresh air filled her bedroom. The long, white, frilly curtains moved back and forth from the night air. She shivered, pulled the blankets up around her neck, but kept her eyes fixed on the window. For several minutes she stared into the night. She was too afraid to leave the security of her bed and walk to the window to see if anyone was outside.

Her imagination was running wild. She could hear someone walking around outside directly below her window. The footsteps crunched in the frozen snow. A car door squeaked. Her muscles tensed. She held her breath.

She hated living alone in the big old family house. Quickly, she jerked the blankets over her head, hoping the noise she heard was simply the paper boy with his morning delivery.

CHAPTER TWO

The American Embassy in Budapest, Hungary is located on Szabadsag Ter, next door to the Hungarian National Bank and within walking distance of the Hungarian Parliament building, the Danube River and numerous methods of public transportation. With the continuing increase of personnel assigned to the diplomatic mission, the interior of the building is undergoing constant updates while trying to maintain its stately elegant outward appearance.

At present, The American Embassy contains the offices of the Ambassador, Deputy Chief of Mission, Political, Economic, Administrative and Consulate officers and their sections. It also has several offices for those posted to Hungary that handle daily operation activities.

Jason Martin stood looking out of his office window in the Political Section on the second floor of the American Embassy. He was dressed in designer blue jeans and a blue Iowa long sleeve sweatshirt. A few locks of his dark brown curly hair hung down against his forehead. He shifted his eyes from the Danube River to the Hungarian Television offices. He held his tall thin body straight but both of his hands were pressed firm against the windowsill. His back was purposely turned toward the doorway. A deep frown covered his face.

"Well, the way I see it you don't have a choice," Ray Clark said. Clark, in his late forties, was dressed in the typical diplomatic style with a dark double breasted suit, light blue shirt and matching designer tie covered with lines and circles. His black shoes shone. His grey hair was combed carefully over his ears and forward on top. His hair had been purposely styled that morning to hide his receding hairline.

Clark watched Jason from the doorway, shuffled his feet back and forth, looked at his watch a couple times and finally repeated himself to get Martin's attention. "You're wanted," he said.

"Don't even think it," Jason said, turning and staring at Clark. Jason's dark brown eyes were half closed. He pulled his sweatshirt down over his belt. "You can see I'm dressed and about to leave for the airport." He motioned with his arm. His dark brown leather jacket was slung over his desk chair and his airplane tickets were obvious on the desk.

The lanky Political Chief, ten years older than Jason, looked at Jason and nodded. He didn't say a word, but his expression told Jason his trip to Greece was a thing of the past.

Jason shook his head and held his hands up. "I know I should have left earlier today as I originally planned."

"They want you. Don't blame me," Clark said. He smiled. He motioned with his head toward the hallway. "I have no idea why, but I'm sure it's important."

Jason picked up his coat and flung it across the room. It landed with a loud thud. He threw his airplane tickets in the air. "Damn it, can't they find somebody else?"

Clark shrugged, put his finger to his lips, turned on his heels, looked back at Jason and snickered. He pointed into the air. "That's why your getting paid the big bucks." He turned sharply on his heels and walked back to his office. He shut his door with a bang, deliberately making more noise than was necessary.

Although, the diplomats assigned to the American Embassy knew the truth, the rest of the Hungarian diplomatic community thought Ray Clark was Jason's boss and direct supervisor. Clark was the Chief of the Political Section and Jason was assigned to the section as one of the Political Officers.

Jason watched Clark leave, shook his head and made a face. Each day, Jason saw it become more apparent that Clark resented him and disapproved of having the political section used for a CIA cover position.

Jason wondered if he should say something to the CIA Headquarters' officials, but remembered Clark was due to rotate within a couple months. He just hoped Clark's replacement would be more understanding and work with Langley.

Punching the air, Jason shook his head and walked out of his office. He stopped at the doorway and glanced back at the plane tickets that had landed on his floor. Slowly, he walked down the hallway toward the elevator.

Stopping suddenly, he turned and walked back toward his office. Passing Clark's door, he moved down the hallway and into a storage closet. He pressed his hand against the wall near a light switch. A door opened silently.

He stepped into total darkness. With his right hand, he felt the wall, clicked on a light switch and dim light filtered through the space. He pulled the door shut and walked into a musty smelling windowless hallway.

There were several large empty wooden crates stacked in the corners leaving only an open walkway to a stairway. He took one step at a time keeping his arms tight by his side. The stairway railings were covered with dust.

Silently, he crept up the two floors passing the wall that separated him from the Ambassador and Deputy Chief of Mission offices.

No one in the Embassy ever spoke aloud the location of the Central Intelligence Office within the Embassy. They always nodded upward or pointed. Only the American diplomats posted at the Embassy knew exactly which floor housed the CIA offices.

The stairway ended and Jason turned the knob and stepped out into another dark space. He now was on a windowless, deserted floor. Directly in front of him, the CIA offices were secure behind heavy insulated walls, metal shields and isolated from normal embassy traffic.

He stood in front of a small black keypad box attached to the wall beside a steel door. For a moment, he stopped to remember what day it was and what numbers he had to push.

Turning toward the overhead camera at the end of the hallway, he made a face. He knew his movements were being monitored and taped. His fingers flipped the keypad cover and flew across the pad. He leaned down and breathed heavily into a microphone shaped space. The door squeaked and he pushed it open.

Taking short steps, he walked through a long, narrow, dingy looking hallway. It was purposely designed to look like a deserted storage closet. He entered a dim lit foyer, which contained a small wooden table, electric coffee pot, several boxes of supplies and file boxes stacked to the ceiling.

"This had better be good," Jason said, moving between two rows of stacked cardboard boxes. He walked into a bright large room which had been divided into several cubicles. Moving toward the largest one, he stopped directly in front of an old wooden desk and stared down at the man sitting in a straight back wooden chair.

Tom Bryan, the CIA Chief of Station, looked exhausted. His thin brown hair was ruffled and his eyes were bloodshot. He was dressed in some dark brown slacks, white shirt and a long sleeve dark brown heavy knit sweater. A box of tissue was in the middle of his desk.

The Chief nodded toward a tall thin man walking behind Jason. They both watched silently as the man moved toward an air condition unit and turned a switch. The loud humming increased dramatically.

The Chief shrugged his bony shoulders, smiled, stood and walked to a large map of Eastern Europe. It was pinned to the side of the wall on the other side of the room. He spoke without expression. "We have word that another shipment is coming across. I was sure that you'd want to be there?"

Jason stamped his foot. "Damn, today of all days. I thought they were going to take a rest after the last mishap."

"So, did we," the Station Chief said. "But, our information is solid. Where do you think they're heading?"

Jason ran his hand through his long, dark hair. He rubbed his chin a couple times and said, "Probably one of the empty coal mines in Romania. The weather is too bad to get across to Bulgaria. I don't think the Serbs would even attempt to take a shipment now with the IFOR troops breathing down their necks." He picked up a pointer and touched a few spots on the map.

"Can we stop them from coming across?" The Chief began walking around the small room, pulling his sweater tighter to his chest. He coughed a couple times. His eyes darted back and forth to the map. "We could alert the border guards."

Jason pulled a chair closer with his long leg. He sat, thought for several seconds and said, "They'd only ditch it somewhere in the Ukraine. At least this way, we have some idea where they are going. The Russians would never be able to drive it back without attracting a lot of attention. There are too many satellites centered on that part of the world. How much time do I have?"

The Chief looked at his watch. "Maybe twenty-four hours. What are you going to do?"

"It's too late to stop it, but at least I can try and keep track where it's going. I'm going to make a few phone calls, talk to a couple contacts and see what's in the wind. Then, I'll be on my way. Are there still flights going into Bucharest?"

"Yes, the safety concerns are only about TAROM's internal flights, not the international ones. Shall I have the political secretary get you a ticket?"

Jason stood, sighed and said, "Make a reservation. I'll pick it up at the airport. I need to go back to my apartment first and get a couple things off my computer." He walked toward the door, stopped and stared at the Station Chief. "After I'm finished with this, I'm going directly to Greece for some R&R."

The Station Chief grunted and watched Jason walk toward the door. He had his hand on the telephone, and said, "I'll need a copy of that updated list of sights you've been keeping under wraps. Langley wants it." He watched Jason take another step and added, "Can you cut out the garlic? You know that raises havoc with the breath machine. I've already had to replace two of them. Headquarters is going to start complaining."

There was no answer. The Station Chief was too late, the door clicked and Jason was gone.

CHAPTER THREE

"Jean, this has just arrived for you. It looks important. It's from Langley, Virginia," Sarah said. Jean's secretary stood in the doorway waving a large overnight express envelope.

Jean looked up from her paperwork. Her eyes widened, her pulse quickened. Langley, Virginia was the home of the Central Intelligence Agency. The CIA was Jason's employer.

Holding her breath, Jean stood, smoothed down the skirt of her favorite dark blue suit and reached for the document. Her hand shook as she touched the cold envelope. She exhaled and held the envelope up to the light, fearing the unknown.

She took several short breaths and ran her long fingernail under the white envelope flap. Without even looking at the words, she knew her world was going to change. She needed to be alone.

Motioning to her secretary, she said, "Sarah, go ahead and finish your work. Those files have to be organized today. The auditors are due here tomorrow and they'll want to go over the files with us."

"Are you all right?" Sarah asked. "You look as if you've seen a ghost." Sarah, a tall slender attractive blonde, tugged at her light blue sweater. She rolled her large brown eyes and brushed back her long blonde hair. She thought for a moment and then said, "The files can wait for a few minutes. Do you want me to get you a drink of water or something?"

"I'm fine. Just a bit tired," Jean said. She waited until she heard the sound of Sarah's footsteps echoing in the hallway before she looked down at the envelope.

She knew she had to read it, and pulled at the paper. It was stuck. She jerked it. It came loose and she glanced down at the words. The lines began moving back and forth.

Steadying the paper with both hands, she held it with just her fingertips. Reading slowly, she mouthed the words aloud.

"WE REGRET TO INFORM YOU THAT WHILE ON VACATION YOUR BROTHER, JASON MARTIN, HAS BEEN KILLED IN A CAR ACCIDENT IN BUCHAREST,

ROMANIA. HIS BODY WILL BE SHIPPED TO THE UNITED STATES FOR BURIAL. YOU WILL BE CONTACTED BY AN OFFICE REPRESENTATIVE REGARDING THE FUNERAL ARRANGEMENTS. PLEASE ACCEPT OUR DEEPEST CONDOLENCES."

She read the words again. Finally, they registered. Shaking her head with disbelief, Jean stared at the paper, and opened her mouth.

Her scream pierced the silence of the quiet bank atmosphere. She collapsed into her chair. The CIA letter went flying across the room.

CHAPTER FOUR

Jean slept late. She dressed quickly in an extra large, white, Iowa Hawkeye sweatshirt, comfortable faded blue jeans and her favorite running shoes. The six restless hours of sleep had left her feeling tired, depressed and extremely irritable. Her dark brown eyes were puffed, red-veined and scratchy from crying.

She felt physically ill. The howling January winds rattled the windows and sent cold lingering shivers down her frail slim body. She rubbed her arms and stood rigid, looking around her bedroom.

Her black dress and black nylons still laid where she had thrown them, on the maroon chair in the corner. One of her black shoes was on top of her nightstand. She had no idea where she had thrown the other. The bedding and pillows were laying around the room in a tipsy turvy fashion.

Jean kicked a pillow, left everything where it was, turned around and looked through the frosted window toward Central Avenue. The fresh snow drifts now covered the small evergreens. She looked closer. Something looked out of place. There were fresh tire tracks in her driveway.

She looked around for some sign of human activity. Although it was the weekend, no one was visible. She wondered if a brave neighbor had turned around in her driveway on the way to church.

Tears ran down her face. She wiped them with the corner of her sleeve. She stepped out into the hallway, stopped and listened to the silence.

She glanced toward Jason's old bedroom. The door was wide open. There were papers all over the floor. She walked to the doorway. Some of his dresser drawers were pulled out.

She wondered what someone might have been looking for. Then remembered, she had sent the funeral director up to Jason's room in search of hangers. He should have been more careful.

It felt wrong, but she stepped into Jason's bedroom. Both of the closet doors were wide open and several pieces of clothing were laying on the floor. The room looked messy. She knew she should straighten it, but she just couldn't. It could wait.

She shrugged and crept downstairs to the security of the old kitchen. Usually, the cozy room gave her a sense of warmth and comfort. Today, a cold damp air filled the empty rooms.

She flipped on the lights and passed from room to room. There was a tall pile of telegrams and cards that someone had stacked on the dining room table. They looked too neat.

With her fist, she hit the stack, sending papers flying across the walnut tabletop and onto the floor. She smiled. Now, she felt better.

Flowers were everywhere. Baskets, vases and glasses were filled to overflowing. There was every color and variety imaginable. Her nose twitched. The mixed fragrances were strong, almost overwhelming.

She suddenly felt as if she were going to be sick. Struggling with the taste of bile, she took several deep breaths and looked around. The rooms were neat, much too neat for her liking.

She wished her friends had left the dirty dishes. Today of all days, she needed something to do. Anything to keep her hands and mind busy.

The Sunday Des Moines Register slammed against the front door. Startled, she jumped backward, throwing her arms upward, just missing a tall crystal vase. Shaking, she grabbed the vase and set it in the middle of the table.

For several seconds, she stood, holding on to the back of a dining room chair, trying to regain her balance. She felt uneasy. Something didn't feel right. There was a strange smell, like a sweet woodsy aroma lingering over the dining room table.

She muttered, then moved toward the front door. Through the peephole, she caught a glimpse of a black car. It was just pulling away from the curb. She hoped it wasn't another reporter. Cautiously, she opened the front door, grabbed the paper and hurried to the safety of her kitchen.

For several seconds, she sat with her hands on the table staring into space. Jason's smile kept flashing through her mind. "Jason," she whispered, between deep sobs. "Why? What happened?"

She glanced at the headlines and skimmed over an article about a hazardous waste spill. It was Russian waste material, but the accident occurred on the border of Romania and the Ukraine. Thousands had been evacuated. The drinking water in several towns was in danger.

Immediately, she thought of Jason. He was always telling her that the Russians couldn't be trusted to dispose of their waste materials properly. It was one of his biggest headaches.

Without thinking, she flipped to the obituaries. Her hand smoothed the paper as she glanced down the page. The small printed text bounced out at her.

"Jason Martin was laid to rest Saturday in the Memorial Cemetery in River City, Iowa. Martin, thirty-nine, a graduate of River City High School, received his Bachelors' degree from Iowa State College and his law degree from Iowa University. After completing his military service, Mr. Martin was employed by the Central Intelligence Agency in Langley, Virginia. Mr. Martin was killed last week in an automobile accident while on vacation in Bucharest, Romania. His sister, Jean Martin, his only living relative, resides in River City."

Jean wondered who had given the paper Jason's information. She knew she hadn't. Maybe it was the funeral home. Whoever had, she really didn't care.

She sat staring at the words. Nothing made sense. There were so many unanswered questions. She had to learn the whole truth.

CHAPTER FIVE

The wing of the 747 sliced the feathery white cloud into two smooth sections. The airplane twisted, pushing the clouds apart, making its approach toward its final destination, Frankfurt, Germany.

Jean stared at the fasten seat belt sign until the flight attendant's announcement flowed across the intercom system to the rear of the plane. She sighed with relief. Pressing her face against the cool window, she watched for her first glimpse of Frankfurt through the scattered cloud cover.

Her pulse raced when she recognized the buildings at Rhein Main Air Force Base. Her thoughts flashed back to her last trip to Germany. It was just a year earlier and during happier times.

She heard and felt the wheels drop and watched the ground get nearer. When the wheels touched the runway, she felt an unexpected sense of excitement and looked around at the other passengers. Everyone was preparing to leave the plane. For the first time in hours, she felt she had made the right decision.

When the plane began its approach to the terminal, she could see people standing on the lookout deck. Several were waving. It was obvious some were meeting the planes and others were strictly observers.

She saw a man dressed in blue. It was too far away to recognize him but she sensed it was Michael Cleary, Jason's best friend. He was one of the people she felt she could always trust.

Her eyes got moist. She shook her head, stood, adjusted her gold locket on her neck, sniffed, slipped on her blue wool coat, grabbed her carry-on bag and stepped behind a young mother and baby. She was extremely nervous, but anxious to see Michael and get on with her mission.

Grabbing a luggage cart, she picked out her suitcases, cleared passport and customs and headed directly for the exit. The cart had a loose wheel, so she moved over to the side, stopped and shifted her suitcases for an even balance. Suddenly, a movement caught her attention.

A tall man, dressed in an Air Force Captain's uniform, was waving frantically from behind the roped off area. She smiled and nodded when their eyes met. The familiar figure gave her a warm comforting feeling. She stared. She was surprised that he looked older than the last time she had seen him. There were streaks of silver in his dark hair. Then she remembered, there was over a ten-year age difference between her and Jason, and Michael was a couple years older than Jason.

Guiding the cart, she hurried down the grey carpet, barely avoiding a collision with another passenger. A short, heavily sun tanned man turned and looked directly at Jean.

"Why aren't you more careful?" he shouted.

"I'm so sorry," Jean said.

"Americans," the man muttered. "They think they own the world." He gave Jean a harsh look and rushed off.

Jean felt her face get hot. She stood back until the man was gone. She glanced up and saw Michael walking toward her. She smiled and waited.

"I'm so glad you could meet me," Jean whispered, throwing her arms around Jason's best friend. "Thanks for coming."

"Let me look at you," Michael Cleary said. "You've really grown up. You look great." He held her at an arm distance and continued. "I'm so sorry about Jason. You did know I would have loved to have gone back for the funeral, but it just wasn't possible." He continued to look at her, raising his eyebrows. "You do understand, don't you?" With his right hand, he pushing her long brown hair back from her face and waited for some reaction to his words.

"I understand," Jean said, avoiding his eyes. She hugged him again. "You're like an old member of the family. You're all I have left now." The warmth of his body and the fragrance of his woodsy cologne sent a shiver through her.

"I'm not that old," Michael said.

She stood back, gulped and stared directly into his eyes. "You know what I mean." She took a couple steps, stopped and looked down at the floor. "It was such a terrible shock. I have to admit I'm still quite upset. I'm trying hard to accept Jason's death but it's so hard when I don't know all the details."

"That's perfectly understandable," Michael said, reaching for her arm. "Didn't the CIA tell you all about his car accident in Romania?"

Jean shook her head. "As I explained when I called, all I've been told by the CIA is that he was killed while on vacation in Romania."

She led Michael toward an empty row of seats and motioned for him to sit. He pulled the luggage cart and positioned it directly in front of them. It formed a security fence between them and the other passengers. Jean sat on the edge of her seat and bent her head toward Michael. She spoke softly but distinct. "I had just talked to Jason on Friday morning. He called to tell me he was going to Greece on vacation. He never mentioned anything about Romania, Bucharest or any other such places."

"Come on, Jean," Michael said, half laughing. He rocked back in his seat, straightened the seam on his pants, looked toward her and then out the window toward the planes. "You knew Jason well enough to know that he didn't tell you everything."

Jean smiled, looked away and then back at Michael out of the corner of her eye. Her face was hot. "It wasn't like that at all. He told me he was going on vacation. He would never have deliberately lied to me about something like that."

Michael let his eyes move back and forth across her face. Then, he patted her on her arm. "No, I don't think he would have, but then, he might not have told you the whole truth either. After all, you are the little sister."

Jean jumped up. She felt uncomfortable, turned away from Michael and looked toward the other passengers. She didn't like the way Michael was reacting. He wasn't taking anything she was saying about Jason's death seriously.

"Jean, what's wrong? You're acting weird," Michael asked. He rolled his eyes and had a hint of a grin on his face.

Suddenly, Jean turned and looked around. She had the strangest feeling that someone was staring at her. She pulled her purse close to her chest. Undecided, she took several steps one way then the other, looked around again, but still didn't see anything unusual.

"Come on, let's get out of here," she said, and began walking. "We can talk about it later. Were you able to get me a hotel room?"

"You're going to stay with me," Michael said.

Jean stopped, turned and stared at Michael. Her mouth opened.

"Before you say anything, I insist." He talked fast as if he had rehearsed what he was going to say. "My apartment is off-base. It has plenty of room with two bedrooms and two bathrooms, completely separated and private. I can promise you, you'll be perfectly safe. I'm almost old enough to be your father, for heaven's sake."

Jean shrugged. She really didn't care, but it did surprise her. He nudged her gently with the cart and hurried passed her.

When he was three feet in front of her, he stopped, turned, glanced back and said, "Now, let's get moving. We'll talk on the drive back to my apartment." Without waiting for an answer, he headed straight for the parking lot exit.

"Well, all right," she wheezed. She was out of breath after finally catching up with him. "I'll stay at your apartment."

"Oh, by the way," Michael said. "I'm taking next week off. I have some vacation days I need to use or lose." Before Jean could comment, he added, "Wherever you're going, I plan on going with you."

CHAPTER SIX

A middle aged man, dressed in a grey London Fog, full length overcoat, purposely stood between a large car rental sign and a portable announcement board in the lobby of the Frankfurt airport. He was hidden from the casual glance. His eyes were locked on the lady from Iowa and her companion.

Dale Weaver, the tall, heavy-set man had started his assignment in Langley, Virginia. His original orders were simple. He was to go to River City, Iowa and offer assistance to Jean Martin with her brother's funeral arrangements. He was to answer questions regarding Jason's death, but without giving any specific details or making any direct connection to Jason's employment as a CIA agent.

The assignment was to have terminated with the funeral. However, due to the unavailability of a return flight to Washington D.C., Weaver was forced to spend the weekend in River City. Making the most of the situation, he spent the time relaxing, visiting the nearby lake, seeing a movie and eating a corn fed Iowa t-bone steak.

Purely by chance, Weaver was in a restaurant waiting for his steak, when he overheard a man at the next table mention Jason Martin's death. The man was explaining to the others at his table that Jean Martin was planning a trip to Europe. Weaver casually glanced toward the table and shifted in his seat.

The man was sitting with a group of eight people. Several guests talked as if they personally knew the Martin family. Weaver took his time eating and listening.

As the evening progressed, the older man's voice grew louder. He explained the details of Jean's upcoming trip. Eventually, Weaver learned she was going to Frankfurt and on to Budapest to personally take charge of her brother's personal goods.

After the guests left, Weaver talked to the waitress and discovered that the older man was an employee at Jean Martin's bank, and would be in charge of the bank while she was gone.

Weaver rushed back to his hotel room, and spent the next several hours talking to Langley.

Before dawn, a decision was made and Weaver's original assignment was amended. Now, he was to follow Jean Martin to Europe and stay near her until she returned safely to Iowa.

His orders were specific. He was instructed to observe, but not to have any direct contact. Only if her life was in danger was he to make his presence known.

Weaver was told to travel to Minneapolis by rental car. His business class tickets would be waiting for him at the check-in counter at the Minneapolis International Airport.

The CIA officials were uncertain how Jean might react if she saw Weaver on the flight. Especially, since she knew Weaver as an employee of the CIA.

After the long flight, Weaver was tired, tense, irritable and needed a shower. He glanced around the Frankfurt arrival lobby and scratched his head. It itched from the harsh color rinse he had used to change his appearance.

"I'm getting too old for this shit," he whispered aloud, still watching the couple out of the corner of his eye.

He was wearing a cheap pair of wire frame glasses, and limped slightly. With his new black hair, he didn't think even his wife would have easily recognized him.

He stepped forward and heard men behind him. They were talking in Arabic. He stopped to let them pass, but they purposely walked around him, one on each side. Weaver looked from one to the other. An alarm flashed in his mind.

One of the men, looked directly at Weaver. He had a wide toothy smile. "American?"

Weaver nodded, looked at the second man and walked faster.

"Ah, we thought so," the second man said, keeping in step with Weaver. His eyes moved slowly up and down Weaver's body.

Weaver stopped to let the two men go ahead. They walked in front of him several feet, then stopped. They turned and waited for Weaver.

"So, why are you following the pretty American woman and her military boyfriend?" The toothy man spoke with a heavy

Eastern European accent. He leaned toward Weaver, his face directly in front of Weaver's. He licked his lips and wiped his hands on his dirty jeans and waited for Weaver to answer.

A strong garlic smell made Weaver jerk backwards. He said, "Excuse me?" His eyes moved to a bulge under the man's worn leather jacket. Weaver wondered how the man had passed airport security.

The second man unzipped his leather coat, pushed it open slightly to reveal the gun under his arm. He moved closer to Weaver until his face was within inches of touching Weaver's. "What's that smell," the man asked Weaver, stepping back a step.

Weaver pulled back away from the man. His eyes darted back and forth between the two strangers. Weaver said,"It must be the new men's cologne my wife gave me. If you like it I have the bottle in my bag and you can have it."

The man laughed and moved toward Weaver. He looked directly into Weaver's face and asked, "Why are you interested in that Air Force man and the girl?" He looked like an Arab, but spoke with a British accent.

"I'm not," Weaver exclaimed. He pointed to the plane with his newspaper. "I just got off the plane, I'm going to change some money and pick up a rental car. I have business down in Darmstadt."

"Hear that, Koniev?" the second man said. "The man isn't interested in the couple, it was just our imagination." He pointed to his head and shook his head several times.

Koniev chuckled. He looked at Weaver. His eyes were dark and piercing. "Keep away from them. You could get hurt." He sneered and picked his tooth with his long fingernail.

Weaver was perspiring. He looked around. There were no policemen in sight. A large tour group was walking directly toward him. He looked at the men and said, "Sorry, fellows, you have me mixed up with someone else."

He stepped away from the two men and worked his way into the center of the tour group. For a couple seconds, he was afraid that he had lost sight of Cleary and Martin. He caught a glimpse of them near the exit doors.

Zig-zagging through the tour group, he made his way toward the exit. Taking his rental car paperwork out of his pocket, he held it in his hand and threw away the German newspaper. He glanced back for the two men. They had disappeared in the crowd.

CHAPTER SEVEN

Jean found the walk to Michael's car refreshing. Her legs were aching from the plane ride. She took long steps to stretch her tight muscles and limber up.

"So, Michael, how have you been since I've seen you last?" she asked, once they were in the car.

"Fine, thanks. And you?" When she didn't answer immediately, he frowned and continued. "Can you talk about the funeral? Where any of our old college friends able to attend?"

"Yes," Jean said, without hesitation. She slid back in the seat and tugged on her seat belt. "There were a couple guys that you both knew. They're living in Iowa City and working with the law department at the college. I specifically remember one of them asking about you, but I don't recall his name."

Michael smiled and said, "Was it Jim Langer? I just read in the campus newspaper that he had taken a job at the college."

Jean shrugged. "I really don't know. I'm sure I have their names at home. If you remind me, when I get back I'll find them and send them to you."

"Did you happen to hear from any of Jason's friends from Europe?" Michael asked, keeping his eyes on the road.

"Several, I think," Jean said, trying to remember who had sent what to the funeral home and to the house. "It's hard to remember because I received so many bouquets of flowers from people I didn't know. I imagined they were all Jason's friends. Most didn't have addresses on them, just names. You can look at the list the next time you visit." She was polite but stared at the dashboard the entire time she spoke.

Michael just nodded. Several minutes later, he asked, "Was it a large funeral?"

Jean wished Michael wouldn't ask about the funeral details. She really didn't want to talk about them. Politely, she said, "Very."

Michael said, "How's everything else in River City?"

Jean looked at Michael and smiled. She knew she might just as well tell him what he wanted to know. She had to talk about the funeral some time. "I'm sorry, I was so sharp. Actually, there were several people that talked to me at the funeral home and after the service that I didn't know. Martha told me there were a lot of out of state license plates at the church."

"That's nice. Jason would have liked that." Michael began turning dials on the dashboard. "How about some music?"

"Great," Jean answered. She knew it was Michael's way of saying she didn't have to answer any more of his questions if she didn't want.

For several minutes they rode in silence. When a commercial was on the radio, Jean turned to Michael and said, "You knew Jason well. Do you have any idea what he was working on? Did he talk to you about his work?"

Michael jerked his head in surprise. "Not the least. Didn't the CIA tell you?"

"No," Jean answered. "After I received the official notice, a CIA representative came to assist with the funeral arrangements, but he wouldn't say much. I never really had time to talk to him about Jason. I don't even know if he knew Jason. He was at the funeral home and at the house after the service but all we ever talked about were things related to the service itself."

Michael stopped for a red light, turned and asked, "Were you all alone most of the time?"

"No, not really. Right after the CIA man called, I asked Martha Wilson to come over." Jean wrinkled her forehead, smiled and said, "You might remember Martha. She's the Chief of Police."

Michael raised his eyebrows and looked at Jean. He shook his head and said, "Oh, I didn't know she made Chief. That must be a first for the area?"

"At least, the first for River City," Jean answered. "But, she deserved it. She's well qualified. But, then I don't have to tell you about Martha. Jason told me once that you had a thing for her."

"Hardly," Michael said. "It's pretty hard maintaining a relationship thousands of miles apart."

Jean smiled. "Yes, I suppose so."

Michael said, "Jason and I usually made it a point to stop in and say hello to her whenever we were in River City. But, she was too busy with her police work to take any special interest in me."

"Maybe, I can do something about it when I get back?" Jean said. She looked at Michael and smiled.

Michael shook his head. "Don't bother. So, when did the CIA guy arrive?"

"The day after I received the notice, he magically appeared. His name was Dale Weaver."

Michael looked puzzled. "He did show you some papers telling you who he was, didn't he?"

"Yes, he had an identical card just like the one that Jason had. Weaver stayed at the Holiday Inn, but was at my house some of the time. I introduced him to everyone as a friend of Jason's, but I'm sure most people figured out who he really was. He looked like the typical CIA employee, with his dark nondescript suit and long overcoat."

"Did he treat you all right?"

"Sure," Jean answered. "He was nice enough, but whenever I asked him a question, he'd answer with something that didn't made sense. He looked and acted just like the government agents you see on the television programs. He wore the mirrored sunglasses and neat haircut. But, he had a cold reserved manner. I don't think I ever saw him smile."

Michael chuckled. "I remember saying something like that to Jason once."

Jean rubbed her hands together and giggled. She said, "Whenever I'd say something to Jason about the clones, he'd defend them."

"Was Weaver really any help with the arrangements or was he simply a warm body?" Michael asked.

"I have to admit he was some help," Jean said. "When he was in the house I felt more relaxed, mainly because he answered the telephone and doorbell. That was a big help. Martha provided a plainclothes detective to escort me to all the services. But, I think part of Weaver's job was to keep the reporters away."

Michael's head jerked. He frowned. "Why were there reporters?"

"I really don't know." Jean slid forward and looked directly at Michael. "The local paper ran just a routine article about the accident. But, the phone rang constantly." She thought for several seconds. A concerned look filled her face. "Now that you mention it, Weaver said they were reporters. But, now I wonder if they really were reporters."

Michael kept his eyes on the road. "How long did he stay?"

"I'm not sure," Jean said. She looked at the traffic and wondered if she'd be afraid to drive in such a large city. There were cars everywhere. After Michael turned onto a secondary road, she said, "After lunch, I sent everyone home. Martha locked up while I went to bed."

"Did Weaver go back to Virginia?" Michael asked.

"I suppose so, but I've no idea what happened to him after he left my house. I suppose he's back at Langley filing some type of a report. I really don't know, and really don't care."

Michael sighed. He was silent for several seconds and then asked, "What made you decide to come to Europe? Do you really think you'll be able to find out anything different than what you've already been told? Surely, you must know that your assistance isn't needed to pack Jason's household goods. The Embassy can easily take care of that."

"Yes, I'm sure they can," Jean said. "But, Sunday morning after I read about Jason's death, I decided I had to know what actually happened. That was when I decided to come, and here I am. I'm just glad I had your cell phone number."

"I was surprised, but pleased to hear your voice." Michael unbuttoned his uniform coat and loosened it from around his chest. "It's awful warm in here," he said. "Aren't you warm?" Beads of sweat covered his forehead. He reached over and fiddled with the knobs.

Jean looked at Michael and then down at her coat. "No, I'm just fine. Maybe you're coming down with something."

"No, I guess I'm just tired. It's been a long day," Michael said. He thought for a moment and then continued, "Jean, what actually did the agency say about Jason's job in Budapest?"

"They never said anything one way or the other."

"What did they say when you told them you were going to Budapest?"

Jean sighed and made a face. "Well, I just left a message with the Embassy's Marine Guard that I'd be arriving. I told him I'd call when I landed. When we get to your apartment, I suppose I should call and let them know we'll be in tomorrow to oversee the packing."

"You'd better. I think they'll be a bit upset with your arrival. It could cause some problems."

"That's just too bad," Jean said. "What's the worse they could do?"

Michael thought for several seconds. "They could not let you into Jason's apartment. They could call the Budapest Custom Office and tell them they suspected you were carrying drugs. They could refuse to see you."

"All right, Michael. I get the picture, but I'm still going."

"Well, do you want to drive to Budapest or shall we fly?" Michael asked.

"Which is faster?" Jean turned and stared at Michael. She started chewing on her finger nail.

"Well, to drive it'll take a very, very long day. To fly it'll take about two hours."

"Let's fly," Jean answered quickly. She rubbed her nail against her tooth. "If we need a car in Budapest, we'll use Jason's. Weaver told me it was in Budapest. Do you have a travel agency you use?"

Michael nodded.

Jean sighed and leaned back in her seat. She felt relieved knowing that things were going as she had hoped. Michael would help her. After several minutes, she pulled her coat tighter around her chest.

"Michael, it's really gotten cold in here. I think you turned on the air conditioning by mistake."

"Sorry, about that," he said. He began fumbling with the controls. Something clicked. "I'm still not used to all these gadgets. In a moment it should be warmer."

"That's perfect," Jean answered. "I can feel the heat already."

Michael reached over and touched Jean's hand. "I have to admit it's good seeing you again. I'm sorry the conditions are as they are." He put his hand back on the steering wheel, and winked.

"You always were good to me," Jean said. She was beginning to feel better. "I remember once when you and Jason came home from college. I was about eight or so. I had the biggest crush on you. Do you remember that?"

"You were a cute kid even back then," Michael teased.

"But, now I'm big, and I want people to realize that. I want to be taken seriously," Jean said. She turned back toward the window and held her fist against her chin.

Michael turned off the small road. "It isn't much further," he said. "Aren't you getting tired?"

She grunted and watched as they passed the different stores. Although, they passed a supermarket, there were several smaller stores for bread, milk, meat, fruit and pastries. The difference between Frankfurt and River City was enormous.

Michael turned the corner. They drove past a crowded McDonald's. She shook her head again and realized that the differences weren't really that much.

Absentmindedly, she ran her hand up and down the back of the brown leather seat. It felt soft and expensive. She turned and for the first time took a long hard look at Michael's new car.

He had told her on the phone that he had gone and done it, but she never imagined that he meant that he had purchased a luxury BMW. She wondered how much the car cost and what kind of a salary the Air Force was paying their lawyers.

She studied the dashboard. It was covered with rows of dials and knobs. Jason would have been impressed. She wondered if Jason had even seen Michael's new car. He had never mentioned it.

CHAPTER EIGHT

Two cars behind Michael Cleary's blue sports car was CIA agent Dale Weaver in his rented white Ford. After the couple left the building, Weaver grabbed his bag and headed for the car rental lot. They were only minutes ahead of him.

On the drive to Cleary's apartment, Weaver had time to contact the Frankfurt CIA office. Between traffic signals, he wrote down a description of Cleary's car and address. He also dictated an incident report regarding his encounter with the two men in the airport.

After Cleary pulled into his apartment parking lot on the outskirts of Rhein Main Air Force Base, Weaver slowed, looked around and pretended to be searching for an address. He held his cell phone to his ear, nodding occasionally for the benefit of anyone watching.

The couple was out of the car and walking into the building before Weaver pulled his car to a stop in the lot across the street from Cleary's apartment. He was thankful that he could see the front door to the apartment building from the driver's seat.

Dale Weaver sat in his car, took off his wire framed glasses, rubbed the new growth on his chin and wondered what he should do next. It had been years since he had been an active field agent. Now, he was considerably older, several pounds heavier, and the years behind a desk had slowed his reactions and reflexes.

A black BMW drove slowly into the parking lot. Weaver ducked down and watched the car lights bounce across his windshield. The car went the full length of the lot, turned around and drove out.

Weaver sat up just in time to see the back of the car. It had a diplomatic CD oval sticker on the rear window. He squinted and tried to read the license plate. It belonged to a Russian diplomat.

The car drove out of the parking lot and turned the corner. Weaver jumped out of his car and walked toward the parking lot entrance. He was several feet from the street, when the car suddenly reappeared.

Weaver turned and started back toward his rental car. The BMW turned slowly into the lot and headed toward him. Its headlights spotlighted Weaver.

Weaver shielded his eyes and looked around for someone to help him. There was no one. The BMW sped up.

Weaver moved to the side of the driveway. The car immediately followed. He leaned backward and caught a glance over his shoulder. Two dark figures were in the front seat. The car moved closer. Weaver's heart raced.

His rental car was parked several feet in front of him on the other side of the driveway. There was a large metal dumpster between him and his car. Several waist high cement pillars surrounded the trash area.

Weaver knew he had to get out of the oncoming car's way. He started running. His leather soled shoes skidded on the gravel. He slipped, almost lost his balance, but continued to run forward.

The black car raced toward him. Exhaust fumes filled the night air. Weaver coughed, and dove toward the front of his car. His cell phone flew out of his pocket and fell in the path of the oncoming car.

The BMW's right fender brushed Weaver's left leg. It threw him forward. Weaver bounced against his car and slid forward on the cold gravel. The car whizzed past. Weaver groaned, pulled himself up and crawled into his car.

He flipped the key, shifted into reverse and backed out. His tires spun. The smell of hot rubber saturated the air. Within seconds, Weaver was back on the street. The BMW was no where in sight.

Weaver pulled to the side of the street and rested his head on the steering wheel. He took several long deep breaths. His head ached and his hands were shaking.

For a split second, he recalled how he had gotten involved in the case. Now, he wished the Director had never asked him for this favor. He just wanted to be back at Langley and in his new job as Director of the European Division.

He looked around for a telephone. Whoever had just tried to kill him knew exactly who he was. He couldn't afford to take any chances. His life was in danger.

A telephone booth was on the other side of the parking lot. With caution, he drove back into the parking lot and parked in the shadows. He crawled out of the car. His legs were still shaking.

His overcoat was torn and dirty, and the palms of his hands were bleeding. His wrist hurt. It made a scrapping sound when he turned his hand. Under the dim light, he stood and pulled small pebbles out of the palms of his hands.

Although, he was glad to be alive, he felt awful. His entire body ached. A light went off in the Cleary apartment. He glanced at his watch and decided the couple was in for the night.

Standing in the telephone booth, he kept looking around. His fingers punched the numbers from memory. "Weaver here." His voice was shaking. He pulled out a pad and pen and rested it on the small corner shelf. "Have you made hotel reservations for me?"

He kept checking the entrance to the parking lot. Every time a car passed, his heart raced. With his teeth clinched, he wrote down an address and listened for a few seconds.

"Do you have any information on Michael Cleary?" he asked. He listened, his eyebrows curved and a deep frown filled his forehead. "I want someone to find out how an Air Force lawyer can be driving a new sporty BMW."

He squinted and looked up toward the Cleary apartment and listened again. He stared at the quiet street. Tapping his foot on the cement, he said, "I don't give a damn if it's the middle of the night or Christmas. Someone knows something. I also want someone to check a black BMW with Russian diplomatic plates. And, don't forget I want information on those two men I ran into at the airport. I'll call in the morning for the answers."

All expression left his face. He crunched his teeth together and pressed his lips tight. Carefully, he replaced the receiver.

"Nuts," he whispered.

He pulled a smashed pack of cigarettes out of his overcoat pocket, flipped out a cigarette and lit one. He took a long drag, looked at the crunched cigarette, threw it to the ground and crushed it with his shoe. "Damn it, they've even ruined my cigarettes."

CHAPTER NINE

The Delta flight was on its final approach to Ferihegy II, the Budapest International Airport. Jean gently nudged Michael in the arm. "Michael, look we're almost here."

He smiled, nodded, turned off his laptop computer, and snapped his briefcase shut. "That didn't take long," he said.

"I can hardly believe I'm here. I hope Larry Perkins, the Embassy Administration Officer or someone from the Embassy, is here to meet us. It would be awful to have come all this way and not be able to get into Jason's apartment."

Michael ran his fingers through his hair. "Well, I'll take bets that someone is waiting at the airport. I'm quite sure they want to find out just what we're doing here."

"Perkins sure didn't sound very friendly on the phone last night," Jean said. "He very politely told me that I wasn't needed nor expected to pack Jason's things."

Michael chuckled. "As if you didn't already know that before you left Iowa."

Jean made a face. "Yea, I knew. I just thought he'd be more understanding."

"Ha. Would you be?"

Jean grinned. "Probably not."

"Well, if worse comes to worse, I'll contact Ray Clark. I've met him a couple times when I was in Budapest to visit Jason. I'm sure he'll get us the key."

"Jason never said much about Clark, but he was Jason's direct supervisor, wasn't he?"

"Why ask me?" Michael said. "Jason didn't tell me much about his work here. When he and I were living in Frankfurt, I knew all the agents, from all the different agencies. But, when Jason moved to Budapest he became pretty tight-lipped about who was who. In Frankfurt, I even partied with the agents."

She was surprised to hear Michael use such a sharp tone of voice. "Well, I know you came to visit him quite often. Jason told me that. I just assumed he told you what was going on here."

Michael began fidgeting with his laptop computer case. "I came over occasionally. It was a good chance for me to get out of Germany."

Jean looked away from Michael and watched the plane taxi toward the airport. Suddenly, she turned to Michael and asked, "Do you think I'm doing the right thing by coming here to Budapest?"

"Well, it's too late now. The plane's approaching the terminal." He reached for her hand. "Don't let anything bother you. We can get in and out before anyone knows we're here. The trip will undoubtedly give you peace of mind."

"Maybe, you're right." She tried to be positive, but knew her visit was bound to create some waves. She said, "I'll follow you."

They walked down the narrow metal steps and boarded a waiting bus for the short ride to the terminal building. "When do we get our bags?" she whispered, while they waiting for the other passengers to enter.

Michael said, "Inside the building. Where's your passport? You're going to need it as soon as we get inside the door. You better make sure it's handy."

Jean's hands were shaking. During the trip, she tried preparing herself for whatever was ahead, but now her mind went blank. Finally, she said, "It's on the side of my purse." She rubbed her hands together. "I don't know why I'm so nervous."

"This is all new to you," Michael answered. "It won't take long. We'll be out of the airport in a few minutes."

After the couple stepped into the customs area, Jean spotted a tall, slim man with grey hair. He was dressed in a dark blue suit and was standing alone against a fenced off area. A large cardboard sign with her name printed in big black bold letters was in his hands.

"Michael, look that must be someone from the Embassy. Do you recognize him?"

"Yes, that's Ray Clark. He's the one we think was Jason's supervisor. I'd have recognized him anywhere because he's so tall. I'm over six foot and he makes me look short. Let's go join him."

Michael made the introductions, and guided the group toward the luggage claim area. He stood back so Clark could speak directly to Jean.

"Did you have a good trip?" Clark asked. His tone of voice was polite, but cold and reserved. He stared at Jean. His face showed no expression.

Jean answered, "Considering, all that has happened it wasn't too bad." She felt Clark's cold, reserved manner and shivered. It made her very uncomfortable. "Excuse me. I'll be right back."

She walked toward the restroom, and left Michael to carry on a conversation. When she returned, the two men were huddled together. Jean kept her distance. She didn't feel like small talk.

Michael motioned to Jean. He said, "I'll get the bags."

"I'll help," Clark said, and followed Michael before anyone could object.

Jean glanced after the men. Her gaze wandered over the arriving passengers waiting nearby. Her eyes settled on a black haired man dressed in a green loden coat.

A faint spark of recognition flashed through her mind. She grew tense. He reminded her of someone she knew but she couldn't place who or where she might have met him. Her eyes moved up and down his body. He was so familiar.

Her shoulders relaxed, she turned and let her eyes continue surveying the room. Someone was watching her. She could feel the eyes against her back. This time, she rotated around on one foot, but couldn't see anyone showing any special attention. Finally, she moved toward the carousel.

The men had retrieved the bags and were loading them onto a luggage cart. Clark led the way, Michael pushed the cart and Jean followed. The trio walked toward the custom guards and the lobby.

Clark said, "Hold your passports up like this as we pass." The couple did as instructed and stayed directly behind Clark. When Clark flashed his diplomatic passport, Jean and Michael held their passports high. The Hungarian guards simply nodded without saying a word and motioned the group to pass.

CHAPTER TEN

Before leaving Frankfurt, Weaver had several long conversations with his Frankfurt office. Although, he still didn't know who the Russians or the two men at the airport were, he had been caught up to date on Michael Cleary's official and private life.

He also went shopping for a new European style wardrobe. A Frankfurt CIA agent met him at the airport with his latest travel arrangements. Reservations had been made for him at the Budapest Hilton, directly across the street from Jason Martin's apartment.

On the flight, he sat three rows behind the couple. He had changed the style of his dark hair by combing it down over his forehead and over his ears, keeping with the latest European look. Although, Jean had glanced his way several times during the flight, she looked directly at him but her eyes showed no sign of recognition.

Weaver had just walked into the customs area, when the couple approached the tall man. He moved behind a pillar, and watched the couple talk to the man he suspected was from the American Embassy. Since he knew where the couple was staying, he went directly to currency exchange. Then, he bought a ticket for the trip to the Hilton Hotel from the mini-bus stand.

When his bag dropped onto the luggage belt he walked toward it without looking around. He passed directly alongside Jean Martin who was standing near the area. He felt her eyes on his back when she turned and looked directly at him.

He looked away and glanced up at a clock. For several seconds, he acted as if he were adjusting his watch to Budapest time. With his head down, he stepped closer to the belt.

Out of the corner of his eye, he watched her. His heart raced. His instinct's told him that if he looked at Jean directly, she'd recognize him.

His suitcase was moving forward on the belt, he watched it and the couple. Michael Cleary pushed his luggage cart directly toward him. Weaver bent down and picked up his bag. His heart was pounding. He stood almost paralyzed as they passed.

After the trio left, Weaver walked straight to the Mini-Bus waiting area in the middle of the lobby. He placed his bag on a near-by chair and watched the three Americans walk out the automatic doors toward the parking lot.

Feeling a sense of relief, Weaver absentmindedly glanced around the busy lobby. A short, shabby dressed, dirty looking man, standing near a flower shop, caught his attention. The man looked his way, shuffled his feet, turned and hurried out of the terminal.

The short man stood outside the glass exit doors and looked back directly at Weaver. Weaver watched the man walk toward a black diplomatic car. He didn't recognize the make but knew it wasn't an American one.

Weaver smiled and felt his senses tingle. Langley had warned him that other nations were also interested in Jean Martin. Now, he was sure that Langley was right.

CHAPTER ELEVEN

"Jean, I'm glad I finally have the chance to meet you. I feel almost as if I know you. Jason mentioned you so often," Ray Clark said. He spoke as he was pulling the car out of the airport parking lot.

"I'm sorry I never had the chance to visit Jason here in Budapest. I had planned on a trip for this coming fall." Jean spoke politely, but felt uncomfortable talking about plans that now were immaterial.

"It's too bad we couldn't have met under more pleasant conditions," Clark said. Turning toward Michael, he asked, "Michael, how are you? When were you here last? It was in November around the Marine Ball, wasn't it?"

Michael looked at Clark, turned his head toward Jean and answered, "Yes, I was able to get a few days off during November. I flew in for the ball and then Jason and I spent a couple days at the Balaton, even though it was off-season. I remember we spent a night at a great spa hotel in Heviz."

Clark looked at Michael. There was no humor in his expression. "Did you have fun?"

Michael laughed as if he were remembering a special event. He turned back toward Jean. His eyes sparkled. "It was great fun. But, I always enjoy Budapest. I'm sorry I couldn't be coming back under more pleasant conditions. As you know, I'm a lawyer with the JAG Office in Rhein Main. My spare time also gets pretty tight during the summer months and early fall. That's when most of the rotations are. Seems as everyone is leaving or coming."

Clark nodded and asked, "When did you see Jason last?"

Michael looked sad. "Unfortunately, it was in November. But, I have talked to him a couple times since. Unfortunately, we never had the chance to get together before his death."

"Well, you and Jean are both here now, that's all that matters. As you know, Jason's apartment is located in the castle area. It's a large third floor apartment directly across the street from the Hilton Hotel. I have the apartment key with me as well as his car key. His car is parked in the Hilton garage. I'll show you where."

"Why there?" Jean asked.

"There isn't a garage furnished with his apartment, so the Embassy rented a space in the Hilton for him," Clark said. "I went by his apartment today. He has a cleaning lady. I asked her to freshen everything up and make sure there were clean linens on the beds."

"That was very kind of you," Jean said. She leaned forward against the front seat.

Clark nodded. "The housekeeper said she'd get a few groceries. There's a small grocery store just down the street. I didn't look to see what Jason had on hand, but I'm sure there's something in the house for breakfast. But, I'm hoping you'll both be my guests for dinner tonight." Clark spoke as he drove expertly through the heavy traffic.

Jean heard what Clark was saying but was so engrossed in her first glimpses of the city, that she didn't pay much attention to what he was saying. She hoped Michael taking mental notes.

"What a beautiful city," Jean said, to no one in particular when Clark stopped for a stop light. She could see the Danube directly in front of them. She opened her window and looked out at the freighters moving slowly down the river.

"Yes, it is," Clark said. He drove past several hotels, across the Chain Bridge and up a one-way narrow steep road toward the castle area. He pointed out some of the sights as he passed them.

Finally, Clark pulled up in front of a modern, four story building in the center of a square. "We're here," he announced.

Jean jumped out of the car. Her eyes were wide. "Is this the apartment house?"

"Yes," Michael said. "Pretty spectacular, isn't it?"

"I love it," she said, turning around in a circle as she talked. "I feel as I've been transported back into time. I'm in the middle of a medieval city. The streets are cobblestone and the buildings are old with huge pointed roofs and ornate designs."

"This apartment house is the only other modern building, other than the Hilton, that has been built in the past one hundred years in this area," Clark said.

"Who else lives here?" Jean asked. She pointed toward the modern apartment building that housed Jason's apartment.

"It's owned by the Diplomatic Housing Service. Several embassies rent apartments here." Clark saw Jean frown. "It's perfectly safe. You have nothing to fear."

The sound of a horse caught Jean's attention. She turned and looked across the street where a horse and buggy were parking. "Do they give buggy rides?" she asked.

"Yes," Clark said. "You're in the very heart of the castle tourist area."

"Jason sent me several pictures of this area, but they didn't do it justice," Jean said. "It's simply spectacular. I can hardly wait to explore it."

"You'll have ample time later," Clark said. He glanced at his watch. "Come, I'll take you inside." He picked up one of the suitcases and started toward the entrance.

Jean walked to Michael and took his briefcase which contained his laptop. She looked at him, made a face and nodded toward Clark. Michael rolled his eyes, picked up the other suitcases and kicked the car door shut with his foot. Clark had walked around to the entrance on the side street.

"Look at this door," Jean whispered. She shifted her eyes toward a huge wooden, entrance door. "It's enormous. It must be nine or ten foot tall."

"I'm sure it had a special purpose when it was built," Michael said seriously. He pushed Jean in front of him into the building.

Jean found herself in the middle of a huge room. It was decorated with large plants and pale beige walls. It was designed as a waiting or reception area. A man was sitting behind a small window in an office area near the stairway. She smiled. He looked as if he were going to sell her a movie ticket.

Clark walked toward the window and said, "This is Jean Martin and Michael Cleary. Jean was Jason's sister. They'll be staying in the apartment for the next couple days. Please, advise all the other doormen of their arrival."

The porter's mouth dropped open. He hurried out from behind his enclosure and walked directly to Jean. He was a short, stubby man with a completely bald head. He was dressed in a gray suit that hung on his body.

He took Jean's hand and began kissing it repeatedly. "I am so very sorry," he repeated over and over.

For several minutes, he spoke in broken English telling Jean how nice Jason had been to him. Jean listened while fighting back tears. Politely, she pulled her hand away and brushed off a tear that was running down her cheek.

"Thank you," she said, her voice was very soft.

"Thank you," Michael added politely. He reached for Jean's arm and lead her toward the steps.

"Sorry, about that. I didn't know he was going to carry on so," Clark whispered to Michael. He lead the way up the stairs toward Jason's apartment.

Jean stopped. She motioned for the two men to go on without her. Resting her purse on the stairway railing, she looked for a tissue.

Someone was dialing a telephone. It was coming from the lobby area that they had just left. She turned and took several small steps back toward the lobby doorway.

"Ms. Martin has just arrived," she heard the porter say. His words carried loud and clear through the quiet space. "She's with another man. His name is Michael Cleary."

Jean held her breath. She leaned forward, overwhelmed with curiosity.

"Yes, I will keep you informed," the porter said. "She will be here for a few days. No, I don't know her plans."

When Jean heard the porter put the phone down, she turned away and hurried back up the steps. Her heart was racing. Once again, she was afraid.

CHAPTER TWELVE

In a shabby cottage on the outskirts of Budapest, two men had just parked their rental car. They pulled their long legs out of the small car and stretched. They took off their sunglasses and put them on the dashboard. The sun was setting.

"This car size is ridiculous," the Arab man, Ghassar Nseir, said. "I'm going to trade this kid's toy for a bigger car in the morning. It would even be too small for my children."

The taller man, Leonid Koniev, flashed his toothy smile. "If you want to change the car, you tell him, I'm not going to. Come on, we're late."

The two men walked toward the shack. They saw a shiny black car parked behind a tree, toward the back of the building, away from the street. Nseir said, "He's here. Let me do the talking."

Koniev held his hands up. "He's yours," he said. He purposely stood back and let the Arab enter the cottage first.

"What have you learned?" the older man asked before the two men were inside the house. He was sitting in the middle of the room at an old wooden table. A blanket had been placed over the chair. His dark blue suit, white shirt and paisley tie looked completely out of place in the dingy, musty kitchen. The dim light from the dirty window cast an eerie effect on the room.

"Very little, boss," Nseir answered. "We have been half way around the world and have found nothing. Not even a scrap of paper."

The boss slammed his fist on the table. A cloud of dust flew into the air. He coughed, took out his clean white handkerchief and wiped his face. "That is totally unacceptable. You have spent a fortune and have found nothing. Martin had to have left something about the operation. He knew too much. There has to be a file somewhere. Have you checked everything I told you to check?"

Nseir looked down at the sitting man. "Yes, boss. Koniev, will tell you the same." He motioned for Koniev to talk and moved closer to the table.

Koniev took one step forward. “Boss, he’s right. We didn’t find anything.” He stepped backward, then stepped forward again. His eyes went wide. “But, we did see another American watching Martin and the Air Force dude in the Frankfurt airport.”

“What? Who was it?” the boss asked. He put his elbows on the table and leaned forward. When he realized what he had done, he moved back into his chair and brushed at his coat sleeves. They were covered with a sticky dust.

“Oh, yea,” Nseir said. “We saw this tall man standing behind a pillar. He was obviously watching the Martin lady, but told us he wasn’t. We just scared him. Nothing serious.”

“Did you get a picture of him? Do you have any idea who he was?” the boss questioned, staring at his two henchmen. “I’m paying you for answers. You must have learned something.”

Koniev said, “I think he’s a cop. He looks and acts like one.”

The Arab turned toward Koniev. He said, “No, dummy. The man was some kind of an agent. Probably the CIA or one of the NSA spooks. He acted too stupid to be a cop.”

“What did he look like?” the tall man asked. He brushed something away from his face and adjusted his mirrored sunglasses. “Would you recognize him again?” Nseir looked directly into his boss’s eyes. He could see his own face in the sunglasses. He smoothed his hair with his fingers and wet his lips. “He was about fifty, a bit taller than me, slightly overweight and coal black hair.”

Koniev added, “He colors his hair, or he was wearing a rug.”

“Never mind,” the boss said, waving his hand in the air. He glanced at his watch. “I have to get going. Keep on top of this now that you’re both here in the city. If you see this man from the Frankfurt airport here in Budapest, please, get a picture and call me. How are you both fixed for money?”

“We’re getting low. I used what money I had left to rent this little baby car we have now.” The Arab pulled out a wallet from inside his leather jacket pocket. “But, I still have some of the phony American one hundred bills.”

"Don't pass them yet. Here." The man stood up and handed the Arab a thick white envelope. "But, I want to hear something positive. Did you hear anything about who killed Martin?"

Nseir shook his head. "Nothing. I've checked all my contacts and no one knows anything. It was not anyone from within the Arab community. Maybe it really was an accident."

"Not hardly," the boss answered. "Martin's death was too beneficial for too many people. No, we have to find out exactly what Martin knew about us."

He took a couple steps toward the doorway and turned and said, "Since Martin is out of the picture and can't cause any problems, Yuri is anxious to move another shipment. He's standing by and waiting for the go ahead."

"Why doesn't he just go ahead?" Koniev asked.

"He's afraid something else is going to be coming out in the paper. The last thing he wants is more attention." Without saying another word, the tall man walked out of the cottage, moved around the building and headed for his parked car.

Once their boss had left, Nseir and Koniev took the blanket off the chair. They walked to the cottage entrance. Each man held corners of the blanket. They began shaking it violently. Dust started flying everywhere. They threw the blanket back into the cottage before the dust settled. All traces of the meeting had been eliminated.

CHAPTER THIRTEEN

After showing the couple around the apartment, Clark said, "I'll leave the keys to the apartment and Jason's car here on the table." He pulled out two papers from his pocket. "Jean, I need you to sign these for the packers."

Michael reached for the papers, read them quickly and handed them to Jean. "Just sign your name on the bottom line," he said, after taking the pen from Clark.

Clark glanced from Jean to Michael. It was obvious by his expression that he didn't understand what role Michael was playing. After Jean handed the signed papers back to Clark, he said, "The household goods are scheduled to be picked up by a moving company from Vienna later in the week. I'll have someone from the General Service Office call you about the details."

He walked to the kitchen,"I'll just check and see if the housekeeper has done the shopping."

Jean shrugged and stood in the doorway and watched Clark. He opened and closed several of the cabinet doors.

"There's fresh bread, milk and eggs," he said, when he turned and saw Jean watching him. "Do you have any questions?"

Neither Jean nor Michael said anything. Jean turned and walked toward the coat rack in the corner. Michael began moving their suitcases out of the doorway.

"Well, I'll leave my card here on the table," Clark said. "I've written my home telephone number on the back. Call me if I can help in any way." He walked toward the door, turned and walked back into the kitchen. Within seconds, he was back in the entrance hall. He was carrying a small plastic bag. "How about I pick you both up about eight for dinner tonight?"

Jean looked at Michael, then walked toward Clark and answered for the two of them. "Thanks, Ray, but I think we'll stay in. I really don't want to eat out. If we can't find anything here, we can always go across the street to the Hilton. If it's all right with you, we'll take a raincheck on the dinner."

"As you wish," Clark said. "Now call me if you need anything." He stepped toward the door and turned back to the couple. Holding up the plastic bag, he said, "This is stale bread. I'm going to feed it to the birds. I hope that's okay."

Jean smiled and answered, "That's fine."

Clark turned and left immediately. Jean walked behind Clark and closed the door. She leaned against the door and looked around the entrance hall in Jason's apartment.

Tears filled her eyes. She walked to the clothes rack, pressed her face against one of Jason's favorite coats, and took a deep breath.

She sniffed, stepped back and looked at the pile of things Jason had stacked in the corner. With her hand against her mouth, she began walking through the apartment. Everything reminded her of Jason. She felt as if he was going to walk through the door any minute.

Returning to the entrance hall, she stood and stared into space. She had an uncanny feeling, she was in the right place at the right time.

"Jason," she whispered, running her hand over his favorite leather jacket. She slipped the soft jacket on her shoulders. Unconsciously, her hands automatically went into the pockets. She felt a piece of paper. Taking it out, she read it and her mouth dropped open.

Holding the paper tightly with her fingertips, she ran into the living room. "Michael, I found this paper in one of Jason's jackets. What do you think it means?"

Michael heard Jean, glanced toward her, turned and finished pulling the drapes wide open. He opened the window, leaned out and took a deep breath. He walked away from the window and reached for the paper. He read aloud. "Files named BMW, EPA, Bank Accounts, Stolen items."

"Well?" Jean questioned. She stood with her hands in the jacket pockets waiting for Michael to say something encouraging.

"Beats me," Michael answered. He made a face. "Looks like a list. I doubt if it really meant anything."

"Do you think we should show it to Clark?"

Michael laughed, wadded up the paper, tossed it on an end table and walked toward the kitchen. "He'll think we're crazy if we go showing him every piece of paper we find in this apartment. I wouldn't doubt if he's already had the apartment checked. I'm hungry. Do you want a sandwich or something?"

Jean opened her mouth to contradict Michael, but walked over and picked up the paper. With care, she smoothed out the paper and put it in her pants pocket. She considered telling Michael about the porter's telephone call, but something warned her to keep that information to herself. At least for the time being.

CHAPTER FOURTEEN

After Weaver arrived at the Hilton and checked into this room, he decided to take a familiarization walk around the castle area. His main purpose was to locate the Martin apartment while it was still daylight.

Before leaving the hotel he asked a clerk for directions to the address. He was surprised to learn the apartment was almost directly across the street. Looking around the busy lobby, he walked toward the gift shop.

Remembering the dirty looking man at the airport, he stood and watched the lobby through a large ornate wall mirror directly behind the front desk. He needed to make certain no one was paying special attention to him. Every few seconds, he took a couple steps, but kept his eyes fixed on the mirror.

No one caught his attention. Feeling secure, he studied the hotel layout map on a pedestal frame by the gift shop. With his route in mind, he walked down the long elegant red carpeted hallway through the lobby, passing a portable coffee bar and toward an antique shop on the North end of the building. He stopped for just a moment and picked up the USA TODAY which was on a table near a grouping of leather chairs.

Glancing at the headlines, he continued down to the end of the hall. No one was in sight. He looked around. Without hesitating, he moved a large green rubber tree plant several inches to the right and located a hidden exit door.

Taking a deep breath, he hoped an alarm wouldn't go off. He pushed the door slowly and quickly slipped out into the small courtyard. Now, he was at the back of the building, partially surrounded with a high stone wall.

He darted down a narrow pathway and found himself on Tancsics Utca, one of the main streets in the castle area. He stopped, glanced up and down the street. For several seconds, he stood and watched taxis leaving their passengers off directly in front of the hotel entrance.

He walked across the street. Keeping close to the buildings, he headed toward Mattias Church. It was on his left, directly in front of him at the corner of the main square. Acting like a tourist, he stood for a moment and admired the area. All the time completely aware of who and what was going on around him.

No one was watching, so he crossed to the statue in the center of Szentharomsag Square. After several minutes of looking over the statue and reading its plaque, he turned completely around and memorized the scene.

With everything fixed in his mind, he turned down the side street and immediately was in front of the Martin apartment building entrance. Keeping with his role as a tourist, he stopped and looked in the Herend shop window next door. Then, he moved back across the street to look at the apartment from a distance.

Taking his time, admiring the construction, he was able to count the windows he imagined to be those of the Martin apartment. If he needed further clarification, he'd get that information from the CIA Station Chief at the Embassy.

Preparing himself, he walked the entire block, becoming familiar with the house numbers, courtyards, exits and black areas. He walked back to the church, and stood in the shadow of the front entrance. Hidden from casual glances, he looked up at the windows he had pinpointed earlier.

The lights were on and the drapes were opened. Although it was January, he saw one of the windows was wide open. He continued to watch until he became cold and decided there wasn't anything further he could do.

A sudden movement in front of the apartment building caught his attention. He slipped back into the church doorway, taking off his wire framed glasses to watch.

A short, stubby, bald-headed man walked out the apartment door. A coat was thrown over his shoulders. He walked to the corner and stopped. Suddenly, a black foreign make car drove up and stopped on the same side of the street. The man walked toward the car.

For several minutes, the short bald man stood by the driver side. Weaver could see the short man's mouth moving. He couldn't see the face of the driver. The short man began waving his arms as if he was arguing.

Weaver debated about walking past the car to get a better look. He decided to take the chance and stepped out of the shadows. Instantly, the car sped away. The short man hurried back into the apartment building.

"Damn," Weaver said, stepping back into the shadows. "I didn't even get the license number."

Walking back to his room, Weaver realized that if the CIA wanted to know everything Jean Martin and Michael Cleary were doing, it would take more than just him.

He glanced at his watch. It was time to check with Frankfurt and see what they had found out. His body still ached.

CHAPTER FIFTEEN

The sound of running water woke Jean from a sound sleep. It had been quite late when she finally crawled into bed. They had eaten in the apartment, spent quiet time listening to Jason's CD collection and watching "Hellfighters", a John Wayne movie.

Jean sat up and looked around her. It took a moment to realize exactly where she was. Jason's presence was everywhere. For several minutes, she sat looking at his things and enjoying the serenity.

She heard Michael walking around. Then, his singing in the shower drifted through the vents and into her bedroom. She smiled when he attempted a high note. It was almost as if he were her brother. He was easy to talk with, and as Jason's friend, he knew most of her faults.

When the shower stopped, Jean looked at her suitcase. It was spread open on top of the dresser. She jumped from bed, grabbed Jason's robe from behind the door, and moved toward her suitcase.

After she slipped the robe on, she wondered where Jason's clothes were that he had taken with him on his fatal trip. She hadn't seen any packed suitcase in the apartment, nor had Clark mentioned one.

Jason's car popped into her mind. She wondered if he had left it at the airport or the Embassy when he left. She added the questions to her mental list she needed to ask Clark.

"Jean, are you up?" Michael called "It's almost nine. I'm finished with the bathroom if you want to use it. I'll go start some breakfast. How about eggs and whatever else I can scrape together? Is that okay with you?"

"That's fine. I won't be long." Jean started digging through her suitcase for a pair of jeans and a sweatshirt. She was glancing out the bedroom window as she spoke. The people in the courtyard below were bundled in heavy coats. The temperature had dropped.

After her shower, with a towel wrapped around her wet hair, she followed the smell of bacon and coffee to the kitchen. "I can't believe we slept so late. Can you?"

Michael finished taking the bacon out of the skillet. He put it on a plate covered with a paper towel. "Good heavens, it was late when we went to bed. That combined with your trip and jet lag, yes, I can believe it. How did you sleep?"

Michael looked completely refreshed. He was casually dressed in brown corduroy slacks and a soft wool beige sweater. He had found an old apron of Jason's and had it tied around his waist.

"I'm feeling much better. I have to admit I felt out of place when I woke up in Jason's bed and looked around the room at all of his things." She sat down and poured herself a cup of strong black coffee.

"Hope it's not too strong for you," Michael said, glancing at Jean's full cup of coffee.

"No, it's fine. Michael, speaking of Jason's clothes, I have no use for most of them. I just want some of his sweatshirts. Would you like to go through the rest? If there is anything you want, you're welcome to it."

Michael nodded. He used the spatula in his hand to point to a plate. "I'll take a look after breakfast or later in the day. First, let's eat. Everything's ready."

"It smells wonderful. You really amaze me, I didn't know you could cook like this?"

"You have to learn to cook when you live alone or you starve." Michael passed Jean a plate overflowing with eggs and bacon. "It's way too expensive to eat out all the time. Remember, Jason was a great cook."

"Yes, I do," Jean said.

"Where do you want to start?" Michael asked, after he finished eating. He stood and starting to clear away the dirty dishes while Jean finished her breakfast.

Jean put down her silverware, stood and looked at Michael. "I don't understand the intelligence world and only knew the bits and pieces that Jason told me."

"It's really quite simple," Michael said. "An agent is assigned to a posting. He often uses a fake name and occupation. Every day, he spends his time between his cover assignment and his intelligence office. Normally, the cover assignment relates somewhat to the intelligence world. Such as political, consulate, economics or administration. He reports directly to his real boss, who in Jason's case was the CIA."

Jean handed Michael the dirty dishes and reached for a dish towel. "You said Jason told you all about his being with the Central Intelligence Agency when you were both stationed in Germany. Did he do most of his spying, investigating or whatever you want to call it under a cover? Or, was it from his work at the Embassy, or at night when he attended the various social functions? Did he wander around on his own?"

Michael finished rinsing the dishes and nodded, "Whoa. I think it was a bit of everything. These days, intelligence agents get their bits of information from all sorts of sources. Just like I do when I'm trying a legal case."

"That makes sense. I just thought if we knew something about his work, we'd have some place to start."

Michael untied the apron, folded it and put it back in the drawer. "I'm sure the CIA doesn't want you or I, for that matter, coming into Budapest and blowing what might be left of Jason's CIA cover."

"Probably not," Jean answered. "Weaver didn't say anything about Jason's job here. Hell, he wouldn't even let me view Jason's body before the funeral."

"You're kidding! Did he give you any reason why?"

"None. He said that it was for the best."

Michael laughed. "I'm surprised you didn't insist. You're usually pretty strong willed."

"I just wasn't up to arguing with him," Jean answered. "I think Clark had something to do with Jason, but do you know if Clark is CIA? I have no idea."

Michael poured himself another cup of coffee. "I personally don't think so. I don't think Clark is anything but a State Department officer. Jason once told me to be very careful when

I was in Budapest. He said I shouldn't tell anyone that he was with the CIA."

"I've never told anyone," Jean replied, "but my friend, Martha, guessed."

Michael laughed. "She probably did a background investigation report on him."

"Well, everyone in River City knows now if they read his obituary in last Sunday's Des Moines Register. It undoubtedly took some of them by surprise. I know that no one at the bank knew. Not even Paul."

By noon, Michael and Jean had almost completed sorting and piling the things in the living room. They only had the desk and a stack of books to go through. Two garbage bags had been filled with old newspapers and magazines. Michael insisted that nothing be thrown away until they had gone through them.

"I'm getting tired of this," Michael said. He stood up and stretched his long arms and legs. He brushed pieces of lint off his slacks. "Let's go for a walk and get some fresh air. I really need to go stretch my legs after all this sitting and shuffling."

While Michael went into the bedroom to get ready, Jean stood and looked out the window. She noticed the doorman from downstairs was standing by the statue in the middle of the square. She pushed the window open so she could have a clearer view.

He was talking to someone. Jean leaned forward. The other person's face was shadowed. Getting cold, Jean pulled the window shut. The sound of the window closing echoed through the air. The porter turned and looked directly toward Jean's window.

She jerked her head backward, and held her body away from the window. For some unknown reason, she didn't want the porter to know she had been watching him. Stretching her arm, she caught the drape cord and pulled it. It was stuck. She pulled harder, it finally came loose.

Jean took a deep breath, leaned back toward the window, spread the drape apart and looked down at the square. The porter was no longer there. She did see a woman, with long brown hair walking toward the church. She had no way of knowing if that was the person the porter had been talking to.

"Are you ready?" Michael called from the hallway. "I'm going to go down and take some pictures. I'll meet you downstairs."

Jean turned, and bumped against the drape. It shook. Something fell off the rod and landed on the floor directly in front of her. She bent over and picked it up. It was a computer disk. Holding the disk tight, she glanced up at the top of the curtain. The drape was attached to the wall by a small wooden casing.

"Michael," she called, but heard his footsteps outside the apartment. Something seemed to be stuffed inside the casing. She pulled an easy chair close to the window. Crawling up on its arms, she stretched and felt inside the casing. Her fingers hit something hard.

Shifting, she reached into the casing and pulled out a folded envelope, and jumped off the chair. Turning the disk and envelope over and over in her hand, she looked around the room.

Suddenly, she remember Michael and hurried to her bedroom. Tucking the items in a corner of her suitcase, she started for the door. She stopped only long enough to grab her coat, pick up the apartment keys and her small purse.

Buttoning her coat, she hurried down the steps and stopped short when she heard voices. Creeping down the remaining steps, she moved toward the lobby. Michael and the porter were huddled together. Hidden in the shadows, she stood and listened.

"You don't need to tell Ms. Martin about this," Michael said. "I'll take care of it."

"If you are sure," the porter answered.

She heard the porter shuffle back to his area. It was the first time that Jean noticed that the porter was limping. She coughed and moved out into the hallway.

Michael glanced her way and walked toward the door. He finished buttoning up his jacket. His camera was still in its case.

Jean saw Michael slip something into his coat pocket, but she hadn't been quick enough to see what it was. Nodding toward the porter, she hurried after Michael.

Within seconds, the couple was out the door and walking across the street toward Mattias Church. They stopped and looked up just as the church bells began ringing.

"I never realized the church bells were so loud before," Jean said. She glanced back at the apartment building. The porter was standing in the doorway watching them. He had a cellular telephone in his hand.

CHAPTER SIXTEEN

Dale Weaver had been keeping an eye on the apartment all morning from his room inside the Hilton hotel. He had moved to a corner room which overlooked the square and gave him a direct view of the Martin apartment. He could see who entered and left the building, as well as all three windows of the apartment that face the square.

Weaver finished his cup of coffee and set it on his nightstand. His table was full of newspapers. Each one was spread open to the sports section.

The television in the corner was turned to CNN. Weaver glanced at it every once in a while. The remote was on his pillow.

His cell phone and black scrambler box were also on his pillow. They were connected and ready for use. He had already talked to Langley three times since he woke, and the day was still young.

Two empty and four full Coke cans sat on his window sill. He preferred diet drinks but the hotel was out. The gift store clerk promised she'd send a six pack to his room as soon as she was resupplied.

Weaver wore faded blue jeans and a light blue Virginia sweatshirt. He didn't plan on going outside his room without his loden coat. For now, he was barefooted.

His hands were still sore, and his legs were black and blue. He ached so much that he had gotten up before six and gone to the exercise room. The swim, spa and exercise hadn't help, now he was stiffer than ever.

The weather had turned bitterly cold and he was just grateful that he didn't have to stand outside and watch the apartment. The best news of the day was that he would be returning to Virginia soon. An agent who has just finished an assignment was scheduled to relieve him.

The morning passed slowly. He watched the apartment for some sign of activity and caught up on the sport results. When the porter walked to the middle of the square, Weaver leaned on the window and drank another coke.

The porter and the young woman spoke for several minutes. The young lady gave the porter a kiss, the porter gave the woman some money. Weaver was convinced she was the porter's daughter.

After, the porter returned to the apartment building, Weaver called Langley and ordered some supplies. A digital camera and night vision binoculars were included in his request.

He had watched CNN, read all the sports results and had just flipped to an old Dallas episode. He was thrilled to see the couple walk out of the apartment. They walk toward Mattias Church, almost directly below his room.

He watched until they moved behind the church and were out of range. Immediately, he shifted to the other window on the other side of the room. The couple walked to the fortress wall, stood and looked down at the city and the Danube River.

CHAPTER SEVENTEEN

It was after three when Michael and Jean returned to Jason's apartment. They were cold but refreshed from the long walk and bowl of thick Hungarian goulash. After entering the apartment complex, they waved to the porter.

Jean didn't recognize the man standing behind the enclosure. He was a different one than the man she had seen when she left earlier in the day. But, he obviously knew who they were, because he didn't ask for any identification.

Jean smiled and was surprised when the porter looked away. He kept his head down. It was apparent he was avoiding her.

"Race you up the steps," Michael called from the stairway.

Instantly, Jean turned her thoughts to Michael and pushed the porter's attitude to the back of her mind. "You're on," she called, running for the stairs.

"Let's agree to call it a tie." Jean gasped. They stood bent over laughing, trying to catch their breath in front of the apartment door.

"All right, but I still think I won by a hair." Michael laughed. He put the key in the lock, but the door sprung open. "Didn't you lock the door?"

"Of course, I did," Jean said. She pushed passed Michael and hurried in. "Holy cow, look at this?" she stammered. She just stood and stared.

"What a hell of a mess," Michael said. He walked through the entrance hall and into the living room. "It looks as if a cyclone struck."

"No wonder the porter acted so strange when we came in," Jean whispered. Her eyes filled with tears. "He knew someone had been in our apartment."

For several seconds, Michael stood and shook his head in disbelief. "What's going on?"

"I have no idea," Jean answered.

"We'd better report this. Where's that business card Clark gave you?"

Jean pointed to the small table in the corner. "I stuck it on the edge of the mirror. Is it still there?"

Michael nodded. "I'll call and get someone out here. Maybe we can get to the bottom of this. This is definitely breaking and entering. Can you hang up our coats and I'll call Clark?"

Jean nodded. She was still sniffling when she returned to the living room. It had taken her a couple minutes longer, because she hung up the other coats which had been thrown on the floor in the hallway. "Jean, I don't want you to touch anything. We may be able to get come fingerprints. Clark said he'd notify Security and someone would be right over. He said we should just sit tight and wait."

"I'll start some water for coffee. Would you like some?"

Michael shook his head. "We just had some. You might as well take a seat, sit down and relax. There isn't anything we can do until they've come and gone."

Michael waited for Jean to take a seat, then he began walking back and forth, taking care to walk around the mess. Jean sat obediently. Neither said a word.

Finally, Jean couldn't take the silence and Michael's pacing any longer. "For my sake, Michael, quit that pacing. You're driving me nuts. Surely, we can turn on the television while we're waiting. Maybe we can get CNN and find out what's going on in the world."

Michael looked hurt. "Yes, I suppose that would be fine. You stay sitting, I'll do it." He looked around the floor and located the remote control. Surfing through the channels, he stopped on CNN. They were giving the latest news update. Moving across the room, he sat down by Jean. "I'm sorry I'm making you nervous, but waiting has never been one of my strongest qualities."

"That's okay," Jean said. "I probably shouldn't have yelled at you. We both know this is a mess. Truthfully, Michael, I'm just glad you're here with me and I'm not alone. I think if I were here by myself, I'd freak out. Have you noticed if anything is gone?"

"Hell, who could tell." He threw his arms up in disgust. "We had the room somewhat in a mess from our sorting. Whoever went through the apartment was looking for something specific, but I wouldn't have the slightest idea what."

"It's a real mess," Jean said. She leaned back, closed her eyes and rubbed her forehead.

Michael glanced at her. "It seems funny Jason has kept so many newspapers. Did he always collect newspapers?"

Jean's eyes popped open and she leaned forward. She looked around the room as if she were seeing it for the first time. "You're right I never realized it before. Jason hated clutter. He'd read a paper and then we'd recycle it or burn it right away. We rarely had the previous day's paper in the house when the new one arrived."

"Well, he must have fallen behind in his reading and was going to catch up," Michael said. He leaned back on the sofa.

Jean jumped up. She moved to the papers and ran her hand through them. "Unless, he was looking through the newspapers for something specific. Some of the papers are in German, some Hungarian and some English. I think we need to go through them again, before we throw them away. What do you think?"

"I agree. This is not like the Jason, I knew. Don't say anything to the police and after they leave you and I can go through them with a fine tooth comb. You take the English ones and I'll take the German ones. We can put the Hungarian ones in a pile until we can find someone we can trust to go through them."

"You're right," Jean said. She started to say something else but the sound of the doorbell stopped her. "That'll be the police or Security from the Embassy now." She ran to the door.

Jean stepped back to let Clark enter. His face was flushed. He was followed by an older, grey haired, gentle looking man, who was dressed in jeans and a blue windbreaker jacket with an American Embassy Bucharest emblem over his left side. A tall Hungarian uniformed policeman entered directly behind the two men.

"Jean, I'm so sorry this happened," Clark said. "This is Ed Slate, he's the Security Officer with the Embassy and this is

Inspector Olah with the Hungarian police. Gentleman, this is Jean Martin and that is Michael Cleary. Jean was Jason Martin's sister. You both remember Jason. He was the Political Officer who was killed in an accident a week or so ago while he was in Romania."

After the polite introductions and shaking of the hands, Jean led the group into the living room through the entrance hall. The men gasped when they saw the room.

Jean watched the men's faces as they looked from one to the other. Without saying a word, they moved around the room, surveying the damage. Slate and the Hungarian Officer slipped on rubber gloves.

Ed Slate turned toward Jean. "May we walk through the rest of the apartment? We'd like to see what extent the search took place."

"Of course, but I'm afraid you're going to find that most of the rooms look just like this. Everything has been thrown around but there is very little breakage." From the doorways, she watched their reactions. She soon discovered the Hungarian policeman was the hardest person to show any facial reaction. That didn't surprise her, because she was sure he also was the most experienced.

"Quite a mess," Ed Slate remarked, after they walked back into the living room. "Do you have any idea what they might have been looking for or if anything was taken?"

"We have no idea," Jean said. "Michael and I spent the morning going through the living room and arranging things for the packers. Around noon, we were tired and took a break. We went for a long walk around the castle area, and stopped for a bowl of soup at one of the little tourist restaurants. It was around three when we came back."

"Did either of you notice anything unusual on your walk?" Slate asked.

Jean looked at Michael. He shook his head. She answered, "No. When we walked in, this is what we found. I did notice that when we entered the building, the porter downstairs avoided looking directly at us. I think he knows something. You might ask him."

"Yes, we will. Are you sure nothing is missing?" Ed Slate asked again. His eyes were fixed on Jean's.

"How would I know?" Jean answered. "I told you we just started going through the living room this morning. I'd never been here in Jason's apartment before, I have no idea if anything is missing. I may not be a police person but it seems pretty obvious to me that whatever they were looking for had something to do with Jason's death."

"There is always that possibility, but Jason's death was ruled an accident. Do you have other knowledge about his death?" Slate asked.

Jean could feel her temper rising. "I'm sure it doesn't come as a total surprise to you three that I've never agreed with the Embassy report that his death was accidental. This certainly shows me that there could be more. Don't you agree?"

She looked at each man in turn. They looked at her for a moment and then looked back at the room. It was obvious they each had strong thoughts on the matter, but none of them were going to say anything one way or the other.

Finally, the Hungarian policeman spoke. "Ms. Martin, I'm sorry about your brother's death, but this break in today doesn't prove anything to me except that someone broke into a rich American's apartment. It was in the local newspapers about his accident. It wouldn't be hard for the criminal element in the city to find out where he lived and ransack his apartment."

Slate added. "I totally agree. You probably came home early and stopped them before they took the television and electronic equipment. It appears to be a common burglary. Unless we find something different, that's what I'm putting in my report."

"I'll do the same," the Hungarian officer said. I'll give the Embassy a copy of mine and you can use it for insurance claims if you need too. Gentleman, if there isn't anything else, I'm going to leave. I'll check with the porter and let you know if I find out anything else."

"Is that all you're going to do?" Jean asked. Her voice volume was rising. "Aren't you going to take fingerprints or something? What kind of a police department is this anyway?"

Michael reached for Jean's arm, applied pressure with his touch, and silently told her with his eyes to be quiet for the time being. "Thank you, Inspector," he said. "Please keep us updated on anything you learn." He left Jean and walked the Inspector to the door.

"Jean, the police know what they're doing. We understand that you're upset, but you mustn't take it out on the people who are only trying to help you," Clark said. "Now, since there doesn't seem to be anything further I can do here, I'm going to leave Slate to go over the scene more thoroughly."

Clark turned toward the door. Suddenly, he stopped and turned back to Jean. He saw Jean's troubled expression and added with an irritated tone of voice. "Jean, do you have any thing further I can help you with?"

Jean was furious. She could feel her blood pressure rising. She had taken all the patronizing she was going to take. Putting her hands on her hips, she stared at Clark with all the contempt she felt. "Yes, now that you mention it, there are several things I want answers to. First, I want to know where Jason's suitcase is that he took with him on his trip to Romania? Second, how did he get to Bucharest?"

Her face felt hot. She looked at the men, took a deep breath and said, "Third, I want all of his personal papers, such as passport, wallet and anything else he might have kept at the Embassy. Including his medical records."

Clark looked at Jean, smiled and with a soft kind voice said, "Just what kind of papers are you looking for in particular?"

Jean snapped back. "I know he carried a big black leather briefcase. He told me he never moved anywhere without it. It held all his personal papers, such as insurance, savings accounts, bank account numbers, etc. I want that briefcase."

Clark's smile froze. He nodded and answered, "Now, is that all?"

Jean could feel her heart racing. She took a deep breath. "I have more, but I want those questions answered first."

Clark rolled his eyes and made a face. "Well," he said. "Yes, he usually drove everywhere but, this time, he went by train. He was going to fly but at the last minute he changed his mind."

Jean sighed. "Oh," she said. "And, his suitcase?"

"We've not recovered his suitcase," Clark said. "We have no idea what it looked like. We don't have any record of anyone seeing him with one. The only thing we have recovered was his wallet and passport. Also, we have not found his new gold Rolex watch or anything else he might have been carrying."

Jean snapped back, "Then, he was robbed?"

Clark shook his head. "Hardly, I said we recovered his wallet."

"But," Michael said, "you didn't say if there was any money in it."

"You're right," Clark answered. "If I remember correctly there was a stack of travelers checks and a couple hundred dollars in American money. I believe he had a credit card or two."

Jean said, "Then, it wasn't robbery?"

Clark shrugged and chuckled. "Well, I didn't say that, either."

Jean said, "What a bunch of crap? What about his briefcase and personal papers?"

"Well," Clark said. "I have no idea where his briefcase is. It might be in his office at the Embassy, I'll have to check. As soon as I know something about it or anything about his personal papers, I'll get them to you. Now, if there isn't anything else?" He turned once again to leave.

"What do you know about his car? Where did he leave it? Did he go by himself to Bucharest?" Jean said. She was standing directly behind Clark at the door, staring at him.

"Yes, I believe he went to Bucharest by himself. I think he was going to meet someone there. I don't know all the facts exactly, you might want to talk to our Deputy Chief of Mission. He was completely briefed on the accident. Weren't you told about his accident from the Department in Washington?" Clark asked. He turned and stared at Jean. His forehead was covered with a deep frown.

"Yes, I was told just what everyone thought I should hear. I was told he was dead but nothing specific. Where is his wallet and passport now?" Jean questioned.

"I believe they've been shipped to you. We sent them to Washington along with the body. Which reminds me, the packers are supposed to be here tomorrow. They're scheduled to pack tomorrow and pick up on Saturday morning. Now, that I see this mess, maybe we should ask them to wait until Monday to pack, they can pickup on Tuesday. What do you think?" Clark smiled.

Jean looked at Michael and he shook his head in agreement. "Yes, it'll be best to wait until Monday now. It'll take us a couple days to sort through this again. Thank you for coming. I'm sorry if we took you from your busy work at the Embassy."

"Ed, see you tomorrow. Call me later and tell me if you found anything else," Clark said, shutting the door quickly behind him.

"You two go ahead and do whatever you want to do," Slate said as soon as Clark left. "I want to go over the apartment. You can start cleaning up this mess here in the living room if you want. I think I've seen enough here. Is it all right, Jean, if I just wander around?"

"Yes, that's fine. Michael and I'll be here in the living room. Just help yourself. Call if you need anything."

Ed Slate walked through the rooms again, making notes and looking at the mess. He hummed as he moved. Returning to the living room, he said, "Well, that's it for today. Thanks for letting me look around. I'll call as soon as I hear anything. Enjoy the rest of your time here in Budapest."

CHAPTER EIGHTEEN

Weaver sat watching the couple wandered around the Var. His legs were stiff from sitting and he was beginning to feel hungry. Finally, he saw the couple re-enter their apartment building and decided it would be a good chance for him to grab something to eat.

He was sure they'd be in the apartment for awhile because it had started to snow. It was cold and wet outside. Taking one final look, he saw lights go on in the apartment. He grabbed his coat and headed for the elevator.

Within thirty minutes, Weaver was back in front of his window. A police car was just driving away from the apartment building.

"Damn," he said. He reached for the phone and dialed Tom Bryan, the CIA Station Chief. "What in the hell is going on over at Martin's apartment?"

"Why don't you know?" the Chief asked. "You're the one that's supposed to be watching. Where in the hell have you been? I've been trying to call you for the past half hour. Did you see whoever broke into the apartment and trashed it?"

"I've been gone about thirty minutes or so and just got back." Weaver carried the phone over to the window. "When was the apartment trashed? I must have been looking out the window on the other side. What happened?"

The Station Chief gave a deep sigh. "I only know that Michael Cleary called Ray Clark and told him that someone had gone into the apartment while they were out. Cleary said the apartment had been trashed. He thought the intruders were looking for something specific."

Weaver kept his eyes locked on the apartment windows. "Who's checking it out?"

Bryan answered, "Clark, the RSO and the Hungarian Inspector went right over to investigate. Clark was fit to be tied. He doesn't like being involved in any of this. He's going to give me a nervous breakdown if he doesn't cool it."

"Have you gotten any word back from them?"

"Hell, no man!" Bryan answered. "They're probably still there. I understand this Jean Martin is pitching a fit about Jason's death. Hopefully, Clark will keep his cool and keep her under control. If anything else happens, I could probably pull some strings and have her sent back to the states, but that's really iffy. She's a civilian."

Weaver was a bit upset with the Station Chief's attitude but decided to let it pass. Weaver doubted if the Station Chief had gotten the bureau announcement stating that he was to be the new Director of European Affairs. He smiled to himself and pushed the Chief's attitude and remarks into his memory bank.

"Can you keep me informed when you hear of anything?" Weaver wiped the frost from the window glass with his sweatshirt sleeve. He stared at the Martin apartment windows, but couldn't see how many people were walking around inside the apartment.

Under his breath, he cussed himself for not having stayed in the room. If he had used room service, maybe he would have seen more. It was a lesson he'd never forget.

Bryan said, "I'm still planning on stopping by tonight on my way home from the office. We'll have about an hour to talk before I have to be at the Romanian Embassy reception. See you then."

"Sure," Weaver answered automatically, hanging up the phone. He wondering how long it would take to get the electronic gadgets he needed from Langley.

CHAPTER NINETEEN

Jean and Michael spent the next four hours on the floor on their hands and knees. They arranged and rearranging the mess. Michael placed all the books, records, tapes and miscellaneous items either in piles or back on the shelves.

Jean went back to gathering up the things she didn't want shipped to Iowa. Once again, she started filling the green plastic garbage bags. This time, however, she took the time to divide the newspapers into piles so they could go through them later.

It was evening when they moved from the living room to the bedrooms. Garbage bags were piled up in the entrance hall. There were still rooms and closets that needed to be checked.

"So, what do you say, how about let's stopping and getting something to eat?" Jean asked, after her stomach grumbled for the third time.

"Yes, I guess we should, if you're getting hungry," Michael looked at his wrist to see what time it was.

"I put out some beef patties earlier this afternoon," Jean said. "Let's just fix ourselves a hamburger. Remember we either have to eat the canned goods or ship them. Come on, maybe we'll find something really appetizing." She reached for his arm.

"Fine by me," he said, but brushed her hand aside. "I really should call my office first. I want to check in just to stay in touch. Do you mind if I use the phone? I can always make arrangements to pay for the call later."

Jean walked toward the kitchen. "Sure go ahead. Don't worry about the cost."

"My office has just converted to a voice mail answering system, and if no one is there, I should be able to check my messages."

Jean laughed. "If it's anything like my bank, someone is always there. I'll start the meal. I guess I should also check with Martha and see what's happening in Iowa."

Jean left Michael standing by the window. She wondered how many times Jason had stood in the same spot and watching the tourists in the square below. She walked to the kitchen and heard Michael dialing.

Twenty minutes later, Michael had just placed the phone back on the cradle when Jean walked back into the room. She announced that the meal was ready.

"I'm going to connect my computer to the phone first. I need to check my e-mail," Michael said. "I'll take just a minute."

"That's fine. Do you mind if I watch you? I use e-mail at work and keep thinking I should get a computer at home."

"Not at all," Michael said. He connected the wires and explained step by step what he was doing. "That's all there is to it. It's easy, isn't it?"

"Sure is. I'll leave you to read your mail and I'll check on dinner."

She set the food on the table when she heard his footsteps. "I searched through the refrigerator and cupboards and came up with something at least that looks eatable. Enjoy!"

She had made the table look festive. It was set with china, colorful blue cloth napkins and Jason's sterling silverware. She lit a candle centerpiece and smiled.

"If it tastes as good as it looks and smell, we're in for a treat," Michael said. "Shall I see if I can find a bottle of wine somewhere?"

"I found one and already have it breathing on the counter top. You can do the pouring honors if you'd like." Jean took off her apron and put some things back in the refrigerator. "Let's use those crystal wine glasses behind you in the china closet. They're really beautiful. I know Jason wouldn't have cared."

"I remember Jason telling me about his buying trip to a crystal factory somewhere in the hills of Hungary," Michael said. "These must be the glasses he bought there."

"Yes, I'm sure they are," Jean answered. "I don't remember ever seeing them before." Her eyes grew misty. She turned her face away and reached for a tissue.

Michael looked at Jean for a moment. He reached for the wine and began pouring it without saying another word.

"Jean, do you know if Jason has a storeroom? Some place where he might have kept spare car parts, tools, a hose or such?"

"I think he did say something about a place in the basement. After dinner, let's go exploring. There are more keys on the key chain than just the two for the door. We can ask the doorman, he might know."

They ate slowly, both weary and tired from the events of the day. Finally, when the last drop of wine was gone, Jean pushed her chair back. "Time to get moving. I'll do the dishes and you start going through that pile of German newspapers. It's twice the size of the English pile. After I'm finished, we'll go explore in the basement."

Michael walked out of the kitchen. Jean heard him turn on the CD player. A Garth Brooks song filled the air.

On the way to the basement, they took their time walking down the hallway, reading the names on all the apartment doors that they passed. One door had a storage sign in English. They tried their extra keys but none fit. They worked their way down to the entrance level.

"Let's see what the doorman has to say," Jean said. She stood back and let Michael go past her.

"Do you happen to know if Jason had a storage room?" Michael asked walking up to the doorman who just happened to be standing in the middle of the lobby.

The doorman still acted uncomfortable around the couple. He shifted his weight from one leg to the other and spoke out of the corner of his mouth. "Every occupant has at least one room in the cellar. Some even have two. I believe the American Embassy has two. They're easily identified by the country flags on the doors. You should have keys for them somewhere."

Michael looked at Jean and shrugged. He looked back at the doorman. "Thank you for all of your help. You have been most kind."

Jean stepped back, made a face at Michael and turned toward the steps. She was thankful they weren't going to have to try every door in the cellar. Although the hallway was heated, the cellar was cold and damp. They walked through the dim hallway and both saw the American flags at the same time.

"See if you can find a light switch somewhere," Michael said. "We could use some light about now. I can't see the key hole."

Jean stepped backward and blindly ran her hand over the wall. She felt something brush against her leg. She bit her lip to keep from screaming. A shiver ran through her body. Running her hand back and forth, she found something round. She kept pushing and finally found a button. Light flooded the area.

"That's great," Michael called. He saw a padlock was also connected to the door. "It takes a key for the door and one for the padlock." Within seconds, he found the two that fit. Swinging the door open, he ran his hand against the inside wall.

Jean looked down at the floor and saw a black cat creeping around the corner. She was thankful it was not a rat or mouse and hurried into the room where Michael had disappeared.

The room was stuffy. It was full of empty stereo and electronic boxes, as well as suitcases and trunks. In one corner, Jason had stacked his ski equipment.

"These boxes should be taken upstairs," Michael said. "We can prepack the electronic equipment and just leave them for the packers to seal. Let's take what we can on the way up and then I'll come down and get the rest."

Jean walked further into the room. "We should also take up the suitcases and trunks. They may have something in them we need to check."

"Sure," Michael said. "The packers can get the ski equipment directly from here. Let's see what's in the other room."

Once again, Michael opened the door, reached for the light and stepped into the room. Jean walked in directly behind him. The storage room held the normal supplies for maintaining a car.

"We have car shampoo, wax, extra snow tires, chains, and a couple boxes full of odds and ends which appeared to be extra car parts. There doesn't seem to be anything unusual here." After checking through the boxes, he turned to Jean.

"Should we take all this upstairs?" Jean asked. She could imagine how heavy some of the items were.

"I think we can have the packers come down here and pack from here. Most of the things you can put directly into your garage when you get them home."

"Fine," Jean said. "There doesn't seem to be anything here that would tell us anything. Come on, let's get the boxes and get out of here. This place gives me the creeps."

CHAPTER TWENTY

Yuri Nikitin had just returned to his home after attending a diplomatic dinner at the American Ambassador's residence. He had spent the entire evening boxed in-between the American Ambassador's young blonde wife and an aging American congresswoman. Although the food was edible, Yuri was completely bored. The Ambassador's wife completely dominated the conversation throughout the entire meal. She related every move she had taken while she was a model.

Now, Yuri had a splitting headache. The bitch had completely ruined his evening with her incessant talking. The American congresswoman must have thought that more was better, because she smelled as if she had taken a bath in her cologne. Also, she had drunk too much wine, was slurring her words and kept leaning all over him and patting him on the leg.

Yuri slipped off his suit jacket. It reeked of cologne and wine. For a split second, he debated about taking a shower, but walked into his bedroom and tossed his jacket on a red velvet corner chair by his bed. He looked in the mirror and made a face. His silk white shirt had a lipstick mark on it. He took it off and threw it on the chair. His entire evening wardrobe would have to be sent to the cleaner's before it could be worn again.

Yuri had hoped the dinner would be an informative business affair, but it ended up a huge waste of his time. He had been instructed by Moscow to get the Ambassador's feelings on the Save the Planet Agreement.

Earlier in the evening, he had only a moment to speak with the American Ambassador alone. Just before he could get any response from the Ambassador, the Ambassador left to take a call from the White House.

Dressed in a long red velour robe, Yuri walked to a tall sideboard cabinet, opened the door, and took out a tall crystal decanter of Jack Daniel's. Pouring a large portion into a crystal glass, he rolled his head back and forth trying to release the evenings tensions.

He thought of Nickie and wished that he had told her to stop by. This was one of the rare times that he needed her to massage his aching shoulder muscles. For a split second, he thought of calling her, but didn't want to interrupt her evening with her family.

With closed eyes, he took several deep breaths and exhaled. He picked up the glass, swirled the dark liquor around, took a long drink and walked into the library.

The American made answering machine was announcing that he had messages. He loved hearing machines talk. It was so high tech.

He sat at the desk, pressed a button, and the recording rewound. He leaned back and listened, pushed the erase button after each call and smiled. He stretched, and pushed the surge center button for his IBM computer. All the lights lit up and his monitor screen sprung alive.

The e-mail icon was flashing. More messages. He maneuvered the mouse, clicked several times, retrieved the messages and hit the print icon. Papers rolled out of the printer.

Picking up a remote control, he pushed a button and heard the gas fireplace start. Flames shot up. The room looked alive. He sighed, he loved all of his American modern inventions.

There was a faint touch of metal against metal behind him. He turned his head slightly. Something clicked. His outdoor door opened. He felt a burst of cold air.

He put his hand on his gun and heard the sound of shoes moving across carpet. He smelled the fragrance of a woodsy musk, it filled his lungs. He held his breath, silently swooning with pleasure.

"You've come?" the Russian said.

"Well, you did give me your key and told me to come and go as I wanted," the male voice answered.

"Make yourself comfortable. Do you remember which room is which?" the Russian asked. He slipped his gun back against the side of his black leather chair and took another deep breath of the man's cologne.

"Yes, I believe so. I was in this house several times when your predecessor gave parties."

"Oh, yes, dear Viktor. Well, there have been few changes since then, other than my electronic toys," the Russian answered, moving his hand in a semi-circle. He returned to his freshly printed pages and listened to the man's footsteps.

Several minutes later, the American walked back into the room. He had changed out of his navy suit and was wearing a tight black bodysuit. "I have to be home in a couple hours. My wife thinks I'm at the British Ambassador's reception."

The Russian smiled. "I'll never tell." He turned toward the man and winked. "Have you found out anymore about Martin and any records he might have left?"

The tall American sprawled out on the large oriental rug in front of the fireplace. He reached up and took several pillows out of a large wicker basket. With precision, he spread them out in a circle, perfectly spacing them. Then, he turned toward the Russian and motioned for him with his fingers. "I'm working on it. Beavis and Butthead met with me. They should know something soon."

"Some of the ways of the old KGB were much better. Now we have to use agents that are either rejects or mercenaries," Yuri said. "But, before as a KGB officer, I never would have lived in this luxury. We still have some time. The next shipment will not leave until I give the go ahead." He put down his stack of papers and walked toward the man. "Do you need more money?"

He kicked off his slippers, and untied his robe.

"No, I gave the men more when we met this evening." The American chuckled deeply. "But, I can always use money. I still want to buy that acreage in Southern Virginia."

The Russian laughed. "Yes, I know. That's where you want to have your stud farm."

CHAPTER TWENTY-ONE

Jean yawned and glanced at the time. "I should call Martha now before it gets too late. Iowa is seven hours behind us, isn't it?"

"Yes, this time of year. It'll be mid afternoon. Martha is bound to be in her office. You go ahead and call and I'll finish looking over some more of these papers."

"Are you going to read everything, or just thumb through the pages?" Jean asked as she walked to the hallway for her purse.

Michael moved his head back and forth. "Boy, my neck's stiff. I'm just going to look through things and see what catches my eye. It'll take weeks to go over everything and analyze what Jason might have been interested in."

"Just be careful you don't miss anything that could be important," Jean said. "We can always ship them back to Iowa if we need to."

Michael laughed. "Who are either of us to say what could and couldn't be important? I'm going out to the dining room table where I can spread out in comfort." He took several papers in his hands. "Somehow I think the U.S. government will frown on shipping stacks of newspapers home in Jason's household goods."

"Maybe," Jean answered. As she dialed, she walked to the window with the cordless phone. She watched a group of tourist go into the church and suddenly, she heard loud music.

"There must be some type of concert at the church this evening," she called to Michael. She pulled the window open wide. She kept time to the rhythm as the phone rang.

"Martha Wilson, please," Jean said.

"Please, hold the line," a crisp energetic voice answered.

Jean waited patiently, now keeping time to the music with her foot. Her thoughts turned to Martha. They had gone to school together although Martha was a couple years older than Jean.

They had climbed trees, played softball, gone swimming, hunted frogs and even decided to run away from home at the same time. Over the years, they had shared the good and bad. Martha was even there for her when she broke up with her high school sweetheart and she was the first friend Martha told about her pending divorce.

"Jean, is that you?" the familiar voice asked. "Yes, Martha. I'm calling from Jason's apartment in Budapest, Hungary. You sound as if you're next door. How is everything?"

"Jean, are you alright? I've been worried to death about you, especially when I didn't hear from you right away. Jean, the airline has called here. They've been trying to get in touch with you."

"What in the world for?" Jean asked.

"It has something to do with a person who was on the same flight with you from Frankfurt to Budapest. The passenger died. I never was able to understand just what happened. The airline wants you to call WHO in Vienna. Ask to speak to a Ms. Connie Ducar. She's the person assigned to the problem. Her number is 310-3420 in Vienna. Got that?"

"Yes, I'll call in the morning."

"Now, don't forget. Otherwise, how are you?"

"I'm feeling fine. Neither Michael or I ate much on the flight. It probably didn't have anything to do with us at all."

"Well, what ever happened, it has several of the world organizations worried. How was your flight to Frankfurt?"

"I arrived at Frankfurt alright," Jean said. "Michael picked me up at the airport. I spent the night at his apartment and then the two of us flew here to Budapest."

"Do you feel better about being there?"

"Martha, you know I had to find out for myself. Things have been a bit hectic but we're fine. We're getting the household goods ready so the packers can pack Jason's things on Monday."

"Martha said, "That's good. When are you coming back?"

"I'm not sure. Things are not what they seem here. Today, we had a break in at Jason's apartment."

"Did you say break in as in robbery?" Martha gasped.

"Yes, as in attempted robbery. Nothing appears to have been stolen. Don't worry."

"Jean, what in the hell is going on?"

"What do you mean?"

Martha sighed. "First Jason dies, then you're exposed to God knows what on an airplane flight, Jason's apartment is broken into while you are in Budapest, and now to add to everything else, your house in River City has also been broken into. Your neighbor discovered it this morning and called me."

"You're kidding, my house?" Jean stuttered. Her eyes went wide. Her hands began shaking.

"Now, don't worry," Martha said. She spoke soft and slow. "It happened sometime in the last day or so. I don't believe anything was taken, but they threw papers all over, books on the floor, things generally tossed, but nothing appears to have been broken. They went through your mail. You'd received a package and it was slit open. The sides were pulled back. It looks as if they were checking what was inside."

"A package?" Jean asked. "What in the world did I get?"

"I only just glanced at it, but it looked like some kind of a rug or blanket," Martha said. "Had you ordered something?"

Jean was silent for several seconds. She couldn't remember ordering anything. It was too late after Christmas to be getting gifts. "I can't remember anything. Was it torn or broken?"

"No, I don't think so. The box was sliced and the white thing was pulled partially out."

"Oh, my heavens," Jean shouted. "I bet it was the Flokati rug I asked Jason to send."

"By darn, I think your right. Now that you mention it, it did look like one."

Jean's eyes got misty. Her voice weak. "Martha, can you check right away? If it was, please, take care of it. Did anyone check the return address on the box?"

"I asked my crew too, but I haven't seen the report. I can't tell if they took anything else or not. I looked around the rooms and they appeared to be alright, except for being a bit messy."

"I don't have anything really valuable. Did anyone hear anything?" Jean asked.

"I'm still investigating, but the neighbor said she thought she heard someone outside. She had a case of the flu and didn't get over to check your house like she should have. She also thought she heard a car start, but she wasn't positive."

Jean caught her reflection in the window and gasped. Her face was chalk white. She remembered hearing noises the night Jason called. "Martha, how was Jason's bedroom upstairs? Did they go in there?"

"I can't remember. The house was pretty well searched. Why, what is it you're not telling me?"

Jean chuckled. "You're so darn suspicious. It's just that the day after the funeral Jason's bedroom had things thrown around. At the time, I thought it was someone at the funeral that was looking for hangers."

"So, now you think it was someone searching for something of Jason's?" Martha asked. "Have you learned anything at all? Did anyone tell you why Jason died?"

"Not yet," Jean answered. "They don't really seem to know. They're all hung up on the accident theory. But, I still believe he was killed and it had to do with a case he was working on."

"What does Michael think?"

Jean shook her head and stared at the square below. "I'm not real sure."

"Well, I've sent a fingerprint crew over to your house," Martha said. Her words jerked Jean back to the present.

"Thanks, Martha," Jean whispered.

"Well, don't thank me yet. It may be hard to find anything, because you didn't have a good cleaning after the funeral. There were probably zillions of fingerprints belonging to most of River City in that house."

Jean leaned against the window and let her eyes roam back over the square outside the window. "I can't believe it. A break in there and here both. What's going to happen next?"

"That's another weird thing," Martha said. "There were no broken windows. I think they picked a lock or had a key."

Jean laughed. "Martha, you haven't been drinking have you?"

Martha's voice turned cold. "No, I think they had a key."

"Come now. I had the locks changed after my folks died. I have a key, Jason had one, and you and my neighbor have one. There are only four keys for that dead bolt."

"Jean, listen to what you just said. I bet they used Jason's key."

"Good heaven's, how! Jason's key was thousands of miles away," Jean laughed.

"Oh," Martha said. "Are you sure?"

Jean suddenly grew silent. She really had no idea where Jason's keys were. "You might be right," she whispered.

Jean hesitated for several seconds and considered telling Martha about the Porter, but decided that she was probably becoming paranoid. "Martha, you know what Jason did. Anything is possible with that agency. I'll tell the Embassy in the morning about the break in at my home in Iowa. Can I tell them to get in touch with you if they have any questions?"

"Sure. I don't know what help I can be, but I'm here for you."

"Thanks," Jean said.

"Be careful. Call collect if you get in a bind. Just keep in touch. I worry about you. Also, I saw your "significant other" last night. He said to say "Hi" if you called."

"Give him my best." Jean spun around. She heard footsteps. Michael walked into the living room. "Don't worry, Martha. I'm in good hands. Michael is here with me."

Martha said, "I wish you'd give up this idea and come back to Iowa."

"I'll be fine, don't worry."

"I'll try," Martha said. The line went dead.

Jean watched Michael get another stack of papers and walk out of the room. He glanced at her, but left without saying a word. She sat for a couple minutes and thought about what Martha had just told her.

"Do you have a minute?" she asked, walking into the dining room.

Michael was working on his computer. There were papers everywhere. He glanced up and motioned toward a chair across the table from him. “What’s wrong? You look as if you’ve just seen a ghost?”

“I want to tell you what Martha just told me.”

CHAPTER TWENTY-TWO

While Jean was talking, Dale Weaver sat in a comfortable chair, looking out his hotel window at the Martin apartment. He saw both Michael and Jean make phone calls. He heard a knock on his hotel room door.

"Come in."

"Hi, I'm Tom Bryan," the man said. He stepped into the room and pulled the door partially closed. "We talked earlier. I've brought some things I thought you might be able to use. We received word from Frankfurt that your relief is due in tomorrow."

Bryan extended his long arm behind him and closed the door. His eyes darted around the room. He had a large brown canvas bag slung over his shoulder. His dark navy suit coat was wrinkled from the weight. He took the bag off, set it on the floor and smoothed his jacket. His long slender fingers brushed at invisible fuzz.

Weaver took the bag and motioned for Bryan to take a chair. "I remember meeting you when you were back in Virginia for a Chief-of-Station Meeting. Glad to see you again. Pardon me, if I keep an eye on the apartment."

"I won't stay long. I'm on my way to a diplomatic reception." He stepped into the center of the room and glanced at a mirror. Vainly, he smoothed his thinning brown hair and plucked again at his clothing. He looked at the available empty chairs and rolled his eyes.

"Hope you brought a strong pair of binoculars? My tired old eyes aren't as good as they used to be," Weaver said. "Were you able to get a remote listening device?"

Bryan stepped toward the bed, taking care not to brush his pant legs against the fuzzy multi-colored bedspread. He opened the bag and began unpacking it. With a serious look, he said, "I've a pair of night vision binoculars. This is one of the best made. It's a Nightseeker III. The Moscow office sent it to us."

He handed it to Weaver and watched as Weaver adjusted it to fit his eyes. Bryan stepped back and rubbed his eyes, glancing once again at the mirror.

"All right," Weaver said. A smile covered his face. "It's great. I can see the Martin lady standing near the window. She's wearing a blue figured blouse and blue jeans. She looks worried about something. I can even see that she has brown eyes. What else do you have?"

Bryan pulled out another item. "I have one of the newest wireless transmitting kits. The range is up to 900 feet." He looked out the window and judged the distance between the hotel and the apartment. "I don't think you're that far away. But, you won't be able to use it until tomorrow. My men have to install the base unit first. They'll do that the first thing in the morning. It just connects to Martin's telephone connection point. I've already checked, it's in the hallway right outside of the apartment."

"I don't want anyone to know you're installing it," Weaver said. "How are you going to do it without attracting attention?"

"The Embassy repair men are always at the Embassy apartments. My men will be dressed like the normal telephone repairmen. It's not unusual to see them in the neighborhood. Don't worry, they know what they're doing."

"Let's hope so," Weaver said, without showing any emotion.

"This unit also transmits what's being said in the room. We haven't had a chance to give it a good testing, so let us know what you think."

"That could be really helpful," Weaver said. "Did you bring any portable units?"

"No, we didn't have any. I asked Frankfurt to send one with your relief. He'll probably have some other goodies with him."

"Do you have anything else?" Weaver could see the bag was almost empty.

"I brought some money. Langley tells me you might be running low."

Weaver snickered. "I can always use money. Did you bring both local currency and dollars?"

Bryan took a wallet out of his pocket. "Yes, both. I just need your signature on this paper."

Weaver took the paper, read it and signed his name. He was surprised to see that he was only signing for the money and wondered why the other items weren't on the list.

Bryan counted out a stack of bills both in Hungarian forints and United States dollars. Bryan put the signed paper in his pocket. "Here's a set of keys for the Martin apartment that I had made from GSO's master set. I wasn't sure if you'd need them, but thought you'd want to be prepared. Also, here's a Smith & Wesson 9mm semiautomatic, and a silencer." Bryan put the items on the bed in a neat row and folded the bag.

Weaver looked at the gun and said, "I really don't think I'll need this."

"Langley said you were to have it," Bryan said. "You're to pass it on to your relief." He looked around the room. "Do you plan on staying here after your relief comes?"

"For awhile. We'll wait and see. I want him to take another room. Then, we'll use this one for surveillance and the other for sleeping. It'll be better for both of us. Who's Frankfurt sending, do you know?"

"I believe he's a troubleshooter named Johnny Collins. He's just finished an assignment in Frankfurt. Hope that's alright with you?"

"Yea, Collins is great. I know him personally and would enjoy having him on this. He's very much of a professional."

"However, he's not traveling under his real name. He's in the field undercover and headquarters has decided to keep him under. His cover is Jerry Sullivan. He'll look you up when he gets to the hotel. Is there anything else I can do for you tonight?"

"Yes, next time you come bring me some American food. I'd love a burger or pizza. I've only been here a short time and I'm already tired of the rich European food. Can you do that?"

"Sure, do you want me to go get you a burger now? Burger King has a big place down at the bottom of the hill. It'll only take a few minutes."

"Boy, I'd love it. Get me the works. Sandwich, fries, shake and anything else that's typical American, that is, if you don't mind?"

"Not at all. I'll be back in a few minutes. That'll give you time to go over what I brought and if you need anything else you can tell me. I can bring it by in the morning. See you soon."

Weaver watched Bryan walk out of the room and could already taste a burger. He looked over the goodies and read the brochure about the listening device. He wished it had already been installed because he'd love to hear what was going on in the Martin apartment.

CHAPTER TWENTY-THREE

The small alarm clock buzzed. Jean rolled over and accidentally sent it flying across the room. A crashing sound filled the apartment. Instantly, she jumped out of bed, retrieved the buzzing clock and push off the alarm.

Placing the clock back on the night stand, Jean looked at the clock's hands for several seconds before she realized it was only seven. Somehow between her hours of sleep and waking she had lost all sense of where she was. She stared for several seconds, and remembered that she was in Jason's apartment.

"Are you alive in there?" came a voice from outside the door.

"Yes, I'm fine."

"It sounded like something broke," Michael said.

"That was only the alarm clock. I accidentally sent it spinning across the room."

"I thought at first you had fallen out of bed. What say I treat us to a buffet breakfast at the Hilton this morning? I was reading about it in one of Jason's magazines. The Hilton is supposed to have a daily buffet breakfast that one could kill for. Are you game?"

"Sure, give me about a half hour. I want to wash my hair first. It looks cold out. I'll have to dry it so I don't catch a cold. Why don't you fix some coffee?"

"Will do," Michael answered.

"After I shower, I'll bring the blow dryer to the living room and have a cup with you."

"Sounds great. I already took a shower so I'll wait for you. Coffee will be ready in a bit."

Jean quickly made the bed and sorted through her suitcase for something warm to wear. She had put her clothes back in the suitcase before she went to bed. She ran her hand through the suitcase and suddenly remembered the computer disc and paper she had placed there. She searched frantically.

"Oh, no," she said. She moved the suitcase to the bed and flipped it upside down. Clothes spilled out everywhere, but the disk and envelope were nowhere to be found. She shook her head and stared at the bed.

The window rattled. The strong wind caught her attention. She looked out the window and saw a bus load of tourists hurrying toward shelter. The short porter was leaning against the side of the next building. He glanced up at Jean.

She jumped back out of his view and sat on the bed. Now, she didn't know what to do. Last night, she hadn't told Michael about the two items when she told him about her phone call with Martha. She shook her head, but, now at least, she had some idea what the intruders had been searching for.

"Coffee's ready," Michael called just as Jean stepped out of the bathroom.

"I'll be right there," she answered. She didn't put the suitcase back on the dresser, but spent just a moment straightening her clothes.

By the time, Michael had the coffee settings on the coffee table, Jean bounced into the room, with a towel draped around her hair. She was dressed in blue jeans and a heavy purple sweater.

"Well, look at you this morning," she said, when she saw Michael. He was dressed in designer blue jeans and an Iowa sweatshirt. "I don't think I've ever seen you dressed so casually before."

Michael laughed. "Well, I do have an image, you know."

"Do say?" Jean teased. "Well, what do you think we should do today?"

"I thought we decided to go to the Embassy," Michael said. He had a puzzled look on his face. "You haven't forgotten have you?"

"Nope, sure haven't. I just thought you might have some more ideas. We can go to the Embassy on Monday."

"We need to tell Clark about the breakin you had in Iowa. Since today is Friday, we still have the weekend to go over the apartment. It won't take me long to bring up the rest of the boxes from the cellar and put the equipment in them." Michael stood up and walked across the length of the room. He looked around, put his hands in his pockets and jiggled his coins. "What did you have in mind?"

Jean thought for awhile. "I really don't know. We may not want to put the television set away just yet. It'll be nice to have it for the weekend. At least we can watch CNN."

Michael looked around the room, walked back to the sofa and poured Jean another cup of coffee. He moved toward the entertainment unit. "Do you have a CD player at home?"

"Yes, I do. Why do you ask?"

"I just thought that if you didn't want all of these CD's, I'd buy some of them from you. Jason and I had the same taste in music. He has many that I don't have."

"Go through and take what ever you want," Jean said. "You don't have to pay for them. That's a partial payment to you for coming with me. Just let me see what you're taking. I really don't know why, but I would like to see what all he had."

"That's fine. I'll make a pile of what I'd like and you can look through them. But, please don't feel that you're obligated to pay me for being here. I can well afford to buy them."

"No, I won't hear of it. Why don't you go through them while I finish drying my hair? If I keep holding this dryer like this, it'll take me all morning. I'm going back to the bathroom. I won't be so long that way."

Jean waited until Michael got settled in a chair with his coffee. He pulled a chair over to the stereo unit and smiled as she walked out. Jean knew he would enjoy the music more than she would. Although, she had a CD player, she rarely used it.

"Still hard at work," she asked when she walked back into the living room almost an hour later. Her hair was dry and she was ready to leave. All she needed to do was put on her coat and pick up her purse on the way out the door.

Michael had moved from the chair to the middle of the floor. He had stacks of CD's and cassettes around him. "Jason really had a super collection. I never realized how large it was."

"Glad you'll enjoy them. The ones you don't want just stick in a pile. I'll have them shipped to Iowa. Are you about ready?"

"Yes, I'm going to finish when I get back. This pile is for me and that pile is to be shipped."

The couple walked down the steps and right into the lobby. The short porter was back on duty. He looked at the couple, nodded but didn't say anything.

Jean glanced back as she stepped out the door. The porter was already on the telephone. She raised her hand to knock on the glass, but changed her mind. She wondered who was paying him to spy on them.

CHAPTER TWENTY-FOUR

Weaver had just walked to his hotel window as Michael and Jean started walking across the square toward the hotel. He watched them walk through the hotel door. Instantly, he called the Embassy.

"They're at the Hilton. I bet they're over here for breakfast," he said.

"I'm going to send my men right away," Chief of Station Bryan said. "Can you keep them out of the apartment for about an hour?"

Weaver glanced at his watch. "I don't know how, but I'll try. If they're having breakfast here, it will take them at least an hour. This place doesn't have the fastest service around."

"Do what you can," Bryan said. The phone line went dead.

Weaver thought for a moment. He decided he'd go down to the lobby and see if he could see them. Quickly, he slipped on his wire frame glasses, ran his fingers through his hair, put on his hat and coat and walked out of his room. He decided to wear his coat and hat, to give the impression that he had come in from outside. If Jean recognized him, he wanted her to think he was staying somewhere else in the city or had just arrived in Hungary.

He wasn't hungry and really didn't want anything to eat. He'd pigged out on burgers until almost midnight. All he wanted for breakfast was a cup of black coffee.

Just as Weaver stepped off the elevator, he saw Jean and Michael walk into the restaurant. Taking off his coat and holding his hat in his hand, he followed. He glanced into a mirror and ran his hand over his hair, ruffling it. He hoped it looked as if he had been outside in the winter wind.

Glancing around the room, Weaver headed for a isolated corner table, behind the couple. There he could sit with his back to a wall, and have a good view of the entire room.

Talking in German, he asked the waiter about the buffet. The waiter encouraged him to walk up and view the buffet before deciding. He decided to follow his waiter's advice.

Acting like a tourist, he walked to the buffet table, walked completely around, looking and asking questions as needed. Finally, he walked back toward his table and glanced at Jean and Michael. They had left their table and were walking toward the buffet.

He returned to his table and watched. He knew they would be eating for sometime. They were talking and choosing items from the various tables. Waving at the waiter, he ordered decaf coffee and decided to take the buffet.

Watching and waiting, he sat while Jean and Michael moved slowly among the tables. Finally, when they returned to their table, he got up and went to the buffet. They were too interested in what they were doing to notice anyone else in the room.

Weaver turned, glanced out the window and then at his watch. He saw a white van pull up and stop in front of the apartment building. Two men stepped out. They were wearing grey coveralls. One threw a roll of cable over his shoulder and the other carried a metal tool case.

He watched them walk around the corner and enter the apartment building. A smile covered his face and he motioned to the waiter for another cup of coffee. He was on his third cup when the men got back into the van. Weaver looked at his watch.

For the next fifteen minutes, he sat and pretended to be reading a copy of a USA Today that he took from an empty table. He never looked up but heard Jean's voice as she walked passed. He could smell her perfume. Shifting his eyes, he saw the couple leave the restaurant and walk toward the gift shop.

Weaver signaled for the waiter and paid. As he walked toward the exit, he passed two men sitting near the door. He recognized them immediately from the Frankfurt airport.

He felt their eyes on him. Trying to keep his eyes fixed on the door, he walked right passed them.

"American?" one of the men said.

Weaver kept walking. The man repeated, "American?"

Weaver could feel his heart jump to his throat. He knew if he ignored the two men they could cause a scene. He didn't need that. He turned and walked back to the men's table.

He put his hands on their table, looked straight at the men and said in a low whisper, "What are you two scumbags doing here?"

Both men jerked their heads backward. The Arab started to get out of his chair, but the other man held his arm forcing him to sit down.

Leonid Koniev leaned toward Weaver, smiled his toothy smile and said, "What are you doing here? We see you in Frankfurt airport and now we see you in Budapest. You are still watching the American lady and the military man. Why?"

Weaver smiled wide and answered, "You still have me mistaken for someone else." He turned to leave.

"I don't think so," the Arab said. He took Koniev's hand off of his arm. He turned his body and stared at Weaver. "Who are you anyway? Are you CIA? NSA? Or DIA? I don't think I've ever seen you around Europe before we meet in Frankfurt. I'm sure that I would have remembered your ugly face."

Weaver rolled his tongue around his teeth. He winked and said, "I'm your worse nightmare. I'm DEA working with Hungarian Drug Enforcement. You two look as if you have plenty to hide. Is there any reason I shouldn't take you down to my office now?"

The Russian chuckled. "You also have a good sense of humor. Why don't you sit down and have a cup of coffee with us? I'll buy."

The idea was tempting to Weaver. He would have loved to visited with the two men in a public place like the Hilton Hotel. There they wouldn't create a scene or disturbance.

Then, he remembered his assignment. He took a deep breath and said, "How about a rain check? I have to catch a plane and I can't take the chance of missing it."

Leonid Koniev took out his wallet. He extracted a business card. "Call us when you're back in town. Maybe we can do some business. I know something about the drug traffic that you might be interested in."

Weaver took the card carefully. He wanted to be sure that he could run fingerprint analyzes on it. "Thanks, I will. What kind of business are you two in?"

Koniev said, "You name it. We'll do it."

"Sounds interesting," Weaver said. He glanced at his watch again. "Sorry, but I have to run."

Within minutes, he was back in his room. He was smiling. He glanced at the business card and put it in a plastic bag and stuck it in his briefcase.

CHAPTER TWENTY-FIVE

Unknown to Weaver or the couple, another man was interested in the couple. He was sitting in a black van, parked in the square between the Hilton and the church. The van had been parked in the same place for the past three days.

At casual glance, the van appeared to be empty. But, the driver was in the back of the van, controlling a desk full of listening devices. The sophisticated computer system was monitoring the Martin apartment.

When the couple left for their first walk after arriving in the city, the driver of the van went into the apartment. He used a key his boss had given him. He felt guilty making a mess, but he was only following orders. He had been told to search and take any loose computer disks, small black notebooks, and briefcases he could find.

He hadn't been told what he was looking for, but he only found two items which he thought were worth taking. They both were in a suitcase in one of the bedrooms.

With the items in his coat pocket, he left through a back door and went out through the courtyard. He wanted to check the items before he turned them over to his boss. He thought if they were worth some real money, he'd offer them on the open market to the highest bidder.

As he turned the corner, he walked toward his van and stopped. His boss was standing in front of him with his hand out.

Although, the driver didn't trust his Bucharest connection, he handed over both items. Then, he was ordered to stay with the van as long as Jean Martin remained in Budapest. He was not to leave the van during the day no matter where she went.

When it was apparent she had gone to bed, he could go home. However, he was to be back in position by six in the morning. No exceptions.

He was told that others were assigned to follow her and her companion when they left the apartment. He was simply to monitor the apartment and call a certain number immediately if anything unusual happened.

The driver had no idea who was controlling the assignment, but he suspected it had to be either the Russian Mafia or one of the Arab terrorist groups, probably backed by the Iranians or Syrians. It really didn't matter to him, he was getting a nice fat paycheck.

He took another sip of Coke and flipped a dial. His heat sensing equipment told him that someone had just gone into the Martin apartment.

He knew it wasn't the lady or her companion. He glanced out the window and saw a white van. Instantly, he pulled out his cell phone and dialed a number.

"Someone else is showing interest," he said. "I think it's an American Embassy van, but the men aren't wearing Embassy workmen uniforms. They are dressed like telephone repairmen." He listened for several seconds, nodded his head and hung up.

He moved back to his equipment, made a note in his log book and turned a button. A man's whispering voice filled the van. The driver smiled when he heard the man speaking English.

There was no doubt in his mind that the American Embassy was placing listening devices in the Martin apartment. He wondered why. He sat down and twirled the apartment key on his keychain.

CHAPTER TWENTY-SIX

CIA Station Chief, Tom Bryan was sitting behind his desk in the American Embassy. He had just received word that the equipment had been safely installed. The red telephone rang.

"Yes," he said. He was holding a secure phone which was connected directly to the operation center in CIA Headquarters in Langley, Virginia.

"Where's the list," the man asked.

Bryan made a face and shrunk down in his chair. "We haven't found it yet."

"And why not?" the voice asked. "Haven't your people checked the apartment?"

"Yes, they have. Evidently, Jason had it on him. We may never know." Bryan closed his eyes and swallowed. His throat ached. He felt his forehead. Maybe, he was coming down with the flu.

"The president has a meeting next week at the UN. The Russians are saying the Americans are dragging their feet. Our teams have been in Russia all week. They reported that they couldn't find anything unusual or suspicious. We need Jason's notes. That's all there is to it."

Bryan said, "You should be yelling at whoever in headquarters told Martin that he could operate alone on this. It's not my fault, he didn't send his reports in. We talked about the locations, but he watched what he said. It was someone at Headquarters that made him paranoid."

"That's your story. He told me that he suspected someone there at the Budapest Embassy. He said someone was giving Russia information about our investigative teams. We simply told him to find out what was going on. Maybe he suspected you, that's why he didn't tell you more than he did," the agency man said.

"You guys had him suspecting everyone," Bryan answered. "I'll do what I can do. Now, that Sullivan is coming maybe he'll find something."

"He'd better, or I'll have you transferred to Albania. There just happens to be an opening." The connection broke.

Bryan put the phone down and slammed his fist against the desk top. "Shit," he said.

He stood up walked around the room and stopped in front of a mirror. With his fingers, he pushed the skin away from his eyes and forehead and rotating his fingers against the skull bone. His headache was pounding.

CHAPTER TWENTY-SEVEN

After leaving the Hilton, Jean and Michael decided to wait until Monday to see Clark. Since it wasn't snowing, they wanted to take a walk and finish exploring the castle area. They walked down Tarnok utca toward the museums, crossed Disz ter and took the pathway around the old fortress wall. The wind had died down and sun felt warm against Jean's face.

They stopped near the cable car lift above Clark Adam ter. Jean glanced around. There were so many people around her, that she felt uncomfortable.

"Let's go over by that tree and watch the car go down," she called to Michael above the voices. She needed to get away from the mob of people waiting to ride the cable car down the hill and into the main part of the city.

"It's really something, isn't it?" Michael said.

She looked around to see if anyone had moved near her. "It really is. It's how I picture Vienna but without the hill. It's truly beautiful with the Danube flowing beneath our feet. I've been trying to remember my history about Budapest. Didn't the Turks have a big influence on this city?"

"Yes, for several years. Turkish influence is displayed in the Mattias Church we saw yesterday. The Turks and every other country tried to control Hungary. Finally, the communist were able to succeed."

"I know Jason truly love it here."

"Yes, he did," Michael answered. He looked around the area and continued, "Someday, I'd like to have the time to really tour the back roads in all of the East European countries."

"Have you been to many of them?" Jean asked politely. She turned around and looked again at the crowd. She still felt as if someone were watching them.

"Yes, all but Albania. Each one has its own special charm. Hungary has Budapest, Romania has the countryside, Poland has Krakow, The Czechs have Prague and the list goes on and on."

As Michael talked, Jean turned and stared at him. She had no idea he had traveled so much. She opened her mouth to speak when a small boy ran into her. "Hey," she said. The boy pulled at her arm. She nudged him with her elbow and pulled her purse tighter to her chest.

Michael turned and saw the boy running around the corner. "Are you alright?" he asked.

"Yes. What a rude boy," Jean said.

Michael laughed. "He was trying to steal your purse but you were too quick for him. He saw that you were a tourist and thought you were easy pickings."

Jean looked surprised. "Why, that little monster. The whole time we were walking down here, I've felt as if someone was watching me. It must have been him."

"Probably was," Michael said. "Pickpocketers usually travel in groups. Come on, let's get out of here before another one comes along. Are you interested in taking a tour? I noticed they were available on the other side of Disz ter."

"Sure," Jean said. She hugged her purse and turned around to see if she could see anyone watching her.

"If I remember right, we can cut through behind the museums and walk up that road. Should take us right to the area. The schedule said the buses leave every hour on the hour. Let's go."

"I'd love to. Let's hurry and maybe we can catch the next one. It's about fifteen minutes to the hour now."

Jean was seated on the warm bus, looking out the window waiting for the rest of the tour group to get settled. Directly below her window, the boy who had tried to steal her purse was talking to an older man.

Jean was surprised and punched Michael's arm. "Look there's that boy that tried to steal my purse."

"Where?" Michael asked.

"Over there talking to that tall man in the grey overcoat and the big fuzzy hat. They seem to be arguing about something."

"The man is probably his controller and he doesn't believe the boy. Well, don't worry. You'll never see either of them again."

Jean said, "I hope so." She moved her head and caught a glimpse of another man walking toward the center of the square.

For a moment, she thought she recognized something familiar about him. She wondered if she was getting paranoid. Every where she looked she felt as if someone was watching her.

The sun was setting as Jean and Michael entered the apartment building. They had just returned from their city tour.

"Ms. Martin," the porter called. "I have an envelope for you."

Jean looked at Michael and looked confused. She walked over and took the letter. Instantly, she thought of Martha and her letter bomb warnings.

Carefully, she held the envelope and ran her finger across it, feeling for lumps. She chewed on her lower lip and cautiously, turned the envelope around with her fingers.

Michael laughed. "Boy, you're getting suspicious."

Jean handed it to Michael. "Here, you open it, big boy."

He pressed it several times and bent it in two. "See, no bombs. Here, you can open it upstairs. It's cold and I'm freezing." He nudged her with his elbow toward the steps.

As soon as Michael opened the door to the apartment, Jean threw her coat at him. She ran toward the living room, turning on lights as she went. "Be a dear and hang up my coat for me. I have to see what's in this envelope."

Michael grabbed the coat. "It's great being back in a warm place again. The bus tour was great fun, but that walk back here to the apartment chilled me clear through to my bones."

Jean heard Michael from the living room. She called, "Run your hands under warm water for a couple minutes, or take a hot shower."

Michael moaned and walked toward the kitchen. Jean heard the water running. She smelled coffee and called, "I'll take a cup."

Michael stood in the living room doorway. "Boy, you have good ears. The coffee will be ready in a minute." He walked back to the kitchen.

Jean pulled the paper out of the envelope. She glanced at the words. "Michael, come here!" Her voice was high and filled with panic.

Michael jumped, turned, slammed his hip against the kitchen counter and limped into the living room. "Good heavens, lady, what is it? You sound scared to death?" He rubbed his leg and leaned against the door frame.

"Michael, read this," she stuttered. Her hands were shaking as she held the white notepaper with two fingers.

Michael retrieved the paper and hobbled to the sofa. His eyes moved from her face to the paper. He began reading aloud.

"YOU MUST RETURN TO IOWA. YOUR LIFE IS IN DANGER. IF YOU STAY IN BUDAPEST YOU WILL SURELY BE KILLED LIKE YOUR BROTHER WAS. I MUST SEE YOU TO TALK ABOUT JASON'S DEATH. PLEASE MEET ME AT TEN TOMORROW MORNING ON VACI UTCA. I WILL BE ON THE CORNER BY THE FOLK ART SHOP NEAR MCDONALD'S. I WILL RECOGNIZE YOU."

"Holy cow! Jean, this is serious stuff. Don't you think we should call the Embassy and talk to the Security Officer or Clark. You can't go to this meeting in the morning. You could be killed?"

"What should I do?" Her eyes darted up and down his face. She rubbed her hands together.

Michael leaned back and thought for several seconds. "Actually you have no choice. You have to go. But, I'm going with you. That's all there is to it."

Jean stuck her chin out and pressed her lips together. She stared at Michael. She turned her head toward the window and said, "I'm going. You can come if you like, but remember Jason was my brother. I've told you before I'm going to do everything in my power to find out what happened to him."

"Gad, you're stubborn," Michael muttered.

"Maybe, but don't you see? This confirms what I've thought all along. Jason was murdered for something he knew. He wasn't killed on any vacation in Romania."

"But, the CIA said...?" Michael said.

"I don't care what the CIA or the State Department said. They're trying to cover something up. They are hiding the truth."

Michael handed the paper back to Jean. "Well, it's quite apparent by this note that someone knows something."

"I'll bet that jerk Clark knows, too. Now, let's have a cup of coffee and let me think about this. You can think about it too, but remember I'm the one who will finally make the decision. Understand?"

Michael didn't say a word. He left Jean and limped back to the kitchen. When he returned, Jean was standing in front of the living room window.

"Here. Have a cup of this hot coffee. It'll make you feel better."

"Thanks," she said. She took several sips. Her eyes were frozen on the statue in the middle of the square. Her stomach began to growl and she realized that she hadn't eaten since morning.

"It's getting late. I'm going to put that chicken in the oven. We can talk later."

"I'll finish with the CD's," Michael said watching her leave the room. He held the hot cup between his hands and looked down at the coffee table when Jean had laid the letter. After staring at it for several seconds, he moved to the stereo unit. He shivered, reached out and pulled a blanket off of the chair and wrapped it around him.

CHAPTER TWENTY-EIGHT

Weaver saw the couple start their walk and felt guilty sitting in his warm hotel room. He dressed and finally saw them near the cable car. Staying a safe distance behind them, he watched as they boarded the bus for the city tour.

After the bus left, he checked to see how long a tour took. He went back to his room, caught up on the news, and took a nap.

The sun was setting when he awoke. He jumped up and looked out the window. The Martin apartment was still dark.

He sighed with relief and laid back down on the bed. Suddenly, he heard a door close. He jerked up and looked around his hotel room. His door was closed and locked. No one had entered his room, but he could hear people talking.

He wondered if the people in the room next to his was having a party. Walking to the wall, he pressed his ear against it. There was no noise.

He looked out the window. Martin's apartment was ablaze with lights.

"Well, I'll be," he said aloud. Bryan's men had installed the monitoring device, and it was working perfectly. Weaver pulled his favorite chair back to the window.

He turned up the sound and popped the pull tab from a can of diet Coke. Kicking his shoes off, he put his feet up on the bed and gazed out the window. The binoculars were on the bed beside his arm.

Jean Martin was standing near the window. He took a drink of his soft drink. The rustling of paper filled his room. He reached for a pad and pencil and tried to write down the words as Michael Cleary read them aloud.

He couldn't hear all words clearly, and hoped Cleary would read it again. When he didn't, Weaver went over the message and attempted to fill in the missing words the best he could. He'd have to wait until he had time to replay the tape to get the message in its entirety.

Jean Martin could be in danger. He debated about offering his assistance, but remembered the conditions of his assignment. Hopefully, his replacement would have an answer. This was too big of a decision to make on his own. He reached for his cell phone and dialed Langley.

After hanging up the phone, he noticed the black van parked in the square by the church. He remembered seeing the van earlier. Until now, he thought it was just a delivery van. From his window, something about the van didn't look right.

Just then, he heard someone knocking. He thought the sound was coming from the Martin apartment. After the third knock, he realized the knocking was his hotel room. He glanced at his watch. Probably the maid wanting to turn down the bed and leave the customary chocolate mint on his pillow.

"Well, hello, welcome to Budapest!" Weaver said, opening the door wide. He stepped back and let his visitor into his room.

"How nice to see you again. I got in about twenty minutes ago. Did you get the message that I was bumped from the morning flight?" The man walked into the room and put his suitcase by the door.

"No, but that's alright. I figured you'd get here when you could," Weaver said. He recognized the CIA troubleshooter, Johnny Collins, immediately but hesitated calling him by name because he couldn't remember what his cover name was.

"I wanted to check in with you right away to see what you wanted me to do."

"Jerry Sullivan," Weaver blurted finally.

Sullivan laughed and shut the door behind him. He was at least ten years younger than Weaver. A powerful looking man with strong facial features, a golden tan, short brown hair with a faint hint of grey at the temples. He looked wide awake and fully prepared for a night of surveillance.

"Glad you came by as soon as you did. I'm getting too damn old for this stuff. I've just hung up with Langley. Grab something to drink from the mini-bar or that windowsill. I'll fill you in on what's going on and what your role will be."

CHAPTER TWENTY-NINE

The driver of the black van, shifted in his seat, twisted his shoulders back and forth hoping to release some of the built up tension from being restricted most of the day. His tape machine had recorded everything that went on in the Martin apartment. He hadn't seen anyone recently enter the apartment building other than residents and the watchmen. The note surprised him.

After taping what Michael had read, he dialed his contact number. "Sir, I have something you need to hear." He played the tape. "Yes, sir, I think she's in the living room. My heat sensor only shows one person there. But, there is someone in another room toward the back of the apartment."

He held the phone tight to his ear. The tape recorder was running. The sensor showed no motion.

"Yes, sir. I think they're in for the evening. I'll stay until the lights are off. Yes, I'll be back before seven."

The driver looked at his watch and said a short prayer to Allah. He prayed that the lady and man went to bed early. He wanted to get home and spend some time relaxing.

CHAPTER THIRTY

By the time, Jean got out of bed, she didn't really care who went with her to the meeting. She knew she was going. Michael had tried to convince her to contact the Security Office at the Embassy, but she was still undecided. She had coffee ready and was watching the news on CNN when Michael joined her.

"How did you sleep?" he asked. He was dressed in expensive dark brown docker pants and a paisley silk long sleeve shirt.

"Wow, look at you," Jean said. "You really look handsome."

Michael lowered his eyes and turned around. "I'm for sale," he teased.

Jean started laughing. "I just bet you are. But, I can tell when something is out of my price range."

"They say if you have to ask the price, you can't afford the item." Michael winked and helped himself to a cup of coffee. "Well, how did you sleep? Was it restful or did you have little boys chasing you and grabbing at your purse."

"Don't tease." She put on her best stern look. "I slept amazingly well, considering."

"What time do you plan on leaving for the meeting?" Michael walked to the window, set his coffee cup on the window sill and looked out.

"I thought we'd leave about nine. That gives us an hour to get downtown. We could go over to the Hilton and get a taxi, walk to the cable car, or take one of these mini-buses that stop in front."

"Well, the Vaci street is the walking street, right in the heart of the downtown area. No matter how we get downtown, we're going to have to walk a couple blocks."

"How's the weather look?" Jean asked.

Michael opened the window and stuck his head out. He pulled it shut, but didn't close it completely. "It doesn't seem as cold as yesterday. The wind's gone. The walk might do us good. Let me get a map."

"Walking sounds fine to me."

Michael spread the map out on the coffee table. "Well, it looks as if we walk across that chain bridge, cut past the Forum Hotel and down a side street we'll be on the Vaci. I'm sure we'll see McDonald signs once we get near it."

"So, do we take the cable car?"

"Sure, that's fine."

"Have you ever been down on the Vaci?" Jean asked. She had no idea what to expect.

"Yes, but it was late in the evening. Since this is Saturday morning, it will be jammed. I'm sure that's what the person planned. It'll be hard to follow someone in such a crowd. Jason and I walked it several times and it was always crowded."

Jean was troubled. "Why are there so many people on that particular street?"

"It's the place to be. Also, they have several of the big name shops there such as Levi's, McDonald's, and Estee Lauder. Just to name a few. What we need to do is wear something that both of us can easily see, just in case we get separated? What did you plan on wearing?"

"I could wear that red hat I brought with me. That should be easy for you to spot. What about you?"

"I brought a bright red wool neck scarf. I'll put it outside my coat and wrap it around my neck. You should be able to see it. Now, that we have that settled, what about something for breakfast. Would you eat an omelette if I made one?"

"Sounds great. There's some chicken from last night, maybe you can cut it up and put some in. I don't know what else you might be able to find."

"I'll check. I'll make mixed ones. A little bit of everything that's edible," Michael called as he headed for the kitchen.

"While you're doing that, I'll go through the CD's you want to take back with you. Call me if you need any help."

By nine, Jean and Michael were down in the apartment lobby. Jean motioned for Michael to wait a moment. She talked to the porter and returned holding four pieces of paper in her hand.

"The porter said the cable car doesn't start running until eleven. These are the tickets we can use for that mini-bus that stops right outside on the corner. We each have one for the trip down and back. But, we have to change to a larger bus at Disz ter where we were yesterday, walk to the front of the pastry shop and catch any one of the buses that passes. Those buses will take us down to the main part of the city by the Forum hotel. He said we can get off anywhere down there. Here's your two tickets."

"Thanks. We'd better hurry, since we're taking the bus it may take us a few minutes longer than if we were going to take a taxi. How much were the tickets?"

"I don't know. He gave them to me free. I think he feels badly about our break in and wants to repay us however he can. Let's hurry."

Within seconds, the bus arrived. Although, the bus was full, Jean felt as if Jason were sitting beside her. Twice, she turned believing something was pushing against her leg.

When she stepped off the bus, she felt a nudge against her back. It felt as if someone were pushing her forward. She turned around but there was no one there.

Michael led the way toward the Vaci. They walked quickly, moving down Jozsef Attila utca and turned onto Jozsef Attila ter. Jean kept close to the shops.

"Slow down," she called. Michael was a couple feet ahead of her. She slowed and glanced in the window of the Herend Porcelain Shop. Pausing for a moment, she looked at the famous Herend china.

Jason had sent her a Herend vase. She smiled when she saw an identical one in the window. "Michael, how much is that pink ornate vase there in the corner?"

"It's Herend. They want two hundred and fifty dollars for the small one and five hundred for the larger one."

"You must be kidding," Jean stammered. "Five hundred dollars. That's identical to the one Jason sent me for Christmas."

Michael took her arm. "Well, what can I say?"

Jean felt honored. She said, "He even sent me a book which described the history of Herend."

He patted her arm. "I'm sure he thought the money was well spent."

"Good heavens," she said. "I only sent him a blue sweater."

"I saw it, and I know that Jason loved it. I thought it was beautiful. Come on, we'll be late if you stop and look at everything." He pulled her away from the shop window.

Jean was pleased to hear that Jason loved her Christmas gift. "Michael, I can't believe I'm here. If I were really rich I'd have a twelve place Herend dinner set. It's so beautiful."

"Too feminine for my taste," Michael said, pulling her along.

"I'm coming, don't pull me." She hurried along, but continued to steal a glance at the shop windows as she went.

They passed the Estee Lauder and Levi stores. "I"m really surprised these people have this kind of money. If my money conversion is right, some of the prices are really expensive. I thought Jason said this country was still struggling."

"They are," Michael said. "But, as in all newly developing countries, some people have a lot of money, and there are those that don't have any. Although, Hungary is on the road to recovery faster than Romania and Albania, they're still behind the Czech Republic and Poland."

"These prices remind me of the stores at the Frankfurt Airport. I thought those prices were ridiculous."

"Yes, but you have a lot of the new rich here," Michael said. "They were the first to invest when the country claimed its independence. Watch the people with their cell phones. You see them everywhere, in restaurants, cars and walking on the streets. I find it amazing, because I think it's expensive to pay air time. I don't own one personally, but I have use of an office one."

Jean asked, "Is that the one I called you on from Iowa?"

Michael nodded. "Yes, I usually carry it with me. It's great when I travel. People can get in touch with me no matter where I am.

Jean laughed. "I don't even own one."

"Are they popular in Iowa?'

"Sure. Most people that I know have them for safety reasons. Such as the farmers and those who drive long distances back and forth to work. You have to remember we have pretty hard winters and a phone might help you during a storm or should one be caught at night with car trouble."

"Then, I'm surprised you don't have one," Michael said. "After all you are in charge of your father's bank, aren't you."

Jean punched him in the arm and laughed. "Only because Jason and I inherited it. There is still a lot I don't know. I still answer to the board. Maybe, someday I'll get a cell phone. I know the officers at the bank keep telling me I should have one. How much further do we have?"

"Just ahead of us," Michael said. "Cell phones are like laptop computers to many. To some they are a necessity and to others a luxury."

"Ha," Jean said. "Guess that explains it. You brought your laptop with you. Say, I saw you looking through some of the newspapers last night and making notes in your laptop. Anything I should know about?"

"Hardly," Michael answered quickly. "I was re-warding an opening statement I'm going to have to give at a trial in a month or so. Every once in a while I like to put my thoughts down. I'm getting old and I have a tendency to forget things."

"Sure, you are," Jean chuckled, taking a hold of his arm.

"Speaking of laptops," Michael said. "Where is Jason's?"

Jean stopped and looked up at Michael. She looked troubled. "I really don't know. No one has mentioned it and I haven't seen many disks, either."

Michael kept walking and then said, "The last time I talked to Jason, he said he had just bought a new anti-virus program for his computer. I don't remember seeing an manuals among all the papers."

"I didn't see any either," Jean said. "I know he lived with his computer. He kept telling me I needed to get one at my house and he could e-mail me. He hated writing letters."

"When I was here in November, he even took it on vacation with us. When he wasn't working with one of the programs, he was playing one of his relaxing games. I think it was a Gateway, wasn't it?"

"Yes, it was one of their latest. He told me he ordered it to support the Midwest. Do you know much about computers?"

Michael smiled and answered shyly, "A little bit. I'm sure between the two of us, if we find his computer, we can figure out how to operate it." He stopped and pointed. "Look on that post, there's a McDonald's sign. Look at the people, didn't I tell you this street would be packed this morning. I'm glad we both wore red."

"There's the Folk Art shop, it's on the corner across from that candy store," Jean said. She turned and pointed across the street. "Oh look, that candy store sells Baskin Robbin Ice Cream and Dunkin Donuts. We should stop and get some donuts to take back to the apartment."

Michael pulled Jean over to the side. They stood beside a bench. Several elderly people were sitting down and watching the people.

"We can," he said. "Donuts sound good. The McDonald's sign points to the right, it must be right around the corner."

Jean stepped out a few feet from Michael and looked up and down the street. All she could see was a mob of people, heads bouncing up and down. "I can't believe we'll even find the person we're suppose to meet in this mob. Who do you suppose we should be looking for, a man or woman?"

"I haven't the vaguest idea," Michael said. "Do you see anyone that looks as if they could be watching us?"

Jean stood on her tiptoes. "I can barely see anything. Shall we stand together, or do you want to separate?"

"Let's stay together," Michael said. "But, not too close."

Jean looked around for a spot where she could watch all the intersection. "How about if I stand over there on that side of the Folk Art shop by that big window and you stand behind me by that antique shop. You can still see me. Whoever wants to meet with me, might hesitate if you're with me. But when it looks as if someone is talking to me, come join us. How does that sound?"

"That's fine. See you later." Michael turned and walked passed the Folk Art store and down to the antique shop, taking his time and looking into the shop windows as he walked.

Jean stood on the corner and then walked a few steps around the corner, to get out of the chilling wind. Sheltered somewhat from the traffic, she watched the people. After standing for a few minutes, her feet began to get cold. She began stomping them on the cold cement, trying to keep warm.

CHAPTER THIRTY-ONE

"Cold out today, isn't it?" the tall woman asked. She was dressed in a full length black mink coat. "The sunshine is deceiving. It makes one believe it's warmer than it looks."

"Do I know you?" Jean said.

"No, but I know you. Shall we go for coffee, that might help. There's a nice coffee shop in the Taverna Hotel, just a few steps away."

Jean was surprised to find she was meeting a woman. In the back of her mind, she had thought it would be a man. "Are you the one that wanted a meeting with me?" Jean looking straight into the stranger's eyes.

"If your Jason's sister, yes. Come, let's not call attention to ourselves, let's walk." The woman pointed her leather gloved hand toward the street. She was wearing sunglasses and a large black hat. Her shoulder length blonde hair glistened against the sun.

Jean turned toward Michael. "I have a friend with me, let me signal him and he'll follow. Is that alright with you?"

"Is it Michael Cleary, Jason's friend from Frankfurt?" the lady asked. "I heard he was with you. Signal him to follow me." The lady began walking away from Jean and whispered, "if you trust him."

For a second, Jean thought about what the lady had said. Then, she turned and motioned for Michael to follow. She hurried behind the lady dodging around the people as she went.

On Jean's signal, Michael ran to catch up with Jean. He grabbed her arm.

Jean smiled and said, "We're going to follow her." She motioned with her head toward the lady with the fur coat.

When the lady entered the Taverna Hotel, Jean and Michael stopped for just a moment to look into the window next door. Jean pointed to a dress and Michael shook his head. They didn't say anything to each other but both looked around to see if they could see anyone that was taking special interest in them.

Jean motioned toward the hotel and said, "How about a cup of coffee, or hot wine? This looks like a good place."

Michael nodded and followed her into the lobby. After they entered, Jean saw the lady walk down the stairs on the right. They stopped and read a large menu on a stand directly in front of them.

"That looks good," Michael said, pointing to an item on the list.

"Fine, with me," Jean answered.

He took Jean's arm and went down the steps. After they entered the restaurant, Michael slipped off his coat and reached to help Jean with hers. He shook his head to the waiter and led Jean toward the lady who had already chosen a table. Within seconds, they were sitting with her.

"So tell me about yourself, how did you know my brother?" Jean asked. She was trying to decide if Jason could have had a romantic interest in an attractive woman, who appeared to be ten years older than him.

The lady had a deep, throaty laugh. "Well, we were not lovers, if that's what you wanted to know. I knew Jason strictly on a professional level. Jason attended a cocktail party that my bank gave about a year ago. We began talking and developed a personal-professional friendship. We often met and talked. I had the feeling he needed someone to talk and relax with. Sometimes, he would come to my house for dinner, but I often went to small gatherings in his apartment."

"Oh," Jean said. "I know he mentioned he'd have small dinner parties."

"Yes, he did. Two, three and sometimes up to six people," the lady answered. "He was a great cook. How do you like Jason's apartment? I found it smashing."

"I love the location," Jean said. Her eyes became misty.

"It has an unbelievable comfort in it, and the location is perfect. Of course, I couldn't afford the rent in the castle area on my salary."

"Just what do you do, Ms...?" Jean asked, realizing she had no idea what the her name was.

"My name is Marta Lenard. I'm a vice president with the Budapest Commercial Bank. Although, I speak fluent Hungarian, I'm Austrian. My parents left Hungary in 1956 during the uprising."

"So you met Jason, through the Embassy?" Michael asked.

"Yes, as I said he attended one of our cocktail parties. We give them often for clients and embassy officials. We often invite the Americans, British, German and Austrian Political and Economic officials. These countries control most of the hard currency which flows through Hungary. Oh, yes, I forgot the French. They also come. Sometimes, we spread out and invite other nations, too. Depends on who and what we are honoring at the time."

"So, you met Jason and spent time with him. Do you know anything about his death?" Jean asked. She really wasn't interested in the background of their relationship.

"Yes, as I said we talked often. We had something come up at the bank that I called Jason about. He came over that evening and we talked. Two weeks later he was dead. I was told he was on vacation in Bucharest when it happened? Do you believe that?"

"No," Jean answered quickly. "I've always said there was more to his death than a simple accident." She leaned on the table and stared at the lady's eyes. "Do you know more?"

"Maybe and maybe not. I suspect what he and I discussed might have contributed to his death." The lady looked back and forth at Michael and Jean. Her eyes grew moist.

"Why?" Michael asked. He stared at the lady.

"It's just a gut feeling," the lady answered quickly. "I feel awful thinking that I might have some way contributed to his death. I cried for days when I heard about his death."

Jean stared at the woman. "Well, what did you talk about?" Her voice quivered. She has struggling, trying to control her excitement.

"First, let's have a cup of coffee or such. This could be a long day," the lady answered, signaling for the waiter to return.

After giving drink orders, the lady insisted she treat everyone to a hot bowl of goulash soup. Jean and Michael agreed that warm soup would help fight the bitter cold when they went back outside.

"Well, let me begin from the beginning," the lady started, after the coffee was placed in front of each of them. She took a drink and said, "As I said earlier, the bank had a problem. We discovered that . . . ugh, ugh." The lady bent forward in her chair. Her coffee cup fell to the floor in a crash.

Michael jumped up and rushed to the lady's side. He placed his finger against her neck, searching for a pulse. He screamed "Someone call an ambulance."

Jean sat paralyzed. She watched the activity around her as if she were in a daze. She muttered, "No, not now."

Michael reached for Jean, and pulled her against him, to keep her from falling over. She was shaking. She felt very cold. He pushed Jean back in her chair and ran for her coat.

Quickly, he draped her coat around her. Then, she began to cry. Leaning her back in her seat, he reached for the woman's purse from the table and shoved it into Jean's coat sleeve.

Several waiters rushed toward the table. They looked at the woman. One of them said, "The ambulance will be here soon. How is she?"

Michael shook his head. "I think she's very sick."

One of the waiters stepped forward, and felt the woman's pulse. He jumped back and gasped, "This woman is dead."

CHAPTER THIRTY-TWO

Jerry Sullivan transferred his clothes to Weaver's room. Weaver had caught an early bus to the airport and promised to keep in touch from the third floor of CIA Headquarters in Langley, Virginia.

Jerry Sullivan had just stepped out of the shower, when he heard Jean and Michael talking. While he listened, he dressed and began to form a plan on how to watch the couple. He had been in Budapest several times, so knew the quickest way to the Pest side of the river.

Eating a hard breakfast roll, he watched the couple leave the apartment building. He knew exactly where they were heading. Stuffing the rest of the roll in his mouth, he grabbed his coat and headed for the elevators.

Timing was crucial. He checked the large clock in the hotel lobby. Signaling for a taxi, he pulled his overcoat around him, jumped in, and told the driver to leave him off between the Forum and Marriott hotels on Apaczai Janos utca.

It was a few minutes to ten, when he stepped from the taxi and started to weave his way through the steady stream of Saturday morning shoppers. He kept a close watch on the people he passed. Within minutes, he found himself standing on the corner in front of the State owned Folk Art shop across from the Dunkin Donut store. The street on his left lead to McDonald's.

He checked his watch. There were still a few minutes to wait. Leaning against the side of the Dunkin Donuts store, he checked the landmarks, just in case he needed to leave in a hurry.

A large clock on the side of the Levi building showed it was almost ten. He began walking back toward the corner and saw Jean Martin. She was standing directly in front of him. He recognized her instantly, both from the picture Weaver had shown him and by her red hat.

Earlier in the morning, he had heard the couple talk about what they would be wearing. With the mob of people, Sullivan was grateful the couple had decided to wear something quite obvious, it helped him keep track of them.

His eyes moved over the area. He found Michael Cleary, standing about ten foot in front of him. Cleary was wearing his red wool neck scarf.

Sullivan took a small camera from his pocket, and playing the role of a tourist, stepped back and began taking pictures. He took several of Jean Martin and Michael Cleary. Keeping his camera in front of his face, he tried to get as many different angles as possible.

As he turned, to include the fountain, his eye caught a woman dressed in a mink coat approach Martin. Watching her actions, his instincts told him this was the person who had sent the message. Walking around, he continued snapping. Several Japanese tourists gathered near him and took out their cameras.

Minutes later, Sullivan was back on the Vaci after leaving the Taverna restaurant. His face was flushed. He leaned against a building and waited for several minutes before he heard an ambulance stop in the back of the hotel near the garage area. Several policemen ran down the Vaci and enter the hotel lobby. Inching his way to the telephone booth on the corner, Sullivan dug out some small Forint change and dialed Budapest Station Chief Bryan's cell phone.

"Yes, may I help you," Bryan's voice blared into Sullivan's ear.

"It's me, Sullivan. I want to report in now because I'm not sure what or when I'll have another chance. Weaver's gone. I'm downtown on the Vaci near the Taverna Hotel. Martin and Cleary were met by a woman. I got some pictures."

"When can I get them? Who's the lady?"

"As soon as you want, and I have no idea who she is. She's dressed in a full length mink coat. Is between 35 and 40, blonde shoulder length hair, stylish dresser and nice looking. She's about 5'7' or so, maybe an inch or so taller. Looks very professional. I'd say she's a business woman or diplomat by her dress and appearance. Anyway, the three of them went to the Hotel Taverna. I followed. They all went to the coffee shop down the stairs."

"Can't you put this in a written report?"

"Sure, but you should know what happened." Sullivan's voice was sharp. He continued talking for several minutes giving Bryan a detailed report.

"Holy cow. Right there in the Taverna?" Bryan said.

"Yes," Sullivan answered. "You had better let Langley know."

"What's going on now? Where are you?" Bryan asked.

"Well for the past several minutes, I've been standing outside, across the street watching what's happening. An ambulance is just pulling away. Several policemen and women have gone into the hotel. I haven't seen either Martin or Cleary come out."

"Stay there."

"I plan to. The Vaci street is packed with shoppers, but I'll stay until I see them leave. Someone is liable to contact the Embassy." Sullivan walked closer to the phone booth. He had been standing outside it as far as the cord would allow.

"What a god awful mess this is turning into? You have no idea who the dead woman is?" Bryan asked. He sounded desperate.

"No idea what so ever. As I said, I took several pictures of her."

"I'll be right down and get the film. Where are you now?"

Sullivan took a step back out into the street. He looked up and down. "I'm on the corner of Regiposta and the Vaci, by McDonald's. If you're coming right over, I'll stay in the area. If I'm not exactly in the same spot, I'll be watching for you. In the meantime, I'll take the film out of my camera. See you soon."

Sullivan walked back toward the hotel. This time he chose a different bench on the other side of the street. He liked Jason Martin and thought about the Flokati rug he had bought in Turkey for him. He wondered if Jean had ever received it. He had mailed it a couple days before he heard that Jason had been found dead.

CHAPTER THIRTY-THREE

Inspector Olah walked down the steps of the Taverna Hotel. His eyes widen. "Oh, it's you two. So, we meet once again."

Jean Martin was still feeling queasy. She took an immediate displeasure with the Inspector's remark. "Listen here, Inspector, what ever it was your name is. Don't start in with us. We were just sitting her talking to Marta when she slumped over and died. This has nothing to do with us. Are we free to go now?" Her eyes flashed with resentment and her words were sharp and harsh.

"My, we are testy today, aren't we?" the inspector laughed. A broad smile covered his face. He motioned for Jean to sit down. "No, Ms. Martin you are not free to go. Nor is Mr. Cleary. You both are being held as suspects in this woman's death."

"Suspects?" Jean cried and then started laughing. "You must be kidding."

"Not at all. Now, as you Americans say, cool it and relax." He turned away from the couple and moved over to an officer.

Jean watched the two men talking. She looked at Michael and whispered, "What are we going to do? He can't possibly believe we killed this woman."

Michael answered, "Apparently he does think we had something to do with it. We can't do anything for the time being."

Inspector Olah walked back to the couple. He took out a notepad and said, "Now, I've been told that you both told the first officer what happened. I want you to tell me again. Although he understands English, we don't want any questions unanswered. So start from the beginning."

Jean opened her mouth.

"Oh, just a minute," the Inspector said, holding up his hand with the notepad in it. He turned to the group of policeman behind him. "I need that recording machine. Who has it?"

He looked toward the steps. A policeman ran down the steps and handed a machine to the Inspector. Then, Inspector Olah set the small tape recorder on the table directly in front of Jean.

"Now, you can start," the Inspector said, holding his notepad posed and ready. "I will stop you if I want you to give more details. Oh, by the way, we have taken the liberty of contacting the American Embassy on your behalf. We expect someone will be here soon. Now, please begin."

Jean looked at the Inspector. She was ready to tell him they would wait for the representative from the Embassy to arrive, but knowing she had nothing to hide, began talking. She purposely took her time, talking slowly as if she were talking to a child. When she came to a word she didn't think the Hungarian would know, she stopped and spelled it for the recorder.

After Jean had told her story, Michael began telling his. The Inspector remained silent. He made an occasional note but didn't interrupt either of them.

After an hour and a half, Inspector Olah stood, and turned to the policemen who were standing behind him. The entire coffee shop was empty except for several policemen and the American couple.

"Now, you're free to leave. I've been told that Mr. Slate, the Security Officer at the American Embassy, is waiting for the two of you at the top of the stairs. Would you like him to come down and talk to you now?" His eyes fixed on the couple as he spoke.

"Yes," Jean answered, "Have him come down here. We might as well stay here where it's warm. It shouldn't take but a moment to talk to him. You can give him a copy of what we just said, can't you, Inspector?"

"Yes, I'll make him a copy. We, Hungarians, always like to work closely with Embassy personnel. I will call you if we need anything further. How much longer do you plan on staying in our great country?"

"At least until Tuesday or Wednesday. My brother's household goods are being packed on Monday and picked up on Tuesday. We may leave on Wednesday or later Tuesday. I really can't say now."

“Thank you for cooperating with me. Slate will be right down.”

Michael walked to Jean and helped her up. He left her standing alone while he went to retrieve his coat from the nearby coat rack. Slate was walking down the steps.

“Morning, Michael. How’s Jean taking this?” Slate asked.

“How in the hell do you think she’s taking this? We were talking to this woman and all of a sudden she dropped over dead,” Michael answered. He glanced at Jean out of the corner of his eye.

“Yes, I’m sure I’d be a bit upset. I’ll drive you both back to the apartment.”

Michael nodded. He turned to Jean and said, “Are you ready?”

“Let’s go.” Jean started toward the steps. “Let’s get out of here.”

“My car’s parked on the side street by McDonald’s. It’s just a couple blocks. You may want to bundle up. The sun is gone and the air feels like snow. It’s quite cold. The wind has also picked up.”

Michael leaned toward Jean and whispered, “Do you have the purse?”

Jean nodded and motioned for Michael to follow Slate. “You lead and we’ll follow,” Jean said. She silently prayed that the lady hadn’t died in vain.

“Let’s go,” Slate said. “Don’t stop and talk to anyone. There may be some reporters standing around upstairs. I’m sure the police are still in the area. Stay behind me and don’t let yourselves get pushed around.”

Jean and Michael filed out directly behind Slate. Neither paid any attention to who they passed, and kept their eyes locked on one another’s backs. They heard people calling them, but they kept on walking. Finally, they were in the middle of the Vaci, and out of the range of the reporters.

When they got to the corner, Michael tugged Slate’s parka sleeve and motioned for him to stop. Michael ran into the Dunkin Donut shop and returned with a bag.

After reaching the car, Slate started the car and turned the heater on full force. Jean sat in the back cuddled in a corner. Michael sat in the front with Slate. No one had said a word since they left the hotel.

"Now, tell me what happened. We can sit here for a few minutes and let the car warm. At least here, I know the car isn't bugged. I can't say the same thing for your apartment. Who wants to start."

Michael glanced at Jean. She nodded and he started telling Slate almost word for word what he had told Inspector Olah. By the time, he finished talking the car was warm. Michael loosened his coat. Slate immediately reached for the heater control and turned the knob.

"Jean, do you have anything to add?" Slate asked.

"No. You knew didn't you, that Jason worked for the CIA?"

"Yes, I knew that," Slate admitted. "I'm finally inclined to agree with you that Jason's death was no accident. I spent a few minutes with the Hungarian police and they promised to get back to me on the cause of Ms. Lenard's death. They suspect it's some kind of poison, but not sure what kind. It was in the coffee. Did either of you drink any of the coffee?"

"No. Neither of us did," Michael said. "I held mine in my hands, mainly to get my hands warm."

"Marta was the first to take a drink. My cup was still on the table. Will the police check our cups to see if they contained poison?" Jean was still shivering and was looking at Michael as she talked.

"Yes, they'll go over everything in the lab, too. They did some checking already in the coffee shop. Do you remember seeing anyone in the room that looked suspicious or questionable? Anyone that seemed to be interested in what you three were saying or doing?" Slate turned around in his seat and watched the couple's eyes.

"No, we were too busy listening to Marta. The waiter came by a couple times. A man went by while we were waiting for our food, I guess he was going to a restroom."

"Could you identify him?" Slate asked.

"I hardly noticed him. How about you, Jean?" Michael asked.

"No, I saw the man, but couldn't tell you much about him. But, I can tell you he wasn't an American. He looked more like a Turk, with darker skin."

"When did he pass you?"

Jean said, "I saw him walk by when the waiter was taking our order for drinks."

"Was he on the way to a restroom?"

Michael rubbed his face and said, "Could have been."

Jean thought for several seconds. "Now that you mention it, I remember seeing him pass just when the waiter brought the coffee. The waiter stopped to let the man past."

"Was the waiter holding anything?"

"I think so," Jean said. She thought for a few seconds. "Yes, he was holding the tray of coffee cups."

Michael said, "I remember the waiter stopping to let the man go by before he put the dishes on the table." He stopped for a moment, frowned and then smiled. "Now that I think about it, there really was a lot of room. We sat in an area where there were no other tables around us."

Jean leaned forward on the front seat. "I think the man purposely walked near our table. His position caused the waiter to stop and let him pass before he continued. Don't you agree, Michael?"

"I can't be sure. You had a better position to see the man than I did. I do remember the waiter having to wait before he could serve us. But, you're probably right. That man could very well have had something to do with the murder. It was only a short time later when Marta fell over."

"I can hardly believe that he would put something in her cup," Jean said, sliding back on the seat.

Slate frowned. "How did he know which cup would be Marta's?"

Jean sighed. "That's a good question. Do you think he put something in all of the cups?"

Michael raised his hand. "Now, just a moment. We're only guessing. Let's leave that to the police."

Slate was silent for a couple minutes as if he were collecting his thoughts. "Now, I have a message for you direct from the Ambassador. Jean, he wants you to go back to Iowa immediately. Michael, he wants you to go back home to Frankfurt. He said Clark will take over the handling of Jason's things. He wants the two of you out of the country as soon as possible."

Jean gasped. "Can he do that?"

Michael shook his head. "Probably."

Slate said, "The Ambassador asked me to tell you that reservations have been made for the two of you, tomorrow morning on Delta's early morning flight. I've been ordered to take you to Jason's apartment and you are to stay there the rest of the day."

"I'm not going anywhere until I know what happened to Jason," Jean said. She pressed her lips together.

"The Hungarian police will post a policeman outside of your apartment door, and one in the street outside of your apartment," Slate said. He continued talking as if Jean hadn't said a word. "I'll pick you up at six in the morning for your flight? Do you have any questions?"

Michael looked at Slate and said, "What is it the Ambassador is afraid will happen to us?"

Slate wiggled in his seat and wiped the dashboard with his glove. He didn't answer.

Jean said, "Can he order us out of the country?"

Slate knew Michael was a lawyer. "Well, Michael, can he?"

Michael thought for several minutes and answered. "Technically, the Ambassador could order me from the country, because I'm a government employee. But, he couldn't order Jean to leave. He could have her passport taken away, but that's pretty far fetched."

Slate said, "I suppose I should have worded the Ambassador's request differently. I should have said the Ambassador strongly suggests you both leave the country, not orders you to leave."

Michael smiled and answered, "That's better. Tell the Ambassador we'll think about it. We'll talk about it when we get back to the apartment. Is there anything else you're not telling us?"

"No. Just be careful. Remember whoever is behind this will stop at nothing. Now, I'll drive you home. Any place you need to stop first?"

"No, but if you're driving, let's take the long way back. We took a tour yesterday, but I'm sure there's a lot we missed. Just pretend you're our tour guide and tell us about the city as you drive."

The stores were all closed so the traffic was very light. Slate drove through the narrow streets on the Pest side, winding along the trolley tracks, past Parliament and to St. Stephan's Cathedral. He stopped for a moment, while a wedding party passed in front of them.

He pointed out the government buildings, American Embassy housing and crossed the Danube on Margit bridge. On the Buda side, he crept along the narrow streets and back up to the castle area. The sun was down when he parked in front of the castle apartment.

CHAPTER THIRTY-FOUR

Jerry Sullivan stood near the corner of Vaci and Regiposta after he gave Tom Bryan the film. He watched police come and go, and watched as the television and news reporters flocked to the scene to investigate.

An older gray haired man came rushing down the street by way of McDonald's and ran into the hotel. The man, dressed in Wrangler blue jeans and wearing a parka obviously purchased from Land's End, appeared to be an American on official business.

Jerry wished Bryan had still been in the area, so he could have learned the man's identify. Within minutes, the man returned followed by Jean Martin and Michael Cleary.

Jerry smiled. His suspicions were confirmed. After the trio passed, he waited for a couple minutes to see if anyone else showed any interest. When no one appeared to be following, Jerry followed at a safe distance, until he saw the group enter a car.

Glancing at the license plate, he immediately recognized the white oval CD on the back window and the American Embassy DT-01 license plate number. Memorizing the number, he continued walking toward the Marriott Hotel. There he caught a taxi back to the Hilton.

On the ride back to the Hilton, he was nervous. He was anxious to get back to the hotel to monitor Martin's apartment. He only hoped the couple planned to stay in their apartment.

He stepped from the taxi a block from the hotel. It was very cold and there were few people on the street. With his head down, he moved his eyes from side to side.

He saw the black van parked in the square. There was steam coming off the roof of the van. He stared at the vehicle and saw a small antenna attached to the rear of the van. It was moving slowing in a circular path.

Jerry stepped to the edge of the curb. He thought he was imagining things. The antennae moved again. He walked casually toward the van. Taking his handkerchief out of his pocket, he walked to the van and tied the handkerchief around the antennae and a side view mirror. He chuckled and walked back to the hotel. Whoever was watching the Martin apartment would have to get out of the van to remove the handkerchief. He intended to be watching from his hotel room with his camera.

CHAPTER THIRTY-FIVE

It was early evening and Yuri Nikitin had just returned to his apartment. Although it was Saturday, he had spent the day working in the Communications Center at the Russian Embassy on Andrassy ut.

Several minutes earlier, he had walked out of the Embassy, caught a bus on the corner of Andrassy ut, rode two blocks, walked down to the underground, and caught a train to Deak ter. For several minutes, he stood in the square by a coffee bar and drank a cup of hot coffee.

The coffee bar was located on the same corner as the Budapest Police Department. Normally, he wouldn't have bothered stopping, but today the police station was buzzing with activity. He asked the waiter what was happening.

No one seemed to know, so Yuri drank his coffee and walked to another small coffee bar near the Kempinski Hotel on the opposite side of the station. There, he learned the details of Marta Lenard's death.

He stopped at a Julius Mendl grocery store near the Vaci, picked up some groceries and walked the rest of the way to his home on Nador ut, across from Szabadsag square and the American Embassy. After taking off his heavy grey parka, he carried the plastic bags into the kitchen.

He smiled, rubbed his smooth chin and flicked on the CD player. An Elton John tune flowed through the speakers. He walked to the kitchen, put away some of the groceries and decided to change out of his work clothes.

Within minutes, he was dressed in skin-tight Levi's, light blue knit turtle-neck long sleeve shirt and soft brown leather slippers. He was humming to the music. Walking to the refrigerator, he took out several pieces of vegetables and fruit. While, he was cleaning carrots, he heard a key click in his front door.

He wiped his hands on the towel he had tied around his slender waist. Hesitating for just a moment, he walked to his desk, took out his Smith and Wesson and walked toward the entrance hall.

"How nice to see you again," he said. He winked and nodded his head. His gun pointed directly at the door.

"It's nice to see you again," the American said. "What's with the gun? Have you started playing games without me?"

Yuri smiled and cast his eyes toward the floor. "I wish I were," he answered. "Come in."

"I'm on my way home. I thought you might be interested in something that happened today."

Yuri motioned with his hand. "Please, come let's open a bottle of Bull's Blood that I just bought. Would you like a sandwich?"

The American took off his parka and hung it on the hall tree. He wiped his damp shoes several times and followed Yuri into the kitchen. "I only have a few minutes. My wife is expecting me home for an evening meal. She thinks we should eat as a family on the weekends."

Yuri set the gun on the kitchen counter top. "Oh, yes. The little wife," Yuri said. "And, how is the wife and kiddies?" He took out two glasses and opened the wine. He handed the cork to his guest.

The American took the cork, smelled it and smiled. "They are just fine," the American answered. "I love this wine." He looked around the room. The kitchen was ultra modern with white tile, ceramic and aluminum. Everything was spotless. "Do you have a cleaning lady?"

The Russian laughed and waved his hand. "Of course, do you think I'd clean this huge barn by myself. Nickie comes in at least twice a week and when I'm entertaining, she comes more often." He handed the American a glass of wine.

The American took the glass and walked through the rooms. He went into the living room and stood with his back to the fireplace. He glanced around the room, his eyes settled on the large wicker basket full of pillows. He waited until the Russian was seated before he spoke. "Someone killed Marta Lenard today."

“Oh no! You’re joking! Where? Who? Why?” the Russian questioned. He was leaning forward in his chair, waiting for every word the American was going to say.

“I”m not sure. The facts are still confusing. She was in the Taverna Hotel restaurant talking to Jean Martin and Michael Cleary when it happened. I learned about it from the Embassy.”

The Russian leaned back, took a long drink of the wine, looked directly at the American and said, “Well, it’s not all bad. She was getting to be a pain in my side. One day last week, she even called the Russian Ambassador to ask him about the influx of hard currency that was showing up at her bank.”

The American looked confused. He hadn’t heard that. “What did the Ambassador say?”

The Russian stood, took several sips of wine and walked directly in front of the American. “I wasn’t there, but I imagine he told her that she was always putting blame on Russia. He told me that she had a similar complaint a couple years before.”

“Was it about hard currency too?” the American asked. He backed up and leaned against the fireplace mantel.

“I believe then it was something about American fifty dollar bills. I don’t remember for sure. I wasn’t here at the time and I only heard Viktor say something about it once.”

He set his wine glass down on the mantel and reached for the remote control. He pressed a button and the flame shut up out of the fireplace. His eyes moved up and down his guest’s body, but fixed on his jeans. “Are you sure you can’t stay for a while?”

The American looked at the wine, the fireplace and the pillows. He smiled, “Maybe for an hour or so.” He looked at his watch and set the glass of wine on top of the mantel.

When the American was ready to leave the apartment, the Russian asked, “Been shopping lately?”

The American shook his head.

The Russian walked to his desk, opened a drawer, spun a lock and walked back to the American. He was carrying a thick white envelope. “Have fun,” he said and patted the American on his butt.

The American smiled, winked and walked out the door.

After the American left, the Russian walked back into the living room. He opened a drawer and pulled out another remote control. After pushing several buttons, he opened the doors to his large entertainment unit. The television and the video player were running.

The Russian curled up in his oversized recliner and began watching the tape. He smiled every time the American's face appeared. Two hours later, he rewound the tape, dressed and with the tape in his parka pocket went back to the Russian Embassy. He knew it would be copied and on it's way to Moscow on the next available flight.

CHAPTER THIRTY-SIX

Shortly, after hearing the couple leave their apartment for their meeting on the Vaci, the driver of the black van called his controller. He had to use one of the pay phones inside the Hilton Hotel. His controller had warned him never to use his cell phone to call him again. They were not secure.

"They're on their way to the Vaci for their meeting. While they're gone I'm going to stretch my legs, have a coffee and take a leak. I'll be back in an hour." He hung up before his controller could voice any objections or give him additional instructions.

The controller sat in his living room after receiving the call and started to worry. Ever since he had heard about the proposed meeting, he wondered if he shouldn't be trailing along behind the girl to see who she was going to meet. Finally, unable to control himself any longer, he turned to his wife and said, "Honey, I need to run an errand for a while. I'll be back in a couple hours."

While the driver sat and drank his coffee and enjoyed a pastry at the famous Ruszworm Cafe, the Controller was driving his car toward Disz ter and the Vaci.

Some time later, when the driver, returned to his van, he saw the monitoring needles on his computerized voice equipment, going wild. He didn't realize he had been away from the van so long. Hurriedly, he put on his earphones and began to listen to the voices from the apartment.

The voices he heard were not those of the couple. Someone else was in the apartment. When the talking stopped, he removed the tapes and inserted fresh ones. The used tapes he put in an envelope and sealed it.

Looking out of the van, he saw two men walking down the street away from the apartment. He knew they weren't the ones in the apartment because they were walking too slow. He checked around the area. Nothing seemed out of place.

He stepped out of the van and walked directly to the Hilton Hotel and to a public telephone. "I have another tape for you," he said to an answering machine. "I'll drop it off at the usual place this evening." He hurried back to the van. He'd take the envelope along with any others he had by the end of the day to his drop off point. Feeling full and relieved, the driver settled back and waited. There was only silence. It was getting dark. He kept checked his equipment, making sure everything was working properly.

Finally, he heard a door open. The couple had returned. For a moment, he thought of his Controller. He had never seen the man when he wasn't wearing some type of a disguise. But, it didn't matter who the Controller was. The driver was only working for the money.

CHAPTER THIRTY-SEVEN

Although, Slate was kind enough, Jean was glad he dropped them off in front of the apartment building. She was relieved to hear he wasn't going up to Jason's apartment, because he had to get home to his family.

"Well, it's true that the police have put body guards on us," Michael said. He was standing at the window and looking out on the square. "I saw three from the time we left the car until we got into the apartment."

"Do you think the police think someone is going to attempt to kill us?" Jean asked. She walked to the other window, opened it and leaned out trying to see if she saw any more policemen hiding behind any of the trees.

"Come on, I'm sure the Hungarian officials really do care about our safety," Michael said. "Inspector Olah told me that he is afraid someone might take a shot at you."

"Well, it's a shame we'll never know what Marta was going to tell us. It had to have been important." She shut the window. A cold shiver ran through her body. Although, she was shaken by Marta Lenard's death, she felt comfortable in Jason's apartment. Now, she knew what Marta meant about the comfortable feeling of the apartment.

Michael shut his window. "How about some coffee? We can eat some of the donuts I picked up."

"Sounds fine. Do you need any help," Jean asked.

"No. You sit down and take it easy. It won't take me but a couple minutes."

Jean sat for several minutes, then stood and walked around the room. She frowned and called to Michael. "What was it I said we had to do when we got back to the apartment? I can't remember."

Michael walked out of the kitchen, and stood in the doorway. He said, "I couldn't hear you clearly. Did you just ask what I was to remind you of?"

Jean nodded.

"I'm not sure. Let me think for a moment. Oh, yes, the computer. We were going to try and find Jason's computer and any of his computer materials. You start looking for them. I'll join you as soon as I finish in the kitchen."

Jean muttered as she walked. "Well, we've pretty much gone over this room and didn't see it. I'll look under things. Jason was always putting it down and he might have slipped it under something so no one would walk on it."

Jean got down on her hands and knees, and looked under all of the living room furniture. She started at one side of the room and carefully, as if she were looking for a needle, moved around the room.

Finally, she found a box of computer disks stuck behind a row of books on the bottom book shelf. She moved closer to the shelves, and one by one, went through each of the books.

The smell of brewed coffee filled the apartment. "It's finished," Michael called.

"Great," Jean said.

Michael walked into the living room, carrying a tray with all the coffee fixings. A plate of mixed fresh donuts was stacked on top of the cups.

"Shall we let it cool a bit?" he asked. He walked over to Jean, and sat on the floor. "Now, what is it that I should be looking for?"

"Anything unusual," Jean answered, not taking her eyes off what she was doing.

He began on the other side of the book shelf going through each book as Jean was doing. They didn't say a word, but worked quickly moving each book off the shelf and checking the space.

"Look at every single piece of paper," Jean said. She noticed a small slip of paper had fallen out of a book that Michael had moved.

"You mean like this," he said. "This says that someone bought something at a grocery store. It's a receipt."

"Well, maybe not that," Jean muttered. "What's the date on the receipt?"

Michael held it up and said, "Hard to tell. But, whatever someone bought it wasn't expensive. It's for ten something or other."

"Toss it," Jean chuckled. "We've got enough stuff going back to Iowa already. I don't need scraps of papers."

"Didn't think so," Michael laughed. "Let's break for the coffee. One room neither of us has actually looked at closely is the dining room."

Jean said, "Shall we do it now?"

"Whoa, slow down, it will wait. " Michael said. "We also need to check Jason's car."

Jean's eyes flashed, "You're right. Jason often kept the computer under the passenger seat. It might still be there. I think I'll go right now and look. You go ahead and drink the coffee. I'll be right back."

"Now, just a minute. Let's both drink a cup of coffee and have something to eat. Then, we can both go to the car. Remember I want to see if my CD is there."

"Sorry, I forgot all about that CD. When did you let Jason borrow it?"

"Am not sure, I brought it with me one of the times I stopped by," Michael answered quickly.

Michael reached for Jean's hand and helped her up from the floor. She stood, wet her lips and started for the sofa.

"Darn, I forgot to call that WHO number in Vienna." She playfully slapped Michael's arm. "I thought you told me you'd remind me?"

"Don't worry," Michael said. "I'll call them from the Embassy on Monday. I'll probably get through faster than you anyway."

"You're a good friend," Jean said. "Now, pass me one of those donuts."

Jean hadn't realized how hungry she was. She looked at Michael and smiled. He was so considerate. In the midst of a crisis, he remembered a small thing like the donuts.

"Let's brainstorm for a few minutes. I want to see what we might be missing," Jean said. She leaned back and closed her eyes and started reviewing everything she knew from the moment Jason called her to the day of the funeral. Several minutes later, she said, "The other thing that was really strange was when Weaver insisted that it be a closed casket funeral. He wouldn't even let me see Jason for the last time. It would have helped me deal with his death."

"What was his reasoning?"

"He just said it was for the best. I never did get to tell Jason good-bye. In fact, I couldn't tell you for sure the casket even held Jason's body. All I have is the CIA's word." Jean looked troubled. She asked, "Michael, what if it wasn't Jason's body in that casket? What if Jason is alive somewhere?" Big tears began to roll down her face.

"Good heavens, don't even think like that." Michael jumped up and went to the kitchen for the box of tissue. He handed her the box, sat beside her on the sofa and put his arm around her. He said, "Now, enough of that. It'll only make things worse."

After taking a deep breath, Jean answered, "I'm fine. You pretty well know the rest. The funeral was a week ago today."

"Now, what do we know about Jason's last days?" Michael asked.

Jean wiped her eyes, and twisted the tissue in her hand. She told Michael what she had been told. Then, she was silent for several seconds and said, "Why would Jason be so concerned what happened at Marta's bank? Why her's specifically?"

"We'll have to ask Clark. He's the only one that might know." Michael took another donut and offered the plate to Jean. She refused a donut but took a refill on the coffee.

"Did Jason seem worried about anything when you talked to him last?" Jean asked.

Michael looked at the floor and thought. He wiped his fingers and answered, "We talked about people we knew and where our friends were. Jason was planning on going back to Iowa this summer for a reunion. I told him I thought I could make it. We planned on staying at your house and at the lake for some water skiing and fishing. Nothing exciting."

"It's useless to speculate," Jean said. "We just have to get through the weekend and then get on with things."

"I agree, all it does is upset you," Michael said. "Let's just get everything ready for the packers and get on with our lives."

"I'm for that," Jean said. She got up and started for the kitchen with some of the dirty dishes.

Michael reached for the tray, stopped and said, "I almost forgot. What did you do with Marta's purse? We should check it."

"Oh, I forgot all about it. I put it in the sleeve of my coat. Just sit, I'll get it."

Within seconds, she returned with the small black purse in her hand. Handling it carefully, as if it were fragile, she took it to the coffee table and turned it upside down, spilling the contents on the table.

"Do you think we'll have to turn this over to the Hungarian police?" she asked, making a scary face.

"We really should," Michael said. "It could be evidence. Let's see what's here first."

"Why don't you let me look through it?" Jean said. "After all you're a soldier of the court. I'm sure this is illegal."

Jean took a pencil and pushed the items from one another. They saw the usual items from a lady's purse: lipstick, comb, tissue, loose change, small billfold, assortment of keys on a key chain and several small pieces of paper.

Michael reached for a paper and Jean lightly slapped his hand. She took each piece of paper and carefully spread them out, one by one on the coffee table. Then, she opened the billfold.

Carefully, she went through every piece of paper, read it aloud, and placed it on the table. Her eyes grew misty when she held Jason's business card. She turned it over, and saw Jason had written his home telephone number on the back. She placed it on the coffee table.

Finally, everything was placed for the couple to evaluate. Silently, they studied each item. Michael got his computer and began making a list and notes on each item.

After they looked at the items thoroughly, Jean asked, "Do you see anything that is relevant?"

"Nothing jumps out at me. The business cards, you can put back in the wallet. I made a list of who's they were. The pictures seem to be friends and family. You can also put them back, as well as the money. That only leaves a couple pieces of paper. Look at this one, Jean. What do you suppose all those numbers mean?"

"I have no idea, looks like a combination or such. No. These are numbers from some type of currency bills. We do this at the bank. She was keeping a list of some type of currency. Let me look at them closer. These numbers are from United States bills."

Michael made a face. "They just look like numbers. How can you tell they're American?"

"That's my business," she snickered. "See the letter and the eight digit number and another letter. That's how the USA distinguishes their bills. My guess is that they are from one hundred dollar bills or higher. Most people wouldn't keep track of smaller amounts. But, why would she have a list of one hundred dollars numbers?"

"Would it be something that is required by the government?"

"Don't think so," Jean said. "My bank doesn't. But, then we don't deal with foreign banks very often." "So, let's say you're right and these are numbers from one hundred dollar bills, why would a Hungarian bank vice president be carrying them?"

"Maybe it's stolen?"

"Might be," Michael said. "Could be counterfeit? Or maybe it's not bills, but treasury notes, traveler's checks, bonds, or some other form of legal tender. What do you think?"

"Could be any of those. Come to think about it, I did read that the U.S. was having problems with black market groups like the Russian Mafia, drug money, or such. I think someone was traveling to Iran and was caught trying to smuggle in a suitcase of large bills. Would the CIA be involved in something like that?"

"I don't know," Michael answered. "You read about the CIA being involved in almost everything. If it did concern a former Russian country or an Arab one, I can see where the CIA would be right in the middle. Then, too, maybe the CIA was passing the money for some type of a sting operation."

"Now, that seems the most likely."

"It could be that Marta's bank got caught in the middle of it. Some business put the money in the bank and she told Jason about it."

"Do you think we should tell Slate what we suspect?"

"Let's think about it. I'm really tired. What say we take a break?" Michael began clearing away the dirty dishes.

"Leave everything until later. We'll have plenty of time later tonight. You look exhausted. Why don't you take a nap for an hour or so?"

Jean opened a living room window. She stood and looked out at the tourists milling around the statue. Suddenly, she felt exhausted. She needed to just rest for a few minutes. She stuck all of Marta's things back in the purse and took it to the bedroom with her.

CHAPTER THIRTY-EIGHT

Jerry Sullivan returned to his room in the Hilton Hotel several minutes before Jean Martin and Michael Cleary returned to Jason's apartment. It gave him time to call room service and incorporate a small tape recorder with the equipment he had already set up. All the equipment components fit into an empty VCR casing.

While he sat eating his sandwich, he tested the new recorder. The couple amazed him. They had gotten close to the truth, by using a logical approach.

He settled back in his chair and opened the latest USA TODAY. The phone rang.

"Yes," he answered with one ear still listening to the apartment and his eyes glued to the paper.

"This is Bryan. How are you?"

"I'm just fine. I've a tape for you that is most interesting. Should you be out and about tonight, you could stop and pick it up. It I'm not here, I'll leave it in an envelope at the front desk with your name. I'm sure it'll be safe."

"That good, huh? Well, we found out what killed the bank lady. It was a poison called Dayak. It's a fairly unknown poison for this part of the world."

"I think I've heard of it. Doesn't some African tree group use it?"

"Something like that. It's made from a substance that the primitive societies in Borneo use. I couldn't find out much about it other than it is deadly poisonous and the primitive people use it on the tips of their blowguns and darts. It can be made into either capsules or drops. My computer was down so I wasn't able to access the Internet to see what else I could find."

"How hard would it be to get it here in Budapest?"

"Extremely hard. The police think it was used in liquid form. That way it is the fastest action and most potent and deadly. One of the Hungarian lab men had seen it once before, otherwise we may not have known what it was.

He had worked a case back in the late 80's that some former Russian KGB assassin used it in Hungary. That was when the KGB were still very active. Interesting, isn't it?"

"Sure is. That's the Russian connection. So what do we know about this former KGB agent?"

"We're checking. We all know the KGB is no longer the KGB but the Federal Security Service and they're operating under two separate departments, the foreign and internal branches. I suspect we're looking at the foreign intelligence side. They're known as the SVR now."

"It really doesn't matter, they are still the KGB to almost everyone," Jerry said. "Has anyone talked to our Moscow office?"

"I just got off the line. They tell me that the old KGB active agents have been divided between the two organizations. That means the agents are very much alive and kicking. Still as deadly as ever."

"We both know some of the old agents took retirement and have become mercenaries for the big money? Could it be one of them?"

"You're right. Some went to the different terrorist groups such as the Abu Nidal's, PLO, Hizballah, and Hamas. Leaders like Arafat or Hussein are recruiting. It could easily be either of them. They could be anywhere."

"Doesn't sound encouraging. Did you see the ad in the Solders of Fortune for their services? I read in the New York Times that some were even acting as security consultants to various countries and big companies. It has to be for the money, I'm sure."

Jerry laughed. "And the thrill. Keep me posted. I'm going to be here unless they leave the apartment. I heard that Slate, the Security guy at the Embassy, told the couple to go home. He said the Ambassador ordered it."

Bryan answered with a soft chuckle. "I haven't heard that but it doesn't surprise me. The Ambassador doesn't like anyone that creates waves."

Sullivan said, "Well, don't buy their plane tickets yet. Remember, Cleary is an attorney. He knows just what the

Ambassador can and can't do. Jean insists she's staying at least until the packing is done. Say, did anyone check Jason's car? The couple can't seem to find Jason's laptop computer. Do you know anything about it?"

"Yes, we have it," Bryan said. "I sent it back to Langley. Jason had the files under some kind of a password and we couldn't get into it. Maybe the whiz kids in headquarters can. We'll send it to Jean when we have erased or copied everything off the hard drive, but first we want to see what's there."

"Are you going to tell her you have it?"

"Maybe, if she asks, but not until she does," Bryan said.

"She also said she was going to try and find out who Jason's CIA boss is here in Budapest. Are you going to help her?"

"How did she say she was going to find out?"

"She said she was going to call her friend, Martha someone. This Martha is the Chief of Police in River City, Iowa."

"Let Jean go through whatever channels she wants to," Bryan answered. "If she finds out who Jason's direct boss was, that's fine with me. But, I'm definitely not going to volunteer any information to her. I don't want to have to appear someday before a Congressional subcommittee over this. It's hard telling what connections she has. After all, she is the President of a bank."

"Well, she appears to be determined," Sullivan said. "I don't think she's going to just go away. Someone, at some period of time, is going to have to tell her something. Maybe, if we just told her now, she'd go back to Iowa and keep out of this."

"I'll talk to Weaver about it. This kind of a decision has to be made at the top. I'm not going to be a fall guy. Headquarters knew how explosive this problem was before Jason was killed, but they still insisted on sending him into Romania."

"Can things get dangerous?" Jerry asked.

"Sure, if she goes to Romania. Those people are spooked. Then, too, she's liable to get herself killed."

"Well, get ready. She said she's going to the Embassy on Monday and talk to the travel lady about Jason's travel arrangements. That sounds to me, like she's going to follow them."

"Jerry, Weaver and I talked about putting you into the picture. Maybe you should introduce yourself to her and tell her you're going to Romania. She might go with you, if, she thought you were going to be a friendly face."

Jerry was quiet for a few seconds. He asked, "What are we going to do with Michael?"

"We could pull some strings in Frankfurt and have him recalled. It would be easier for all concerned if we controlled the situation, rather than having an inexperienced woman control it."

Jerry sighed. "Yes, look what's happened so far. It's a shame that the bank lady was killed."

"The other side is getting restless. We may have to tame them."

Jerry said, "Let me think about it. We'll talk when you come over later this evening. Why don't you plan on coming after ten? They'll be home by then. They don't seem to be party animals."

"All right, I'll be over after ten. Let me have some time with the family and I'll be over after the kids go to bed. If you have to go out I'll go up to the room. I still have Weaver's key."

"See you then," Sullivan said. His mind was already planning some way to get close to Jean Martin.

CHAPTER THIRTY-NINE

Jean woke from her nap with a slight headache. She searched through Jason's medicine drawer for some type of a pain pill. She pushed and pulled various bottles, holding them and shaking her head.

Her fingers touched something hard taped to the bottom of the shelf. Using her fingernail, she probed the covering loose and pulled it out.

"Oh, my heaven," she shouted. "It's a gun." Her hands were shaking and she placed it carefully on the counter top.

"What's wrong?" Michael called. He ran to the bathroom and pushed the door all the way open.

Jean didn't say anything, she just pointed to the small pistol.

"Is that all?" Michael laughed. "I wondered where Jason kept it. Where did you find it?"

Jean looked shocked. "You knew he had a gun?"

He picked up the gun and spun it on his finger. "Sure, we used to joke about it."

"I didn't know that," she stuttered.

"He probably thought you'd react like this. He's had it for years, ever since he became a spook." Michael took the weapon and checked to make sure it wasn't loaded. "I'll take it if you want me to."

Jean walked out of the room. "Please, I don't want to see it again." Her headache was gone.

For several minutes, Jean stood at the living room window and looked down on the square. She could hear Michael rustling around in his bedroom.

"So, are you ready to finish checking the rooms?" She asked without looking at him. Her voice was sharp.

"Any time you say," Michael answered.

They spent the next four hours preparing Jason's apartment for packers. Jean had thought it would be relatively easy, but as she went from drawer to drawer, she was surprised to see Jason had so many things.

Finally, feeling stiffness in her arms, Jean said, "I've just about had it for today, how about you?"

"I agree, I hate to admit it but I'm getting hungry. Those donuts have worn off and I'm craving something solid."

"I forgot to tell you, I found two beautiful steaks in the freezer and took them out earlier this afternoon. There's a small table top barbecue out in the hall, but I haven't seen any charcoal. Did you?"

Michael thought for a moment. "Yes, there's some below the sink in the kitchen. Why don't you sit down and I'll bring you a glass of wine? Then, I'll get the grill going. After all, you fixed the chicken last night."

"Won't argue with that," Jean said. She didn't like cooking anyway. "I believe there's some salad fixings in the frig."

"I'll check."

"I'll start through the stack of English newspapers. Okay?"

Michael pointed to a pile of papers in the corner. He said, "I still have those to look through." He headed for the kitchen.

Jean pulled an easy chair closer to the English stack. She sighed and wished she was all finished. There were so many that she was tempted just to throw them all away without checking them.

She barely had flipped through the first paper, when Michael appeared with a glass of white wine. She said, "Thanks. This is going to take hours. Do you really think it's worth the time?"

Michael looked at the stack and back at Jean. "What do you think?" He stared at Jean with his hands on his hips and waited.

"Oh, I suppose so. But, there are so many."

"You're just tired," he said. "Once, you get into it, you won't mind doing it." He turned and went back to the kitchen.

"I don't think so," Jean muttered. She had always hated doing research. She took the glass, climbed off the chair, and made herself a nest among the papers. Starting with the paper on the top of the pile, she spread it out and began going through the items, page by page. After finishing with each newspaper, she placed it in another pile. She continued adding to the finished pile, as she progressed paper after paper.

Jean could hear Michael going back and forth from the small balcony to the kitchen. She could hear him humming as he worked. After almost an hour, she stood and stretched.

When she moved from the papers, a paper fell to the floor from the pile she hadn't checked. Instantly, her eyes caught an item someone had circled. "Bingo," she sighed.

She jumped up, almost spilling her wine, and ran to the kitchen, waving the paper in her hand. "Michael, look at this article with a circle around it."

"Did you circle it?"

"No, dummy, Jason probably did."

Jean spread the paper on top of the place settings Jason had already arranged for their meal. She stood back so Michael could read it.

"Well, this must have something to do with him. It says a Russian black market gang is operating in Hungary and Romania. They seem to be dealing in hard currency, weapons, toxic waste and almost anything illegal." He shrugged and looked at Jean, "So?"

"Don't you see? This could be the connection to Marta. But, what do we do now?"

The smell of something burning caught Michael's attention. "The steaks," he said and ran out of the room.

Jean stood and reread the long article again. She looked at the date. It was early December. Weeks before Jason died. She looked up when Michael came back into the room. He was carrying a plate of grilled meat.

"It might be just a tad over cooked, but should still be very good. I used my special seasonings." He motioned for Jean to remove the paper and take a seat.

Jean folded the paper and said, "I need to wash this newsprint off my hands first. I'll be right back."

Michael had just finished setting all the food on the table when she returned. She pulled a chair out and sat down. She was too excited to eat.

"I have a gut feeling about this," she said, helping herself.

"You're probably right, but I can't possibly imagine what we can do." Michael said. He stacked his plate full.

Jean glanced at his plate and was pleased to see that he still had an appetite. She didn't.

"I don't know, but I'm going to Romania," Jean said. She took a bite of the steak and nodded her approval.

"Jean, we can't run all over Europe." He put his fork down, rested his arms on the table and looked directly at her. He kept his eyes on her face while he continued. "You can't possibly do anything until after the household goods are packed. Personally, I think you should follow the Ambassador's advice and go back to Iowa. Let the government and police handle this. Next thing we know, you'll be on someone's hit list."

Jean laughed. "Hardly, I can't possibly be a threat to anyone. I'm a nobody."

"Yea," Michael said and continued eating. He didn't look at Jean, but concentrated on his food.

Jean waited until she saw he had his mouth full before she began talking. "You're right, we can't leave until Tuesday evening. We can probably catch a train then. There isn't any reason in the world why I can't go. Are you with me or not?"

"Did you hear anything I just said?" he said after he swallowed. His eyes were half open. "You're going to get yourself killed."

Jean laughed. "I rather doubt that. Who would want to kill someone as sweet and kind as I am?"

Michael sighed and shook his head. "I'm not sure I can get the time off. My vacation will be up the middle of next week. Aren't you going to talk to the Embassy first?"

Jean shrugged, stood up and walked out of the room. She left Michael staring after her. Within seconds, she returned with her glass of wine.

"I'm tired of being treated like a helpless female," she said, standing in the doorway. "I'll talk to the Embassy on Monday. I'm going to try and call Clark now."

"He's probably getting ready to eat dinner. Maybe you should call later."

"It's fine if he's eating. Then, he can't talk long. Where's his business card?"

Michael pointed to the entrance hall and started toward her.

She motioned for him to stay and finish his dinner. "You can put the rest of my steak in the frig. I'll eat it tomorrow." She walked out, picked up the card and went into the living room.

Holding the cordless phone, she walked to the window, looking out and dialed Clark's number. She turned slightly when she heard Michael's footsteps.

He stood in the doorway, watching and listening. She motioned for him to take a seat, but he shook his head.

Jean explained to Clark what had happened earlier in the day. She asked him all the questions she had stored in the back of her mind. As he answered, she nodded and made mental notes.

Finally, Michael walked back to the kitchen to finish his meal. He looked up when Jean entered.

"Do you want to hear what he had to say?" she asked.

He didn't say anything, but motioned toward a chair.

"Well, he doesn't seem to know where Jason's computer is but said he thought someone at the Embassy had it, and that I should contact Tom Bryan. Clark didn't say who Bryan was, but I think Bryan is CIA. He said I should go to the Embassy on Monday and talk to the travel section regarding Jason's trip to Bucharest. It seems he's all ready told them I might be stopping by."

"That's one for our side," Michael said.

Jean smiled. She was pleased Michael wasn't angry with her. "Clark said he had already heard about our activities today. Evidently, he knew Marta Lenard and was sorry to hear of her death. Clark wasn't sure what Jason could have been talking to her about, but maybe this Bryan fellow could tell us. If it has to do with the CIA, Bryan is the one."

"Well, that helps some. When are you going to call Bryan?" He leaned back in his chair and watched Jean's face.

She looked around. "Did you see any telephone list or such here when you were going through the things in the living room? Clark said we should have an Embassy employee list with their home phone numbers here somewhere?"

"I didn't see one, but I did notice a yellow page big telephone book, but it looked as if it were for the city of

Budapest. You might try in your room. Isn't there an extension phone there?"

"To tell you the truth, I don't think I've really noticed." Stopping to refill her wine glass, Jean took the glass with her and went to her bedroom. Although she had spent the past two nights in the room, she still felt as if she were invading Jason's privacy.

Her suit case was back on the bed. She stood and looked at it for several seconds. She ran to the kitchen. "Michael, someone was in the apartment while we were gone today."

"How do you know that?" he asked.

"Come, I'll show you." She took him by the hand and lead him into her bedroom. She pointed to the bed. "See, my suitcase is on the bed."

"So?" Michael questioned.

"So!" Jean said, stamping her foot. "I didn't put it there. I put it on the dresser last night and I slept in the bed. I didn't put it back on the bed when I left this morning."

"Oh, maybe you forgot you did," Michael said.

"Damn it, I know what I did. I didn't put it on the bed. Someone was here," Jean insisted. She put her hands on her hips and walked around the room. "Did you see anything else that might have been changed from the time we left until the time we got back?"

"I really wasn't looking. There was no reason to suspect someone had been here. Do we report it?" Michael asked.

Jean shrugged. "They'll think we're crazy for sure, or they'll have us out of town on the first plane. No, let's just wait and see what happens next."

"I'm going back to the kitchen. Are you going to be okay?" Michael asked.

"Yes, I came in to see about a phone list. I'll be fine. Go finish eating," Jean answered. She saw the phone list under the phone. She picked it up, but something told her to look through Jason's drawers.

Taking a big drink of wine for courage, she began pushing his clothing aside, and digging to the back of the drawers. The top drawer remained the last one to check. There was the usual boxes of cuff links, assorted coins and toilet articles. She moved some of the odd items aside. An old sock was taped to the back.

She pulled it out, took it to the bed, and shook it. A box of computer disks fell out. Her heart quickened. She opened the box and found several labeled disks.

She wished she had Jason's laptop. Michael had his, but she wasn't sure she wanted to tell Michael about her discovery. Leaving the box on the bed, she went back to the drawer.

First, she tried to take the drawer out, but it seemed to have something catching it. She felt around. There was another sock. It was stuck, she jerked on it.

This time she found a cassette case, containing six small audio cassettes. Quickly glancing at them, she could tell some had been used and some were new. She didn't remember seeing a small cassette player in the house, but thought Jason probably had one in his office. She placed the cassettes on the bed, and once more returned to the drawer.

Now, she was able to remove it. There was nothing else that caught her eye. She put the drawer back and took the two items and placed them in her suitcase under her sweaters.

Turning back toward the bed, not sure what she was doing, she pushed with all her strength against the mattress. As children, they often hid things there. The mattress slipped to the floor.

Jean gasped. A small black case was laying on top of the box springs. She climbed on the springs and grabbed the case. Sitting on the box spring, she opened it.

She felt a strange calmness and walked to the kitchen with the black case. Maybe, Michael would know what the papers meant. She certainly didn't.

CHAPTER FORTY

Jerry Sullivan had dozed off during the afternoon while listening to Jean Martin and Michael Cleary talk. The inactivity in a warm, closed room, caused his eyes to flutter and then close. Fortunately, just before he fell asleep, he had changed recording tapes.

The sound of Jean's voice talking louder than normal, brought him back to consciousness. He twisted his shoulders and rolling his head back and forth to release the tension which had built up in his neck. Lifting his aching right arm, he vowed never again to fall asleep in the chair. It was too painful. He had added extra cord to the listening device, so he could lay in bed and monitor the apartment.

Jerry bolted upright when he heard Jean talking. "What in the hell is she talking about?" he asked aloud, knowing he was the only person in the room. He wondered if something important had been discussed while he was asleep.

Quickly, he pulled his chair to the window, and listened as the couple talked about what Jean had discovered in Jason's room.

He took out his cell phone and called Bryan.

"Are you coming by?" he asked. He didn't bother identifying himself.

"Yes, if you want."

"I do," Jerry said.

"The kids are in bed. It's just a matter of minutes at this time of night if I drive down Matyo utca and turned onto Istenhegyi. I'll be there in five to ten minutes."

Jerry hung up without saying another word. He waited patiently. He flipped on CNN and got caught up on the latest world happenings. He heard a knock and glanced at his watch. It had taken Bryan almost fifteen minutes.

"Hey, come on in," Jerry said as he held the door.

"So what's new?" Bryan asked.

Jerry motioned for Bryan to take a seat. "Listen to this. This is the best so far today. Can I get you a drink? It might take sometime."

"No, thanks. I'm fine. Give me the control, I'll run through it myself. I can play the whole thing tomorrow or Monday at the office." Bryan took off his coat and shoes. He pulled the only other chair toward the bed, sat down, put his feet on the bed and settled into a comfortable position.

"Sure, you can fast forward over some of the places," Jerry said. He handed him the control and explained just how it worked.

For the next two hours, the two men sat listening to the tape. Jerry walked around the room and occasionally glanced toward Bryan. They learned about the black case which Jason had hidden between the box springs and mattress.

"Damn, I told my people to check everywhere," Bryan said. He made notes in his little black spiral notebook.

"Could something be in Jason's car?" Jerry asked.

"I hope not. But, after hearing this, I really don't know." He looked troubled. "I wonder what happened to Jason's little black address book. He used it to keep track of all his foreign contacts. He also used a small black spiral notepad which he kept notes in, just like the one I'm using."

"Did they look for it in Bucharest?"

"I can't remember. Seems someone was looking but not sure who. I'll have to check the files," Bryan said. He made another note in his notepad and handed the control to Sullivan. "Start it, while I make a couple more notes to myself."

Sullivan pressed the remote and walked toward the window. The black van was just pulling away from the curb. He turned to tell Bryan about the van, when Bryan yelled.

"Stop it there. Did she say she found some papers?"

Jerry rewound the tape, and replayed the part in question a couple times before the men were sure what it was Jean was saying. They finally decided she said she had found a list which covered a couple pages.

Bryan said, "I think she's found the list we've been looking for." He sat up on the bed.

Jerry made a face. "So?"

"You're right, it really could mean almost anything. But, I have to see it. If it's what I think it is, we have to get it and send it right away to Virginia."

"That might be easier said, than done," Jerry said.

"I think she'll give it to me, if I ask her," Bryan said. He frowned and looked at Jerry. "Don't you?"

"She doesn't know you from a load of hay. What makes you think she'll give it to you? I think you're dreaming." Jerry watched Bryan's smile disappear.

"You're right," Bryan said. "I'll have to think about this."

Jerry asked, "Did you know Jason had a gun at home?"

Bryan rolled his eyes and nodded. "It doesn't surprise me. Most of my agents have weapons at home with them. Hell, I even have one."

Being a troubleshooter for the Company, Jerry knew most of the people he dealt with had several weapons that they kept easily accessible. Jerry moved back to his chair, sat and looked at Bryan. "When did you talk to Jason last?"

"He called from the train station right before he left for Romania. He told me he'd be back with proof that an Embassy employee was working with the Russians. I told him it was ridiculous."

"So, you didn't actually send him there?"

Bryan moved his head back and forth, then rolled his eyes from side to side. "Well, I did and I didn't. Earlier in the day, he agreed to go, but after he went back to his apartment, he called and had mixed emotions about the trip. We had an argument. We talked about the Russian Mafia and their role in the various black market activities in the area. He said he was sure that they were getting inside information from someone at our Embassy. I told him he was wrong. He insisted I was only seeing the forest and not the trees. He was great for saying things that didn't make sense."

"Did he give you any idea who he suspected?"

"No," Bryan said. "He hinted it was an officer assigned to the American Embassy here in Budapest. Someone who knew how things operated and who had an insight into who did what in the government. I never took him seriously, because it would mean that one of the officers I worked with was a traitor. The thought is unbelievable. I remember asking Jason how high the officer was, and he smiled and told me to wait and see."

"What do you think now?" Jerry questioned.

"Now, I really don't know. It wouldn't be impossible. Hell, look at the traitors and spies through history. Most were people no one suspected."

"Did the agency do any checking on Jason's hunch?"

"Not to my knowledge. I did some preliminary, but decided it was ridiculous."

"And, now?" Jerry asked.

"Tomorrow I'm going to start a full blown investigation into the lives of the Embassy officers. I'm going to ask Langley to check bank accounts and pull all security clearance information. The Ambassador will have a fit if he finds out I'm doing this, so not a word to anyone. Let's approach this as if there is a traitor among us. All right?"

"Fine, with me. I don't know any of them anyway, and I sure as hell would feel better if I knew if there were someone working against us. Did Jason give you any idea if it were a man or woman?"

"I had the feeling from Jason that it was a man, but I'm not going to overlook any women officers. We'll go under the assumption that it could be anyone."

"Great. Now, how about my making contact with Jean? I need to establish a relationship with her. That's only way I'll be able to keep track of her. But, we have to do something with Michael. Can you get him recalled to Frankfurt?"

"I think we can do something. You're going to have to make Jean's acquaintance very carefully. She'll be on the lookout for anyone who can do her harm. What say we get Michael out of the picture by Tuesday morning? Then, we can stage something with Jean, you can protect her, invite her to dinner and casually drop the news that you're taking the train to Bucharest Tuesday night."

"I don't want to waste time. The sooner the better."

"This will have to be planned carefully. She'll smell it, if it doesn't appear natural."

"They're both going to the Embassy Monday to talk to the travel section," Jerry said. "I have an idea. I'll be there. We stage a purse snatching, I'll get her purse back and be the hero."

"That's fine, but how do you get Michael out of the scene?" Bryan said. "He'll see right through that."

"He'll have to be eliminated," Jerry said without blinking.

"Good heavens, man. We're not going to kill the guy."

"No, just leave it to me. The less you know the better off you'll be," Jerry said. "I've done it lots of times. He'll never know what hit him. It's painless. How about that?"

"Don't kill him. It will have to be bad enough that he'll have to go back to Frankfurt for medical attention."

"Shouldn't be a problem. I have a couple ideas we can use," Jerry said.

Bryan scratched his head. His eyes sparked. "I can probably help find something that will work. Getting him to go back to Frankfurt will be a given, considering he can't be seen by a foreign doctor. The military have strict regulations on that. I'm tired and by morning it may sound stupid. Let's think about it over night. I'll go along with almost anything within reason."

Jerry walked Bryan to the door, and secured all the locks before he went to bed. Checking once again, that his machine was functioning correctly, he turned off the lights and was asleep within seconds of hitting the pillows.

CHAPTER FORTY-ONE

On Monday morning, Michael made a quick trip to the corner grocery for fresh bread. They had time for a leisurely breakfast. They were not expected at the American Embassy on Szabadsag ter until after ten.

"What shall we have this evening," Jean laughed. "Do you want to take pot luck on some of those canned goods over there that don't have any labels?"

Michael shook his head. "Give them to the housekeeper or porter. Let's have the pork chops tonight and if we don't eat the chicken breasts, we can give them away."

"Well the housekeeper is going to be thrilled with that pile over there." Jean looked at her watch. "She's due any minute. She called while you were showering. I asked her to stay with the packers today while we're at the Embassy."

"That's great. I wasn't too excited about going to the Embassy and leaving the packers here by themselves."

"How long will it take to get the household shipment to Iowa?" Jean asked.

"Well, if it runs true to form, it could take three to six months. You aren't in any hurry for anything are you?"

"No, I just wondered. Actually that's a good time. It'll be spring or summer and easier to unload. Want some more coffee?"

"No, I think I'll start clearing everything off and stack the dishes. While I'm doing this, why don't you take a trash bag and empty all the garbage cans. Then, I'll take the trash out."

Jean stood and brush the hard roll crumbs off her slacks. She loved the hard rolls but they were really messy. "We've still an hour before the packers are due. Can you think of anything we need the cleaning lady to do until the packers arrive? You've more experience along these lines."

"I guess she could clean out the medicine cabinet. She can toss most of the stuff in the trash. I don't think you want to drag it all the way to the states."

Jean started out of the room, turned and asked. "Where's that box of things we brought back from the car last night?"

"It's in the hallway. I went through it after you went to bed and tossed what I know you aren't allowed to ship. It's ready to go. The papers are on the hall table. You might want to put them in your suitcase."

"What about the car papers? Will I need them to get the car into the states?"

"More than likely. The car manual and all the papers relating to it are all there." He turned and wiped his hands on a towel. "Have you decided what you're going to do with Jason's car?"

"No, I haven't. Probably end up selling it. A Mercedes is just too expensive for me to maintain. Besides, I have my Ford. His car is way too flashy. Besides, I've always believed in buying American."

Michael chuckled. "Actually, Jason wanted one that was sturdy, reliable, easy to maintain and speedy. I guess that's why he went with the Mercedes."

"Yes, he loved his speed," Jean sighed.

"Don't forget to put that pile of papers that's on the coffee table in your suitcase. There's the car insurance policy and maintenance records. You should contact the insurance company and see what's covered."

"Did you have a chance to read any of it?" Jean asked. "You know how I hate legal papers."

"I glanced over it and the policy is in effect until next October. From what I read, the policy covers the car in transit, which means marine insurance. But in case of death, I'm not really sure. You can call them later today or when you return to the states."

"Thanks. See that pile of papers by the waste basket. That's the English pile, and they can be tossed out. Where are the other piles?"

"I put the German stack in the trash already. The Hungarian stack, which is only a couple, I thought we'd take with us this morning."

"I'd best get busy. Time's flying." Jean left Michael with his hands in soap suds. She made a mental list as she walked, trying not to forget anything that needed to be done before the packers arrive.

"Michael, are you about ready?" Jean called. She glanced again at the clock on the wall. She had just finishing talking to the cleaning lady.

The door bell rang.

"It's probably the packers," Jean said. "I'll take them around."

Jean opened the door and two men walked in. They said they were from the moving company and showed identification cards. She walked them around the apartment and then, turned them over to the housekeeper.

"They're here," Jean said. She was standing in the hallway waiting for Michael but something didn't feel right.

"Yes, just need to grab my coat," Michael answered. He set down a bag that held the newspapers. He looked at Jean. "What's wrong?"

She shook her head and turned to the housekeeper. "Now, don't let the packers near our suitcases," she said. "Also, don't forget to take the batteries out of all the remote controls and wall clocks." She turned and followed Michael down the hallway.

Jean buttoned her coat and patted her chest. She was carrying the black case, computer disks and cassettes. She knew the one place they would be safe was on her.

The short porter was standing by the entrance door. Jean nodded and followed Michael out the door. She stopped, adjusted her gloves and glanced through the window at the porter. He was holding the telephone. She smiled.

CHAPTER FORTY-TWO

"Can you tell me who knew about Jason's travel arrangements?" Jean asked the tall Hungarian lady. They were sitting in the travel office of the American Embassy.

"Actually, Mr. Martin never contacted me personally. They were always made through his secretary. I was told that Mr. Martin picked up his train tickets to Bucharest at the station the night he left. His office made his return plane arrangements." The lady frowned. "I've already told Mr. Clark all of this."

"Yes, I know," Jean said. "We appreciate your helping us. Now, let me get this clear. The secretary that worked for both Jason and Mr. Clark made all of Jason's arrangements for his trip to Bucharest and return. Is that correct?"

"I'm not positive, but that is the way he usually worked."

"Did she also make his arrangements to Greece?" Jean asked.

"No. Actually, Mr. Martin's trip to Greece had been postponed. Mr. Martin made those arrangements himself. He was originally scheduled to go to Greece on vacation but called and said he would have to cancel them. I never knew why."

"Did Jason bring his tickets back to you?"

"No, his secretary did. The tickets are still here, I was going to ask you what I should do with them. Since Mr. Martin paid for the trip out of his personal account, I can't do anything with them until someone authorizes it."

"Can you turn them in for cash?" Michael asked.

"I can try, but it would be best to turn them in for credit. It is less confusing."

"But, since Jason is dead, I'm sure the tickets could be cashed in and the money given to Jean," Michael said.

"As I said, I can try," the lady said. She looked at Jean and asked, "Shall I send the cash to you?"

"If you have a problem, please just give it to Mr. Clark. I'll ask him to send it to me." Jean leaned on the counter and thought for several seconds. "Do you have any record of his travel arrangements to Romania?"

"It is just by chance that I do have. Mr. Martin's tickets were made with a government credit card. They sent the bill to me since I made all the arrangements and I kept a copy for my files. I'll run you off a copy. You'll see that he was leaving by train and had an open ticket for his return."

"I didn't know you could get a plane ticket with an open date like that," Jean questioned.

"Yes, we do it often. The Officers may go by rental car, train or such and they call and I confirm their flights back."

"Thanks," Jean said. She twisted her hands together. Finally, she felt she was getting somewhere.

"I have never seen the airplane tickets for his return flight. The Embassy had to end up paying for them because they were never canceled. Have you seen them?" The lady typed a few things into a computer and started printing the schedule.

Jean glanced at Michael and watched him shake his head. "No, we've never seen them."

"Here's the report. Would you like to look at it a minute? I'll be right back." The lady handed the paper to Jean and walked out of the room. She returned almost instantly and asked if Jean had any more questions.

"I'd like a print out of Jason's trip to Greece, if it's no trouble."

"No problem at all. Mr. Clark said I should help you with whatever questions you have. Ms. Martin, I am so sorry about Mr. Martin. We all liked him and were very sad to hear of his accident. He was always so friendly and always had time to say hello to everyone. He was a very nice man."

The lady spoke slowly and compassionately. Tears where in her eyes. She handed Jean the printout, shook her hand and waited for the couple to leave the room.

Jean smiled. "Thanks. He'll be greatly missed."

Michael reached for Jean's arm and turned to thank the woman. He escorted Jean out of the office. Jean clutched the printouts in her hands.

Jean led the way down the Embassy hallway toward the Marine Desk. She heard footsteps and turned. Ray Clark was hurrying to catch up with them. He was dressed in a dark suit and white shirt. Jean turned away to keep from smiling.

"Did you find out everything you wanted to know?" Clark asked.

"Actually not. Do you have a moment?" Jean asked, still holding the printouts.

"Sure, let's go downstairs to the Embassy snack area. We can sit and talk. You can have something to eat if you'd like. It's not quite lunch time, but the Neals are there. I'm sure that Linda can find a sandwich or such."

"I'm not really hungry," Jean said. "But, we'll join you."

"Now, what is it you want to know?" Clark asked as soon as the trio was seated. He turned to Linda Neal and ordered a ham and cheese sandwich and three soft drinks.

"I just found out that the Political Secretary made Jason's travel arrangements for this trip. You gave me the impression that he had made them himself. If things operate in an Embassy as they do in the business world, and if the Political Secretary made his reservations, then he was on official business. Am I right?" Jean placed her elbows on the table and stared directly at Clark.

"Well, in a way yes, he was." Clark answered after a long silence.

"Official business. All the reports issued by the government said he was on vacation. What gives?" Jean demanded. She was struggling to keep her voice level down. Michael was shaking his head at her. She frowned and took a deep breath.

"Well, we believe it was an accident, and it is less complicated, within the diplomatic community, if we stated he was on vacation," Clark said. His face had turned bright red. "Until it's proven differently, Jason Martin's death will be listed as an accident. However, the Bucharest Embassy is still doing an investigation."

"So, who can tell me truthfully why Jason was in Romania, can you?" Jean asked.

"No. Not officially. I only knew he was going." Clark answered looking around the room to see if anyone was sitting near enough to them to overhead what he was saying.

"Well, who can?" Jean demanded, her voice level went higher with each word.

Clark began to sweat. It was obvious that he knew exactly who was behind Jason's trip to Romania but didn't want to be the one to say. He glanced up and smiled. Tom Bryan had entered the area.

"Tom, come join us," Clark called. "I want you to meet some people."

"Well, who do we have here? Welcome to Budapest." Bryan smiled, extending his arm.

Clark made the introductions and told Bryan a bit about his two guests. He also told Jean and Michael a bit about Bryan.

"Nice to meet you both," Bryan said politely. "Ms. Martin, I'm so sorry to hear about Jason. You cannot image how much we'll miss him. Captain Cleary, it's nice to meet you. Please accept my condolences. Now, if you will excuse me, I have an appointment in the Consulate." He turned and left the room as suddenly as he had appeared.

Jean watched Bryan leave. She glanced back and forth between Clark and Bryan. They looked like they had bought their suits in the same store. Even their ties were similar. She wondered if government employees were given discount shopping somewhere. The thought made her chuckle.

She said, "What does it mean that he's a political agent and assigned to this Embassy as a special assistant?"

Clark looked at Jean and took a drink. He turned and stared at Bryan's back, and checked his watch. He swallowed the rest of his soft drink in a long gulp. "Sorry, I have to be running. I have a meeting with the Ambassador and I'm almost late. Can you find your way out?"

By the time, Jean and Michael left the Embassy, Jean was totally confused and irritated. "What was that all about?" she asked Michael.

"Let's sit down here and watch the world go by," Michael answered. He pointed to an empty bench in the park in front of the Embassy. When they were seated, he asked, "What do you mean?"

Jean was silent for a few minutes. She looked at Michael, shook her head and said, "Well, do we know everything now?"

"Hardly," Michael said and nudged her arm. "Other than seeing his itinerary, we don't know squat."

"Come on, let's get out of here. This place gives me a creepy feeling."

They started across the park. Jean shivered, she felt she was being watched. She turned a couple times, to see if anyone was following them.

Suddenly, out of nowhere, a tall, dirty man pushed against her back. For an instant, she was confused. Something tugged at her arm. She looked down and saw the man with a long blade knife. He was cutting the strap to her purse.

"Michael, help me!" she cried. She grabbed for her purse, but the tall man shoved against her. She fell to the ground.

Michael turned and saw Jean as she fell. The tall man was running away, and he was clutching Jean's purse. He ran straight across the park, toward the Embassy.

"Are you all right?" Michael asked, helping Jean to her feet.

"I think so," she muttered, brushing her coat and slacks off. "My slacks are all muddy. He has my purse."

People started yelling. There was a loud commotion.

"Look someone's chasing the thief," Michael said.

"I hope he gets my purse back. I have everything in there," Jean sobbed.

"Don't worry," Michael said. "Let's walk toward the corner. We might need to identify the thief."

Jean froze. She stared at Michael and finally said, "It happened so fast, I couldn't tell you anything about him. He was dirty, that's all I know."

Within seconds, A tall middle-aged man, wearing a dark blue parka, began walking toward the couple. He was carrying Jean's purse.

"Sorry, about this," the man said, holding the purse out for Jean.

Almost in tears, Jean answered, "Thank you. My purse has my passport and money in it. I was holding it close to my body but I never thought anyone would come up and cut the strap. Thank you, again."

Michael also muttered a thanks to the stranger. Brushing Jean's coat off, he stepped back and shook the stranger's hand.

"Well, you don't look any worse for the incident. By the way, my name is Jerry Sullivan. I was just coming out of the American Consulate door when I saw this dirty man running past. As he ran, I saw he was carrying a purse and I ran after him. Lucky, I guess. Anyway, here we are."

"Thank you, so very much. I'm Jean Martin and this is Captain Michael Cleary. We also just came from the Embassy. That man must have been waiting for an American to come out of the building." Jean said. "I'm only thankful that nothing was taken. So you're an American, Mr. Sullivan?"

"Yes, I'm a business man doing some work here in Hungary for a computer company. I was just checking with the Americans on what I have to do to go to Bucharest. Don't want any problems at the border. Before I left Washington, I was told that the Romanians had relaxed their visa requirements and Americans no longer needed visas. I just wanted to be sure. How about you?"

"Well, our story is a bit more complicated," Jean answered, feeling Michael's arm on hers. "Why don't you join us for a glass of wine? We'd like to thank you for your help."

"Yes, please do," Michael added, politely. His face showed no expression.

"That's great," Sullivan said. "I could use a bowl of soup or something. This morning I had so many things to do, I didn't have time for breakfast. I'm staying at the Hilton. How about you, where are the two of you staying?"

"Actually, we're staying in a private apartment, just across the street from the Hilton. What a coincidence," Jean said. She followed Michael as he lead the way to a small restaurant across the street near the Hungarian Television Offices.

They sat for over two hours, eating, drinking and talking. By the time, they left the restaurant, Michael was very quiet.

"I don't feel too good," Michael said.

"What seems to be wrong?" Jean asked.

"My stomach," Michael said. "Also, my head is really aching." He stepped out on the side walk and started weaved from side to side.

"Michael, I think you've had too much wine," Jean teased.

Jerry Sullivan took a hold of Michael's arm. "Here, I'll help you."

"Let's catch a taxi," Michael said. "I really don't feel well."

"Was it something you ate?" Jean asked. "Your face is really white."

"I don't know. I need to lie down."

Jerry said, "Just lean against me for now. I'll help get you back to your house."

"No," Jean said. "We'll be fine. We'll get a taxi and once we're home, Michael will be all right."

"Well, I insist on going back to the Castle area with you," Jerry said. He held Michael with one arm and waved at a passing taxi with the other.

Jean looked at the stranger and shrugged, she knew she would never be able to handle Michael by herself. She followed Jerry without an further hesitation.

The taxi ride helped Michael feel better. He sat in the front seat, rolled down the window, and turned his face toward the cold air.

"It was probably that extra glass of wine that you insisted on drinking," Jean teased.

Michael only grunted. "I really don't think so."

Jean and Jerry sat in the back seat. They talked about Jerry's family and business. Jean enjoyed the conversation. She was glad to talk to someone other than those connected with the American Embassy. The older man made her feel safe. He spoke proudly of his wife and children. It reminded her of Iowa and how much she was beginning to miss it.

Michael and Jean said goodby to Jerry Sullivan at the Hilton Hotel. Jerry handed Jean one of his business cards, "I've written my hotel room number on the back. You be sure and call me and tell me what time to meet you for lunch tomorrow. I'm going to be free until I get the train to Romania."

"We will," Jean said, helping Michael. They walked across the square and directly to the apartment.

CHAPTER FORTY-THREE

The packers were just finishing as Michael and Jean entered the apartment. The cleaning lady came rushing to them, relaying the events of the day. Jean walked around the apartment shocked at how empty it was.

Boxes were piled around the sides of the rooms, leaving just enough space for the men to walk through. "We'll be back in the morning," the supervisor said. "I have to make an inventory list and then load everything into a cargo container. We'll seal it right here. The customs inspector will be here, too."

Michael said, "Be sure someone looks over the inventory list in the morning. You don't want to be short when your boxes get to Iowa."

"Michael, don't you worry now. You go rest, I'll talk to the cleaning lady. I want to make sure she takes all the bags with her."

After thanking the cleaning lady and sending her off with several full plastic bags, Jean went to the living room where Michael had stretched out on the sofa.

"Michael, where do you hurt?"

Michael could barely talk but answered in a whisper, "Jean, I really feel awful. Do you have anything in the apartment for an upset stomach?"

"I rather doubt it. Everything would be packed. Shall I call Clark at the Embassy and see if we should get you to a doctor?"

"No, do we have any soda water in the refrigerator or soft drinks?"

"Yes, there's a couple soft drinks and some mineral water. Both have fizz to them. That might help. You just lay quietly and I'll get it."

She wondered what could be wrong with him. All three of them had eaten the same food and neither her nor Jerry seemed to have gotten sick. "Maybe he's just got a touch of the flu," she said aloud, as she poured both a glass of mineral water and a glass of Bubble-Up.

Michael drank both glasses quickly, alternating them as he drank. Suddenly, he said, "I'm going to be sick to my stomach." He rushed to the bathroom.

Jean sat on the sofa and listen to the sounds from the bathroom. They were awful. She reached for the phone and called Clark. After talking to him for a couple minutes, she hung up the phone and went to the bathroom door.

"Michael, are you all right?" she called. Not hearing an answer she called again and again. Frantic, she opened the door. Michael was slumped over on the floor. He was unconscious. His face was chalky white and his pulse was very weak.

Shaking, Jean ran back to the phone and called Clark again. She opened the door to her apartment, and rushed back to the bathroom. Michael hadn't moved. She ran back to her bedroom to get a blanket, but found they had all been packed.

She thought for a moment and then ran to the hallway and got her coat. After she covered Michael she sat down and held his head in her lap until she heard the ambulance arrive.

Racing to the living room window, she threw it open, leaned out and calling to the ambulance men below. "Up here. Come up here. Got around the corner and come up the stairs. Hurry."

She motioned with her arms. Seeing them run, she ran to the top of the stairs and yelled at them. When she saw them in the hallway, she ran back to Michael.

By the time, Michael was in the ambulance, Clark had arrived with Tom Bryan. Relieved, Jean explained what had happened, but as she spoke she started to ramble.

Clark said, "Don't worry, we'll take care of everything. We'll let you know what's going on."

"I'm going with him," Jean insisted. Tears were running down her face. "He needs me."

Bryan pushed Jean gently into the living room. "There is nothing you can do for Michael now. Do you know anyone here in Budapest that you can get to come keep you company? I really don't think you should be alone."

Jean sunk back on the sofa. "I really don't know anyone here," she sighed.

"Well, you should have someone with you. Think about it, there must be someone," Bryan insisted. Jean stood and began walking around the room. She put her hand in her pants pocket and felt Jerry Sullivan's business card. She pulled it out, looked at it and said, "Yes, there might be someone."

"Call him," Bryan said. "I'll check back with you later today to make sure you're all right."

"There's a man I met today that's staying at the Hilton. He's an American and would probably walk over and stay with me for awhile. Do you really think that's necessary?"

"Yes, it would be best. Do you know his room number?" he asked.

"Yes, he wrote it on the back of his card." She held her hand out.

Bryan took the card and looked at it. "I'll call him and ask him. Why don't you go splash some cold water on your face? I'll let you know if he's available." Bryan motioned her toward the bathroom.

When Jean returned to the living room, Bryan was walking around the room. He said, "Everything is fine. Jerry Sullivan would be arriving in a few minutes. I'll stay until he comes. Clark will call and let us know about Michael's condition."

Jean didn't know what to say. She thought of poor Michael and everything he had done for her. She walked to the bedroom that he was using and started arranging his suitcase. If he was going to be in the hospital he would certainly want his things. Carefully, she folded the washing that the cleaning lady had done and noticed how perfectly everything had been ironed, even his shorts. Smiling to herself, she wondered what Michael would say when he saw his shorts had been ironed. She reached for his camera on the nightstand.

The ringing of the telephone startled her. She ran to the living room but found Bryan had already answered it and was talking. Setting a box on the floor, she cleared a chair and sat down.

Finally, Bryan put the phone back on the receiver and turned to Jean. The door bell rang. Jean jumped, then realized it was the doorbell and ran to answer it.

Jerry Sullivan entered. Jean burst into tears. Jerry held her for several minutes.

After the men introduced themselves to one another, Bryan said, “Jean, you’d best sit down. That was Clark on the phone. Michael is being taken to the airport and will be flown immediately to Frankfurt.”

“But, why?” Jean sobbed.

“Michael has a top secret clearance. He cannot go into a hospital other than one that’s approved by the United States. There are no such hospitals here in Budapest and because of his job he must be under certain security supervision.”

“That’s ridiculous. What are they afraid he’s going to say?” Jean asked.

“Maybe nothing,” Bryan said. “But, the government doesn’t take any chances. Should something seriously be wrong with Michael and surgery be needed, he would have to be sent back to Germany anyway. This is best for all concerned.”

Jean sat back down on the sofa. “Who’s going with him? Can I?”

“No, I don’t think that’s possible. The nurse from the Embassy will go with him.” Bryan said. He walked to the hallway and returned with his coat. “She has strict orders to call once they arrive at Rhein Main. Someone will let you know how he is. Clark was going to call Michael’s office now and have them prepared for his arrival.”

Jean shook her head. “But, it was simply an upset stomach. They would send him back to Germany because of any upset stomach?”

Bryan walked over to Jean and looked down at her. “We have reason to believe it is more than that. Could be his appendix or maybe his gall bladder. We don’t know. Now, you and Mr. Sullivan have to explain to me exactly what happened. Jean, you said you and Michael had wine and a bowl of soup with Mr. Sullivan. Yet, neither of you are sick.” He looked from one to the other as he spoke.

CHAPTER FORTY-FOUR

By the time Jerry Sullivan returned to his room in the Hilton Hotel, he felt that he had played the role of the American businessman perfectly. He was sure Jean had no idea what he had done.

After Bryan had left Jean, Jerry stayed at the Martin apartment. One thing he had learned from his many years of working as a troubleshooter for the CIA was to keep as close to the truth as possible. He had seen more than one agent get caught in lies which could have been avoided, if they had only used half truths.

He tried to either tell the exact truth about his family, or if he was trying to seduce someone, he took a total no family role. This way he only had to remember the period in his life before he was married. It would have been too hard for him to remember what he might have told someone if he claimed to be more or less than what he actually was.

Neither he nor the Agency had any intentions of seducing Jean Martin. All he wanted was to gain her trust and sex wouldn't figure into that play. After talking to her for a few minutes, he knew she would trust him more if he were the family type with a wife and kids. Loyalty, honesty and faithfulness were her creeds.

After a couple hours of just talking about nothing, Jerry could see Jean's eyes growing heavy. She was having a hard time keeping from yawning. Finally, he thought the time was right and decided to go back to the Hilton.

As he stood to leave the phone rang. He stood up while Jean answered it. "Yes, thank you for calling," she said, after only talking for a minute.

"That was Clark. Michael is in Frankfurt. He's going to be all right, but may be hospitalized for a couple days."

Jerry smiled. "That's great. Do they have any idea what it was?"

"Clark never said. I'm sure we'll hear more about it."

"Well, Jean, now that everything is okay here, I'm going back to the hotel. I'll call you in the morning. Do you want me to stop by and help with anything?"

Jean started to stand, but Jerry motioned for her to stay seated. She said, "If you don't mind. The packers will be here and I'm sure I could use an extra set of eyes."

Jerry nodded. "I'd be happy to. Do you want me to bring you anything?"

"Good heavens, no. I've more food here than I can possibly use." She laughed. "Do you want to take anything back to the hotel with you?"

Jerry shrugged. "What do you have?"

Jean pointed to the kitchen. "Look in the kitchen. You can take anything that's there."

Jean could hear him rummaging around the cans and bottles. He returned carrying a bag. "I took some of the small liquor bottles you had out. I hope that was all right."

"Perfectly," Jean said. "You can take some of the crackers and snacks if you want."

Jerry thought for a moment and said. "I think I will. I'm going to be taking the night train to Bucharest tomorrow night and I can save them for the trip."

Jean's face lit up. She had forgotten that he had mentioned going to Bucharest.

Jerry left, turning the door lock as he pulled the door shut. After he got back in his room, he saw the red light on his VCR flickering. He removed the casing and watched the recording tape revolve. He considered turning the machine off, because he already knew what was going on in the apartment.

He looked out the window and saw one of the lights in the apartment go off. He could tell the lamp light in the living room was still lit. He watched for a few minutes and saw Jean walking back and forth across the room. His eyes frozen on the scene.

As he turned away, his eyes focused on the street below. He saw the black van parked again in the square. It seemed to be the same van that had been there since he had arrived. He didn't remember seeing it earlier in the evening.

His eyes adjusted to the dark and he saw something moving near the van. It was hard to see what it was. Cussing at himself, thinking he might need to get glasses, he tried to make out a dark figure appearing to walk around the van.

Instantly, he knew he had to go outside and check it out for himself. Something was going on and he had to know what it was. He grabbed his coat and rushed toward the elevator. When he stepped out of the hotel, the van was still in its parked location.

Checking up and down the street, Jerry walked around the block. He wished he'd taken a closer look when he tied his handkerchief on the antennae. The van was a black, two-door van, with a rear door. It was a cargo van rather than a passenger van. It had no rear windows.

It appeared to be new but he couldn't find any brand name. Someone had removed any distinguishing features. Even the license plate had been covered with a thick coating of oil and dirt.

No one was around. He walked passed the van, stopped near the rear door, and leaned toward it. A phone rang.

Pivoting around in a circle, Jerry looked up at the nearby windows. He was trying to pinpoint the sound. His ears strained. The ringing continued, in sharp muffled spurts, and then stopped.

His eyes widened. The ringing was coming from inside the van. He felt the metal of the van. It was warm, not cold as it would have been if it had been parked there all day.

Stepping softly, he walked to the driver's side, and tried to look inside. The windows had been shaded. The interior was dark. He leaned his head against the window and felt a strange vibration.

Something was humming. His interest had peaked. Cautiously, he moved around the van, keeping as close to it as possible. Without touching it, he listened to it.

A loud humming sound started and then stopped. Several loud clicking sounds followed. It sounded as if someone were opening a door. Sullivan jumped back and ran for the corner of the church.

He melted into the shadows. From the safe distance, he stared at the van. He saw the small antenna connected to the right side of the van and smiled. Now, the owner had it attached to a company logo.

Looking up, he saw a movement from the Martin apartment window. Jean was standing in front of the window and holding the telephone. She glanced down at the square, turned and drew the drape.

He knew the van was listening to Jean's phone conversation. For several minutes, he thought about punching a hole in one of the van's rear tires, but decided that would only irritate someone.

No, he would wait and watch. He wanted to know whoever was interested in what was going on in the Martin apartment. His gut feeling connected this van to Jason's death.

CHAPTER FORTY-FIVE

After Sullivan left Jean, all she could think about was going to bed. Her eyes stung and were puffy from crying. First, Jason and now Michael, she wondered who or what would be next.

She walked to the bedroom Michael had been using. His suitcase was still on the bed as she had left it earlier. Absentmindedly, she went to it and packed all of his things which were around the room.

She took Michael's suit out of the closet, folded the slacks and put them in the bag. She began folding the suit jacket and felt something hard. Carefullly, she opened the suit jacket to discover what it was. Flipping the pocket inside out, a computer disk fell out. She glanced around and saw his laptop on the night stand. She put the disk by the computer.

Michael had placed the stack of CD's he wanted on the dresser. Judging the stack and the remaining space, she knew she'd have to repack the entire bag. When she removed a pair of shoes in a plastic bag at the bottom of the suitcase, she found a small cassette tape. She slipped it in one of the suitcase pockets.

Finally, she went to the dresser drawer, removed Michael's plane ticket, passport and travelers checks. These she placed on the bed, thinking she'd carry them and give them to him when she went through Frankfurt.

Flipping through the travelers checks she realized Michael had brought a great deal of money. Slowly, she counted the checks. They totaled almost fifty thousand dollars. She wondered why he was carrying so much money.

Gathering the unpacked things, she went to her bedroom and dropped everything on her dresser. In the morning, she'd put it all neatly in her purse or her carry-on bag.

Michael's toiletry bag caught her attention as she passed the bathroom. She picked it up, looked through it and put it on top of the suitcase. Suspicious of what else she might find, she spread out the toilet items and looked at them closely. Nothing unusual caught her attention.

Feeling a bit paranoid, she put the toilet articles in the case, zipped the case shut and carried it to the hall. Clark promised to send someone in the morning to pick it up and ship it to Frankfurt.

As she stood in the hallway, the telephone rang. It was only on the third ring that she realized it was coming from the living room because it sounded muffled and too weak to be in her apartment.

Rushing to the phone, she picked it up and stood looking out the window. "Hello, Martin's."

"Jean, it's Martha. How are you?"

"Oh, Martha, it's so good to hear your voice."

"I thought you might call me," Martha said. "I've been wondering if you're all right or if something else might have happened to you." The line was so clear, Martha sounded as if she were calling from next door.

"I've been a bit busy," Jean laughed. "Since you're paying for this call, do you have a minute and I'll catch you up to date?"

"Actually, River City is paying, I'm calling on official business."

"What's wrong?" Jean stuttered.

"Nothing is wrong now. What I'm calling about is the break in at your house last week. Remember?"

"Of course, I remember. I wasn't too worried. I knew you were taking care of it. Did you learn something new?"

"Yes, we discovered that the break in was done by two out-of-towners who arrived that afternoon on a Northwest flight from Minneapolis. Their flight originated in Washington, D.C. From what I found out they are connected somehow to the Russian Embassy."

"You're kidding?" Jean answered. "Russians?"

"Maybe. I'll have to do some payback favors for that information. They spent the night in a hotel at the lake and left on the Northwest morning flight back to Minneapolis. They connected in Minneapolis and went to National in Washington. We have the names they registered under but they were phoney. The only way we traced them was from the rental car here at our the airport. Once of them showed a passport for identification and a credit card."

Jean chuckled. "That wasn't very smart."

"I'm sure they weren't too worried. Probably thought we were in some hick place. We traced the credit card and passport to Washington. Well, I should say, we didn't, but a friend of mine with the FBI did. Now, the Fed's want to know why these jokers were prowling around River City. Do you have any ideas, Jean?"

"Martha, this gets more complicated with each minute. I have no idea. It has to be connected to Jason. There is no other explanation. Both you and I know he was connected to the Washington, D.C. scene. He is the Budapest connection."

"That's what I told them," Martha said. "How are you?"

"Now, guess what happened here? Michael Cleary had to be medical evacuated from Budapest today."

"Was it something he ate?"

"No one knows for sure. He's going to live but will be in the hospital for awhile. First, the lady we were having a glass of wine with is murdered, then my house in Iowa, Jason's apartment here, and now, Michael. I still don't know where Jason's computer is."

"Oh, speaking of computers. You received a box today from Washington. Shall I open it? I placed it in your kitchen on the counter top. It's big enough and just might contain Jason's computer. Maybe, Budapest sent it to Washington and they sent it here to you as his next of kin. That certainly makes sense, although not much else does."

"Yes, open it. If it's the computer, take it to your office and see what you can find out. Do you have anyone there that knows anything about computers?"

"Yes, a couple. I know a bit myself. I'm sure between the three of us we can find out what if anything was or is on the hard drive. Now, with the modern programs, you can also bring up erased things from the hard drive. I hope the box does contain Jason's computer. It'll be the first solid thing we have on this matter. When are you coming back?"

"I'm probably going to Bucharest tomorrow after the packers leave. Something was going on there and I'm going to find out what it was."

"Are you crazy, girl? You can't go off alone like that. That's it, I'm coming to Budapest." Martha screamed.

"Martha, calm down. I'm not in danger. It'll be all right."

"No, Jean, I'm leaving tomorrow. You stay put until I arrive."

"No. Martha, don't. I'll be fine. I plan on going to Romania with an American businessman I met. How about if I promise you that if I need your help, I'll call you? Do you agree to that?"

"You're really stupid, you know that? What do you know about this businessman?"

"Well, he's married and really a nice guy," Jean said. She read all of the information about him to Martha from his business card.

"Don't go until I can check if he's who he says he is. Do you promise?"

"I'm leaving tomorrow night. Can you get the information by then?"

Martha was silent for a few seconds. "I'll try, but I rather doubt it."

"Well, the trip takes an overnight train ride. After I'm finished, I'll fly from Bucharest back to Frankfurt and home. Should be home by the end of the week or early next."

"Get back here," Martha warned.

"Oh, call the bank and tell them I've been delayed. Don't you dare tell them anything else. Now, I'm going to go to bed. I promise you I'll call from Bucharest. Wait a minute and I'll give you a contact name at the American Embassy there." She set the phone down and ran to her purse. "Call a Mr. Larry Royal. He's one of the consulate officers and was Jason's contact. Good night, Martha."

"Jean, you had better call or I promise you I'll be on the next flight. Remember we all love and miss you."

"Good night, Martha, I love you, too." Jean replied.

CHAPTER FORTY-SIX

By morning, Jean had played and replayed her plan for traveling to Bucharest in her mind. By the time the cleaning lady arrived, the packers were parking the huge transport van. The stack of shipping papers were sitting on the dining room table ready for the proper signatures. Jason's car was outside, ready to be loaded on the truck.

Her suitcases, in Jason's bedroom, were almost packed. Michael's suitcase was sitting by the door. Someone from the Embassy had just called and said that a driver would be by to pick it up.

The doorbell rang. "Come in," she yelled.

"I wondered how you would be this morning," Jerry Sullivan said. He was carrying a white paper bag. "This is for you."

Jean's eyes sparkled. She could smell a pastry of some kind. "You really shouldn't have."

"How could I resist with the Ruszworm pastry shop next door? Did you know it's the oldest such shop in Budapest and has been written up in every tourist book about Budapest?"

"No, I didn't but I can smell their baking from my bedroom window. Will you join me?"

"Probably not, but I'll gladly take a cup of coffee. How are you today?" He took off his parka and set it on the dining room table. It looked to be one of the rooms that packers had finished.

I'm about as fine as one could be under the circumstances." She went to the kitchen to start some water boiling for instant coffee. "How are you this morning?"

He saw the suitcase in the hallway. He wondered if she had changed her plans since he had heard her talk to Martha last night. He said, "Are you leaving?"

She saw him glance at the suitcase and laughed. "That's not my suitcase. That's Michael's. Someone from the Embassy is coming to pick it up." She put her hands behind her back. She was nervous and didn't want Jerry to see her hands shaking. "I've decided I'm not going back to Frankfurt today."

"What?" Jerry said. He walked into the living room. "What does the Embassy say?"

"They don't know," Jean whispered.

Jerry walked toward the entertainment center. He reached down and picked up a small black case. It was quite heavy. He went back to the sofa and unzipped the cover. "Shouldn't you pack this?"

Jean had completely forgotten about Michael's laptop computer. She said, "It's Michael's."

The telephone rang.

Jean spoke for several seconds and then listened. After she hung up, she said, "I'm supposed to leave the apartment keys with the Porter downstairs."

Jerry nodded. He unzipped the computer case and flipped on a switch. The screen came to life. Making a face, he set it on the coffee table. "I just wondered if we should take the batteries out."

Jean laughed. "I wouldn't have the slightest idea. Don't you think it's cold in here?"

Jerry said, "Actually, I think it's rather warm in here. Maybe you're coming down with something."

The doorbell rang. Jean signaled for Jerry to answer it.

He walked back into the living room and said, "It was a driver from the Embassy. He took Michael's bag and said he'd take it right out to the airport."

Jean nodded her approval. She was holding the telephone. She hung up and looked at Jerry. "Michael has been released from the hospital."

"That's good news," Jerry said.

"He's gone home. He left early this morning."

"It must not have been as serious as they thought."

Jean started crying. "Isn't that wonderful. I'm going to call him at his home and tell him that his suitcase will be coming soon. Maybe he'll have it before he goes to bed this evening."

She dug through her purse for her address book, dialed Michael's number and waited for someone to answer. The phone rang and rang but no one answered. Frowning, she turned and looked at Jerry.

"No one home?" he asked.

"Michael doesn't answer." Jean said.

"That's not unusual. Maybe he went to work." Jerry answered.

"Of course, why didn't I think of that. That's exactly where he is. I'll wait and call him a bit later." She got up, took a pastry off her plate and began pacing. "Anyway, I feel better just knowing he's out of the hospital."

The door bell rang and Jean jumped up. She walked through the rooms with the packing supervisor. They went through the final arrangements.

Jerry felt out of place. He looked around the room and knew that if Jason Martin had hidden anything, it was hidden very well. The rooms were in a state of turmoil. Furniture was stacked on top of each other. The packers were loading the final boxes.

Jean walked back into the living room and stood in front of Jerry. "I have something to ask you."

"Sure," he answered quickly.

"I want to go with you to Bucharest tonight. How do I go about getting a ticket for the train?"

"You're kidding! Bucharest?" He looked confused.

"I plan on following Jason's trip schedule. The Embassy gave me his itinerary. He went to Bucharest on an overnight train. When he arrived he met with Larry Royal with the American Embassy. I'm going to do the same. Do you care if I go with you?" Her voice had become more timid and it had lost the strong determination that she showed only seconds earlier.

"No, I don't care. Actually, it'll be fun to have someone to travel with. I've made the trip before and it's very boring. This way I'll at least have some company."

"Great." Jean took a deep breath and exhaled. "So how well do you know Bucharest?"

"I can find my way around fairly well. Maybe I could be of help. My business calls shouldn't take too long. My only restriction is that I need to be back home in the states in five days for my wife's birthday. She's planning a small family get-together and she'd never forgive me if I didn't make it."

"Great, then it's all settled. What time shall I meet you?"

"I'm taking a taxi. I'll pick you up here about nine this evening. That should give you plenty of time to get organized. Is that all right with you?"

Jean shook her head. "That's perfect. Now, run along and do whatever it is that men have to do to get ready for a trip. I'll see you this evening."

Jerry started for the door, but turned around. "Say, I forgot to give the driver Michael's computer. I'll take it back to the hotel and have them send it to Michael. Is that all right with you?"

"Sure, will they do that?"

"Most hotels can make those kind of arrangements. I'll see you later," Jerry said. He grabbed his coat and the computer and hurried out the door.

CHAPTER FORTY-SEVEN

Determined to catch Michael Cleary before she left for Bucharest, Jean dialed his office in Rhein-Main, Germany. "I'd like to speak to Michael Cleary, please." Her voice was strong and determined.

"I'm sorry but Captain Cleary is not in the office today. May I ask who's calling?" came the crisp, brisk response.

"This is Jean Martin. I'm calling from Budapest."

"Captain Cleary should be home by now. He had some personal matters that he had to take care of and doesn't plan on being in the office today."

"Thanks, I'll call him at home. I have his phone number. But, just in case, do put down on his records that I called, so in the event that I'm not able to contact him, he'll know I tried. Is that okay with you?"

"Yes, that's fine. I'll leave a note on his desk that you called."

Jean immediately tried Michael's apartment. The phone rang and rang and just as Jean was ready to hang, a male voice answered.

"Michael, is that you? You sound so strange. This is Jean."

"I'm sorry, Ma'am, but this is Captain Larson. Captain Cleary is here would you like to talk to him?"

"Yes, please tell him that it's Jean Martin." Jean listened to the muffled sounds. She wondered what was going on that Michael hadn't answered the telephone himself.

"Jean, is that you?" Michael asked.

"Yes, Michael. You sound troubled. What in the world is going on? I called the hospital this morning and they said you had been released. When I called your office they said that you had personal things to take care of. Are you all right?"

"Jean, take it easy. I'm fine, or almost. The hospital was just too much. I feel a lot better. The doctors ran tests but they never came up with any thing positive."

"Do they have any ideas?"

"They believe it was a case of food poisoning. Something just didn't sit right with me. Anyway, I left the hospital this morning with Ray. He's with the OSI. We often work together on cases. Anyway, when we got back to my apartment you should have seen it. It was completely in shambles. Someone tore it apart."

"Michael, not you too. Was anything missing?"

"No, it was just a mess. Whoever searched it was looking for something specific. They didn't take any of the electronic equipment. But, then I don't have a lot worth taking."

"That sounds like when someone ransacked my house in Iowa. Do you think these ransacking are related? That makes mine in Iowa, Jason's here in Budapest and now, yours," Jean said, trying to hide her tears.

"I believe all of these break-ins are related and probably done by the same group. It's strange that all three cases are so many miles apart. Did you send those CD's in my suitcase?"

"Yes," Jean said. "Everything was packed. Your suitcase was picked up this morning and taken to the airport. You should have it soon."

"I think you should go back to Iowa. You could be in danger. Do you think anyone at the Embassy could be behind this?"

"I don't think so," Jean answered. "It might have something to do with that list I found. Martha told me last night that my break in was traced to two out-of-towners. Do you want to call and talk to her? She might be able to answer some of your questions."

"Let me think about it. What did you do with that list?"

"I have it. It's safe." Jean patted her chest.

"Did you send my laptop?"

"No, I didn't see it when the driver was here. Jerry Sullivan took it back to the Hilton. He's going to have them ship it to you."

"Oh!" Michael said. "Did you give him my home address or my office?"

Jean couldn't remember having given Jerry any address. "I'm not sure. I'll find out."

"When are you leaving for Iowa?"

Jean made a face. "I know I should go back, but I've decided to go to Bucharest this evening with Jerry Sullivan. We're taking the overnight train. When I arrive in Bucharest, I"ll contact the Embassy. I can't go back to Iowa until I know I've done everything possible to find out about Jason's death."

Michael sighed heavily. "Gad, you're a stubborn woman. Please, contact the Defense Attache Office when you arrive in Bucharest. I'll get in touch with them and see if they can give you some assistance. If I were you I wouldn't put a lot of trust in that Sullivan. Do you know any more about him?"

"No, nothing other than what he told us. At least he's not connected to the Embassy, so shouldn't have any hang-ups. He said he does know his way around Bucharest, so he'll be a big help that way. He's a family man. I don't think he'll hurt me."

"Well, be careful. Whoever is behind all of this wouldn't hesitate for a moment to kill a woman, especially if they're from the Arab world or connected to the Russian Mafia. You be careful. Get something to take with you that you can use for a weapon."

"Michael, you're scaring me. I don't need a weapon."

"I don't think you should go out and buy a gun, but you could carry some kind of a knife or spray of some type. Remember, don't trust anyone. Keep alert. If you have any problems whatsoever, go to the police, any Embassy or any major hotel. Do you have enough money?"

"Yes," Jean answered. "I still have a wad of travelers checks that I haven't used. I bought them before leaving Iowa. I promise I'll be careful."

"Be alert and watch everything around you," Michael said.

"Martha did mention that a box came in the mail. We thought it was probably Jason's laptop. I told her to take it to her office and see what was on the hard drive. How do you feel?"

"I feel a lot better. What I can't do is eat much. My stomach feels sore inside. The doctor said that it would all go away in a couple days or so. Are you going to stop and see me on your way through Frankfurt?"

"Hope so, but it depends on my flights."

"Well, call me."

"I will. Now, don't worry. I'll be fine. You take care of yourself."

"I"ll be waiting for your call."

"See you soon," Jean said, just as a tear rolled down her cheek.

CHAPTER FORTY-EIGHT

The train left on schedule. Jerry Sullivan was settled in his seat. His small bag had been placed on the shelf above him. He took out the package of snacks, opened them and put them beside him on the small shelf by the window.

He opened a paperback novel, flipped through a couple pages and watched Jean struggling with her bags. "Need any help?"

Jean shifted her suitcases a couple times. Finally, she answered. "No, I'll be fine."

He watched for several minutes more, then asked again, "Are you sure you're all right? You don't look as if you're feeling just right?"

Jean chewed on her lower lip, pulled at her large white Iowa sweatshirt and brushed some lint from her blue jeans. "I really hated leaving Jason's apartment. It's so final."

Jerry closed his novel, glanced at her and said, "I doubt if anyone ever told you life was going to be easy."

Jean smiled and blinked several times. Her perfect white teeth reflected the lights from the platform. "You're right," she said. "Life can be a bummer at times. Now, I'll take you up on your offer of help and have you put this suitcase up there on that mesh rack."

"Well, what we don't need is you sniffing for the next twelve hours," Jerry said. His tone of voice was harsh but he winked after he spoke.

"I'll try not to," Jean answered. She reached for a tissue, looked at him out of the corner of her eye and gave him a mischievous smile. "I thought you said the trip only took ten hours?"

"You caught me there." He sunk back on his seat, picked up his paperback book, took a cracker and turned to his page.

"How soon do we leave?" The words had barely gotten out of her mouth when the train started moving.

Jerry laughed. "I'd say any minute now."

She slid toward the window and pushed the drapes all the way open. She leaned forward on the window sill and watched the train leave the station. "I've never ridden on a train before."

"Well, I never would have guessed," Jerry chuckled.

Jean turned and saw Jerry smiling. "Oh, you big tease."

Several minutes later, Jerry said, "Now that we're on our way, I'm going to walk through the cars and see what's happening. For the time being, you can leave the door open if you want. But, once we get out into the country side, you should close and lock it. I'll knock when I get back."

Jean motioned for Jerry to go on his way and turned back to the window. She could hear footsteps in the hallway outside of their compartment and looked up every once in a while. She felt tired and sad.

The lights whizzed past, she wasn't totally aware of what was going on around her. She just couldn't find the inner strength to shake her depression. Jason was the big brother, but he wasn't going to be around anymore to take care of her.

She glanced at her watch. It had been almost thirty minutes since Jerry had left the compartment. She was thirsty. The smell of fresh coffee filtered down the hallway. Stepping out into the hallway, she look back in the cabin and started to pull the door closed.

"What do you think you're doing?" Jerry asked. He was standing behind her.

She jumped backward and fell against him. Stumbling, she grabbed a railing and regained her footing. "You scared me."

"Well, I should hope so. Where were you going?"

Jean backed into the cabin. "I was going to find something to drink."

"Well, we shouldn't leave the cabin empty. There are a couple unsavory looking thugs on this train. I just came from the dining car and thought I'd tell you."

"I'm not worried if they stay off our car," she said. "Did you see a restroom on your excursion?"

"There's one that way. Just between the two cars. Do you want me to go with you?"

“You’ve got to be kidding. If something happens I’ll yell and you can come running. Be sure and put on your shinning suit of armor first.”

“Get out of here,” Jerry said, making a face and literally pushing her out the cabin door.

Jean walked down the narrow hallway and headed in the direction Jerry had pointed. When she got to the end of her car, she saw two men huddled deep in conversation. As she neared the men, she overheard them talking about an American on the train.

She froze, then stepped backward out of their sight. Her instinct was to stop and go back to her compartment, but she didn’t want to attract their attention by running.

Suddenly, the train jerked. She bumped against a fire extinguisher and the men stop talking. She knew they knew someone was nearby. With no other choice, she walked down the hallway toward the men.

She saw the ladies restroom sign directly behind where they were standing. With a smile, she nodded toward the door. The men stepped to one side. She opened the door and entered.

Inside, she leaned on the door, locked it and stood for several seconds. She was shaking. Although, she couldn’t hear what was going on outside the door, she could feel the men’s presence.

She shivered. They scared her. They both had dark features, needed shaves and haircuts. A dirty dusty, chemical smell surrounded them. Their dirty blue jeans clung to their tall, slender bodies. Their black leather jackets were worn but had at one time been expensive.

She hadn’t caught a glimpse of their hands but cringed when she thought of how dirty their fingernails must be. Rubbing the soap back and forth, she scrubbed her hands. For some strange reason, she felt this would keep her safe from the two men.

After she finished, she unlocked the door. It wouldn’t open. It was stuck. She leaned against it and pushed with all of her strength.

The door flew open. Jean tumbled out, landing on the floor in front of the two men. She looked up, smiled and said,"Sorry, about that."

One of the men offered his hand. She looked at it. It was caked with dirt.

She hesitated, then took it and pulled herself up. Without another word, she brushed her jeans off and walked slowly down the hallway. Her heart was racing.

When she got almost to her cabin, she could hear the men laughing. Her face felt hot. They were talking about her. She didn't care. She was safe.

"Are you too warm?" Jerry asked. He glanced at her face, frowned and let his eyes move up and down her body.

"No, I just saw two really scary looking guys. I had to go right by them to use the restroom."

Jerry stiffened. "I bet those were the two I saw in the dining room. Did they look like they might have just jumped off a prison work gang?"

"That's the two. They were wearing black leather jackets and dirty blue jeans."

Jerry got up and looked out the door. "I can't hear or see anything now. They must have gone. Did you hear them talking?"

"I was shaking so, I can't remember. Seems they were saying something about an American on board the train. They had such heavy accents that I only caught a couple words."

Jean sat down on her side of the car, leaned back and closed her eyes. Using her fingertips, she massaged her temple. Budapest was offering too much excitement for her. She longed for the peace and quiet of her hometown.

CHAPTER FORTY-NINE

The constant chugging of the train was beginning to give Jean another headache. She had been checking her watch for the past two hours willing the hours to fly past. Finally, no longer able to control herself, she decided she had to get up and move around. Trying to be quiet, she crept out of her bunk. Jerry appeared to be asleep in the other make-shift bed. She ran a comb through her hair and tried to arrange her things in her bag. She would make her bed after Jerry was up.

She opened the cabin door and looked out. The smell of fresh coffee made her smile. Silently, she started to step out.

"Where do you think you're going?" Jerry Sullivan asked sharply. He turned over with a loud crunching noise.

Jean gasped and dropped her purse. It made a loud clanging sound when it hit the metal rod at the base of her bed. "You almost scared me out of my wits. You could've just rolled over so I knew you were awake. Did you have a restful sleep?"

"As well as can be expected when one tries to put a six foot three inch body into a five foot space. How about yourself?" He pulled himself up and stretched his arms upward. His clothes were not wrinkled.

"I've been awake for about an hour. The constant chugging of the train was giving me a headache. I'm sure it's also just a bit of nerves." She was pleased that she was finally able to talk aloud. It felt good to break the quiet of the early morning.

"I know what you mean. I fell asleep last night listening to the chug-chug and counting the wheel revolves. Train rides always sound more exciting than they actually are."

"Yes, it sounds mysterious and romantic to say one has taken a trip across two countries, but in reality it gets old fast."

"So, where were you going?" Jerry asked.

"I thought I'd get a cup of coffee. From what I'm able to guess, we have another hour until we arrive in Bucharest. Is that what you think?"

"Maybe even longer. We crossed the border a couple hours ago. We just stopped at Braslov and that's a couple hours by car from Bucharest. It should take about that long by train or a bit longer, depending on how many times the train stops to pick up passengers."

Someone knocked on the compartment door. "Conductor," the voice yelled.

"Yes, sir," Jerry answered. He jumped up, unlocked the door and stood in the doorway.

"Tickets and passports, please," the conductor said.

Jean dug through her purse for hers and Jerry pulled his out of his back jean pocket. He handed them to the conductor. "How much longer to Bucharest?"

The conductor took the items, held the passports up to the light, looked at each of them, stamped them with a black stamp he had in his pocket, and handed the passports back. "Why are you visiting Romania?" the conductor asked.

Jerry spoke first. "I'm on business."

The conductor said, "With what company?"

"My own. I"m a consultant for several companies that are expanding in Romania."

"And you?" the conductor turned to Jean.

"Vacation," she answered quickly.

The conductor frowned, squinted and stared at Jean. "Vacation? What in the world for?"

Jean smiled. "Actually, I've heard you have wonderful folk art and craft items. I'm doing some scouting for a friend." When the conductor continued to stare, she added. "I'm going to take a trip to Bran Castle and see what I can learn about Dracula."

"Dracula," the conductor said. "It's all tourist garbage. He was the same as you and me. The tourists like to think he was this evil monster." He handed Jean her passport. He punched their tickets and glanced at his watch. "We have about two more hours or so. The dining car is open." He turned and knocked on the next compartment.

Jerry shrugged. "Well, that answers that. Pretty clever adding that bit about Dracula."

Jean looked bashful. "I couldn't think of anything else. It just popped into my head. Actually, I wouldn't mind seeing Bran Castle."

"Well, maybe you'll have time. I think it's a couple hours from Bucharest. Wait a moment and I'll go with you to the dining room. It'll be better if we're seen together as much as possible. If anyone should be following you, it might scare them off, when they find you aren't alone. It won't take me but a couple minutes to make myself presentable. Okay?"

"That's fine," Jean said. "I don't want any trouble from anyone on the train. Is that a real possibility?"

Sullivan nodded and walked out of the compartment. Jean straightened both of the pull down beds and turned them back into bench seats. She cleaning up her space and straightened out her bag. After shutting the door, she quickly changed out of her sweatshirt into a deep purple t-shirt and soft flannel long sleeve shirt. Although, she hadn't showered or washed her hair she felt cleaner.

"Ready?" Jerry looked refreshed and his slightly grey hair had been combed. He was still wearing the same jeans and turtleneck.

"Let's go." She kicked the base of her pull out bed, grabbed her purse and overnight bag. Something told her to take them with her. Minutes before, she moved Michael's papers from her purse into her overnight bag. Her purse had been too heavy and was making her shoulder hurt.

When they entered the dining room, they were surprised to find the tables almost full. Toward the very back of the car, Jerry spotted an empty table for two. He headed for it. Jean followed.

As Jerry passed the occupied tables, Jean noticed he was watching everyone. For the first time, she wondered if he was really a businessman. He was awfully street smart.

"Just two coffee's for now, please." Jerry ordered as Jean sat down.

She looked around and placed her bags on the empty chair near the window. "It's nice to be among all the activity, after spending the night in silence. I love the idea of people around me. I guess that's why I love my job."

"That's important," Jerry said. "I love my job, too." He rested his elbow on the table, rubbed his chin several times, giving the appearance of someone waiting.

"So, what's the plan once we get to Bucharest?" Jean asked. She watched his eyes move up and down, watching the people arriving and leaving.

"My office has already made me reservations at the Hotel Inter-Continental. I'm sure the hotel will have space for you if you want to stay there. But, should worse come to worse, you can always share my room."

"Where's the hotel located? I'd like to be in the heart of the city."

Jerry grinned. "You're in luck. That's exactly where it is."

"The only hotel I'd heard about was the Sofital. I understand it's quite nice. But, then I really don't know anything about the city and where the hotels are in location to what is in the city."

"Yes, the Sofital is nice but it's out on the outskirts of the city near the World Trade Center. I prefer the Inter-Continental because it's almost across the street from the American Embassy, in the heart of the city."

"Are your appointments downtown?"

"Usually, I make visits to the Commercial section at the Embassy and I prefer being in the heart of the city. I also find that if a person stays in the center of a city, there are more choices for eating. If you stay at the Sofital, you're pretty much stuck to eating at the hotel. Also, the Sofital is a bit expensive and I only allow myself a certain amount for lodging and food. Do you want to stay at the Inter-Con or would you rather see about the Sofital?"

"No, the Inter-Con is fine. They're usually very nice hotels."

"Yes, usually," Jerry said. "I heard this one in Bucharest is a franchise and remodeled a couple years ago. It should be all right. After all, it'll only be for a couple days. Today is already Wednesday and I plan on leaving by Friday. How about you?"

"Yes, I hope to be either in Frankfurt or on my way home by this weekend. I told Michael I'd see him this weekend if I couldn't get a flight directly to the states. I don't think it'll take me over a couple days to find out what I want to know in Romania."

"I hope for your sake it doesn't. From what you told me last night, everyone that had anything to do with Jason's death is already aware that you're in the area."

"At least the Embassy people are."

"Well, if they think you're carrying anything on you that they could be interested in, you could be in danger. Hopefully, you'll be back in Iowa and at work next week."

"That would be nice."

Jerry finished his coffee and glanced at his watch. "We should be getting back to our car and preparing for departure."

Jean set her cup down. "I'm ready." She picked up her bags and followed closely behind him.

As they approached the doorway, Sullivan grabbed her arm and pulled her back toward him. "Be very careful. Walk quickly out the door and down the hallway toward the compartment. I'll be right behind you. Don't stop no matter what happens. Understand?" Jean hesitated for a moment, but felt the pressure of Jerry's hand against her back. When she walked out the door, she passed two men who were trying to enter the dining. They were blocked with the couple's departure.

Jean casually glanced at the two men and felt a sudden chill. Her hands began to shake as she walked forward. Her purse hung over her shoulder and she pulled it closer to her chest. She held it and her carry-on bag with both hands.

She could feel the warmth of the men's bodies when she passed. A strong garlic odor saturated their clothes. Glancing up, she noticed they both had changed their dirty jeans and were wearing clean Levi's and plaid shirts.

She paused for a moment, looked at them but avoided looking at their faces. Quickening her step, she hurried. When she was out of their sight, she almost ran back to her compartment.

Sullivan followed right behind her. Back in the compartment, he leaned firmly against the compartment door, locked and sighed. "Thank God that's over."

"What was that all about? Who are those two men?" She stood directly in front of the window, with the bright morning sun reflecting around her. She watched Sullivan's expressions.

"I'm not really sure. I just felt they were trouble." He looked very serious.

"Jerry, what are you not telling me?"

He chuckled and crossed to his seat. "Thanks for putting this back." He watched her staring at him. "I guess I'm just getting punchy. When I saw those two men I had the strangest feeling they meant trouble. I probably overreacted. That's all!"

"Maybe not," Jean said. "I felt something evil as I passed them. It was really strange, a sudden chill ran down my spine. I don't think I've ever seen either of them before last night, nor do I want to see them again."

She was more relaxed now that the encounter was over. For some reason, she didn't completely believe Sullivan, but she didn't want to pressure him. She needed his help in Bucharest and didn't want to cause any type of resentment.

The faces of the two men were imprinted firmly on her mind. She knew she would recognize them, if she ever encountered them again. The train was slowing. She turned toward the window. They were moving into a populated area.

"Is this Bucharest?" she asked.

Jerry watched for several seconds. "It looks like it."

Just then the conductor walked passed their door. "Your stop is coming up. This is the end of the line. Everyone off."

"Thanks," Jean said automatically.

"Let's go," Jerry said.

When the train pulled into the North Train Station, Jerry took Jean's suitcase and his. They stood by the door waiting for the train to stop. Within seconds, they were off the train, walking through the noisy station toward a waiting taxi.

Jean stepped into the taxi and glanced back over her shoulder. The two grubby men were running toward her. She saw them signaling for a taxi. Her heart raced.

Jerry said,"Intercontinental Hotel, please."

Jean gasped. She was sure the men had heard Jerry. The bag she was wearing around her neck was hurting her. It suddenly felt very heavy.

CHAPTER FIFTY

There was a mixup with Jerry Sullivan's reservation. Jean accepted the delay cheerfully and thought it was norm for the area. She moved from seat to seat, and kept watching the mixed variety of guests. She positioned herself so she could see who was coming in all three of the entrance doors.

Jerry repeatedly told Jean that the clerks were holding up their reservations because they had been told to do so. Jean thought he was being paranoid, but kept a watchful eye for the two men from the train. Several times, Jerry considered leaving the hotel and going to another, but he was afraid it would only attract more attention.

After two hours they were finally shown to their rooms. Jerry said, "I'll meet you downstairs in ten minutes for lunch. Is that all right with you?"

Jean walked into the restaurant exactly ten minutes later. Jerry was waiting by the front door.

"Well, what now?" Jean asked after they had ordered a warm meal. It had been hours since she had eaten something hot. Her stomach knew it.

"Well, I need to contact my office. I still haven't been able to get a hold of my appointment. Are you going to get in touch with that person at the Embassy?"

"Yes, I tried to call him from my room. His name is Larry Royal. I left a message with his secretary that I was here at the hotel and asked him to call. I think I'll stay close to the hotel and wait for his call. Where is the Embassy from here?"

"Just go out the front door where we came in. Directly across the hotel parking lot, on your right, is the National Theater. Directly across the street from the National Theater is the American Consulate. To walk to the Embassy, you simple walk past the Consulate building and walk around the corner. The Embassy is directly behind the Consulate, but you can't get to it without walking around the corner."

"That's weird. Why don't they have a cut through?"

"Security reasons. There's not a public access way connecting the two buildings. It's only been recently that a connection was built for employees. You'll notice all the diplomatic cars parked on the street around the two buildings. The American license plate number for Romania is 156. Any car with that license plate is registered to either the Embassy or someone assigned to the Embassy."

"Great, I should be able to find it without any problem. Where are you going?"

"I need to go down the main street the other way. I'm going to a big building a couple blocks from here on Unirea corner. That's near one of the McDonald's and the Delta Airlines Office. In fact, the meeting I have is in the same building as Delta. It's about a ten or fifteen minute walk from here."

Jean had no idea what she would do if Royal didn't call. It sounded as if Jerry was going to be busy for the rest of the day. She had already checked the television channels and found CNN. That was at least something.

"What say we meet this evening? Just call my room. It's 435," Jean said.

"I'll call when I return. I'm exactly one floor below you in 335." Jerry began shaking his foot and looking around the room. He jumped when a waiter bumped into a chair directly behind him. "This place makes me nervous. I'd advise you not to leave the hotel without leaving word for me where you're going. I hate to sound like a big brother or old uncle, but I'll worry about you."

Jean patted his hand and smiled. With a wink, she said, "Don't worry, I'll be fine. I'm a big girl." Although, she spoke confidently, she really wasn't too sure that she would be.

While they ate, Jean sat so she could look out the window and see the people walking pass. Jerry's seat gave him an excellent view of who was entering the restaurant. They had rearranged their seats to accommodate them. The waiter had just removed their dirty dishes when Jerry gasped.

"What's the matter?" Jean's heart skipped a beat. She thought of Michael and how he looked when he had gotten sick. "Was it something you ate or swallowed?"

Quickly, Jerry tried to act as if nothing was wrong. "Nothing. I just thought of something I forgot to do for the meeting this afternoon. If you don't mind, let's leave as soon as you're finished. I need to go back up to the room and do a bit of work. Are you about ready?"

Jean stood. "I can always call for room service if I need anything else. Shall we go?"

"Yes, let's." He stood and immediately took her arm and escorting her from the room.

The couple had just stepped into the hotel lobby when Jean stopped.

"What's wrong?" Jerry asked.

"There are those two men from the train. Can we go another way so they won't see us?" She turned and faced Jerry, trying to hide her face.

Instantly, Jerry pulled her behind a large pillar. "I'm not sure this is going to work," he whispered. He kept his back to the men and pushed Jean around in front of him. They moved around the pillar as the men passed. Jean could see the backs of the men and could smell their garlic odor.

"Are they gone?" Jerry asked. He had bent himself down to give anyone watching the impression that he was a much shorter man.

"Yes, they went into the restaurant. Let's dash for the elevators. I just want to get out of here. I wouldn't feel comfortable in my room, if I knew they knew that I was staying here."

"Go and I'll follow right behind you. I'll go up to your room with you. I don't want something to happen to you. Be sure you keep your door locked and don't go anywhere without leaving me a message."

They stepped into a waiting elevator and Jerry pulled Jean to a side. He pushed the buttons. "If you want to make an appointment later, I'll be happy to go with you."

"Why do you suppose those two men are here? Could it be a coincidence?"

Jerry stepped off the elevator on the fourth floor, and looked up and down the hallway. "I have no idea why they're here.

Promise me, you won't leave the room unless this Royal person calls or I get back."

"Yes, I promise." Jean unlocked her door and rushed into her room. "I'm fine. You can go now." She could hear Jerry chuckling.

"Well, lock the door," he said after she closed the door. "Then, I'll leave."

She turned the key in the lock and heard his footsteps go down the hallway.

Jean stood leaning against her door. Her heart felt as if it were going to explode. She put her hand to her chest. The pressure of the leather bag hanging around her neck made her realize she was carrying something on her that could well be extremely valuable.

If, she could find someone to trust, she'd turn over the contents to them. She had thought of sending it to Michael in his suitcase, but she was afraid his suitcase would have been searched.

Jason had taken the time to hide it, now it was her job to keep it safe. She would take it back to Iowa and give it to Martha. Martha was the only person she really trusted.

Taking a deep breath, she decided she was going to take control of the situation. She went to the telephone and dialed the American Embassy. "I'd like to talk to Larry Royal, please."

"I'm sorry, Mr. Royal is out of the office at the present time. He's at lunch. Would you like to talk to his secretary?" A cheerful voice asked.

"Yes, please," Jean answered. There were a series of clicks. Finally, she heard a female voice.

"I'd like to talk to Larry Royal."

"I'm sorry Mr. Royal has a luncheon meeting. He isn't due back in the office until later this afternoon. Could I take a message, or maybe I could help you? I'm Sarah, his assistant."

"Sarah, thanks. Yes, please take a message. Tell Mr. Royal that Jean Martin called. I'm Jason Martin's sister. I'm here in Bucharest at the Intercontinental Hotel. I'd like to meet with him."

"I'm so sorry, Ms. Martin, but Mr. Royal has a busy schedule today."

Jean thought quickly. "Tell him that I just left Clark, Slate and Bryan in Budapest and they recommended that I contact him. My room number is 435. I'll be in my room for the rest of the day. Ask him to call or stop by. Thanks, Sarah, for your help."

"Ms. Martin, I'll make sure that Mr. Royal gets your message, but I can't promise you anything. Is this your first visit to Bucharest?"

"Yes, it is. I'm a bit overwhelmed. I really don't know any thing about the city and haven't even looked at a city map yet. Have you any words of advice?" Jean could only hope that by being polite she could win the secretary's confidence.

"Yes, several words of advice. Be very careful walking around the city at night. Be careful of pickpocketers. They are everywhere. This country isn't as westernized as Hungary and things are still unsettled. If you have any specific questions, just give me a call. I'd be more than happy to help you."

"Sarah, you're very kind. I certainly will keep you in mind. Thanks for giving my message to Mr. Royal." Jean felt better. Now all she had to do was sit and wait for Larry Royal's call.

Knowing Royal wasn't going to be back in the Embassy for a while, Jean decided to take a hot bath and try and relax. She unpacked the rest of her suitcase and sat on the bed. After bouncing a couple times, she knew the bed was going to feel a great deal better than the train bunk.

By the time, she had taken her bath and slipped on her robe it was almost two in the afternoon. She glanced at her watch. Her eyes felt heavy. There was time for a nap. She rolled over and closed her eyes.

While Jean slept, she was completely unaware of a soft knock on her door. When the door wasn't answered, the knob turned. The sound of someone trying to insert a key into a lock vibrated through the hallway.

The door opened slightly, but the chain lock only allowed the door to open a couple inches. Silence filled the air. The intruder knew that using force to break the lock would cause more noise and attention than he wanted. Since the hallway was empty, no one heard the door close, nor the footsteps hurrying down the hallway.

CHAPTER FIFTY-ONE

Jean awoke from her nap in a cold room engulfed in darkness. When she laid down, she hadn't covered herself with a blanket, and now she was shivering.

Disorientated, she crawled out of bed. She stood up, pulled her soft lightweight robe around her and looked around the room. It took her several seconds to realize where she was. Looking at her watch, she was amazed to see it was almost five in the afternoon.

She had slept much longer than she had intended. A light was flashing in the middle of her nightstand. Snapping on the bed lamp, she reached for the phone.

"Do I have a message?" she asked.

"Yes, you are in room 435?" the clerk asked. Her voice was expressionless.

"Yes, that's correct. Do you have a message for me?" Jean asked again. She was feeling irritated.

"Yes, you have a message from a Mr. Sullivan. He said to tell you he will be late getting back." The weary voice said in her monotonous tone.

"Thank you." Jean made a face, sighed and hung up the phone. "Nothing from Royal. Wonder what happened to Jerry?"

She slipped on a clean pair of blue jeans and a sweatshirt. Then, she finished unpacking and straightening up the room. Just as she started brushing her hair, she heard a loud knock.

Hurrying to the door, expecting to see Jerry Sullivan, she unhooked the chain lock, unlocked the door and pulled it wide open.

"Hi," she said automatically. When she saw a woman standing in front of her, she looked surprised and jumped back.

"Jean, I'm Sarah. Larry Royal's secretary. Remember!"

Jean recognized the voice. "Yes, of course. I remember talking to you earlier today. Come on in. What can I do for you?"

"I want you to come with me. Now! Grab your coat, purse and whatever else you want to bring. You can leave your suitcase. Mr. Royal is waiting for you downstairs in his car. Please hurry!" The woman whispered. She stepped into the room and shut the door behind her, leaning against it as she spoke.

"What's the hurry? I'd really rather wait until my friend, Jerry Sullivan, comes back so he can go with us. I traveled to Bucharest with him." Jean took several steps backwards into the center of the room. She felt uncertain and confused.

"Hurry, Mr. Royal wants to talk to you. Please get your things. He will explain," the woman insisted.

Jean looked at the middle aged woman. She looked as if she could be Sarah from the Embassy, but Jean had no real way of knowing. "Do you have any type of identification you can show me?"

"Yes, of course. I'm sorry, I should have shown you this when I first arrived." Sarah opened her purse and pulled out a grey identification card. It had her picture on it and stated that she was with the American Embassy.

Jean glanced at the laminated card, reached for it and took it over to examine it under the light. It looked very official. For several seconds, she looked at the card and back at the lady. She spoke quickly, "Okay. Thank you. Just a minute. I'll finish dressing. I won't be a minute. I only woke a few minutes ago from a nap. We brought the overnight train into Bucharest and I didn't get much sleep."

"Hurry. Don't take your suitcase. It would attract attention and you will probably be back. Just grab any valuables that you don't want to leave in the room." The lady continued to stand against the door. She leaned her head against the door as if she were trying to hear if anyone was out in the hallway.

Jean quickly gathered up her personal items. She put on her leather neck bag, look around the bathroom and grabbed her overnight case. She left her suitcase and clothes as they were.

"Well, I'm ready," Jean said. She walked toward the door and took her coat off the chair. "I'd like to leave a message for Jerry Sullivan downstairs at the reception desk."

"That really won't be necessary," Sarah answered. She was already starting to run down the long hallway.

Neither woman said a word until they were out of the building. Sarah led the way. Jean glanced around the lobby of the hotel as she hurried through it. She tried to see if the two men from the train were there. Sarah motioned for her to hurry, so Jean stuck her room key in her pocket.

"Jean, that's Mr. Royal's car," Sarah said. She stood very close to Jean and talked directly into her ear. "The blue BMW. We will walk over to it. Start pretending to talk to me as if we are old friends. You are being watched." She pushed Jean along. "NO! Don't turn around and look. Keep following me. Smile at me, pretend like I am saying the nicest things you have heard in a long time. We are best of friends."

"But, why?" Jean questioned, trying to understand what was happening.

Sarah patted Jean on the back and motioned with her hands as she talked. "When we get to the car, you are to open the front passenger door and slide in. Roll down the window and continue to talk to me. Understand?"

Jean was shaking. She felt as if she were going to face a firing squad. The woman took Jean's arm and steered her toward the waiting BMW. Sarah continued to mutter and Jean smiled.

Jean's smile was frozen on her face, but she did as she was instructed. She was too scared not to. Reaching for the car door, Jean glanced inside the car. Jerry Sullivan was sitting in the back seat. Her mouth dropped open. A man she believed to be Larry Royal was sitting on the driver side.

Jean got into the car. She shut the door, rolled the window down, looked out the car window and continued smiling. She had only said a couple words since she left her room. The car sped away.

CHAPTER FIFTY-TWO

Larry Royal weaved in and out of the traffic. Jean fumbled for her seat belt when the BMW turned the corner on two wheels, squealing its tires. Her hands reached for the door panel and her fingers searched for a safety handle.

She heard the car door locks snap into place. Afraid for her life, she stared ahead watching as the car swerved from one lane to the other. She started to speak but a small red car pulled out from a side street. It was heading straight for her side of the car. Her scream froze in her throat as the BMW missed hitting the car by a hair.

Fixing her eyes on the dashboard, she began to pray. The two men in the car hadn't said a word. Jean didn't say anything for fear she'd cause the driver to lose his concentration.

A large white city bus pulled out, just as the BMW turned the corner. Royal twisted in his seat and looked out the rear window. Jean was sure they were going to hit the bus and grasped the door handle until her fingers went white. She ducked her head down and pulled her knees up.

Expertly, Royal pulled the BMW around the white bus. A large AMFOR tour bus was passing another city bus in the oncoming lane. Jean gasped aloud. She was sure that now they were going to be smashed between the two buses.

Royal pressed the gas, held the wheel steady and pulled the large BMW in front of the white city bus. Jean exhaled. Her sigh flowed through the car.

"Not bad driving, Larry. Where did you learn to drive like that?" Jerry Sullivan asked from the back seat.

"I took that defensive driving course the State Department offers up at Fort Meade. I also took the FBI defensive driving course at Quantico that the Agency recommends for all agents being posted abroad. I must admit it was a bit hairy. But, at least we aren't being followed." Royal smiled to himself in the mirror.

Jean could feel her face getting hot. She turned and looked at Sullivan in the back seat. "What in the hell are you guys doing? Are you trying to get us all killed?" She let go of the door handle and rubbed her aching hands together.

"Jean, I'm sorry. Let me introduce myself. I'm Larry Royal. Sorry, about all of that but Jerry told me you knew about the two terrorist agents that were following you."

Jean's eyes grew wide. "What do you mean two terrorist agents? I knew there were two men on the train that seemed to be interested in us." She twisted around in her seat and looked directly at Jerry. "But, no one told me that they were terrorists?"

"Jerry, I thought you told me she knew?" Royal questioned, looking through his rear view mirror to Sullivan in the back seat.

"Larry, there are a few things that I didn't tell you. You just assumed a couple things. Let's stop somewhere safe and we'll have a cup of coffee. Then, we can explain everything to Jean."

"I think that's a great idea," Jean snapped.

Larry drove for a few minutes. He passed the Sofitel Hotel and was on the road toward the airport. He looked for a place to stop and suddenly spotted a McDonald's drive-in restaurant. He pulled the car into the restaurant lot. "Do you want to go inside or shall we have coffee in the car?" Larry asked.

"Let's go inside." Sullivan answered.

"I agree to that. I need to walk for a couple minutes after that joy ride," Jean answered sarcastically. She glared at the two men.

CHAPTER FIFTY-THREE

Inside the restaurant, Jerry bought three coffees and the trio sat at a table that overlooked the parking lot. Royal kept his eyes rotating from the parking lot to the customers inside the restaurant. Jean sat still for several seconds. She placed her hands flat on the table and took several deep breaths.

"All right. Now, tell me what's going on?" she demanded looking from one face to the other.

"Well, it's like this," Sullivan answered. "To begin with, I went to the Embassy earlier today and met with Larry. I told him why you were in Bucharest. My way of thinking was that if I could help you, then you'd be free to return to Iowa. While I was talking to Royal, I explained about the two men and gave him their descriptions. He thought the description sounded like two terrorist he had learned about in a recent briefing."

Jean thought for a moment and looked at the two men. "So let me get this clear. You, Jerry Sullivan, an American businessman, went to the American Embassy and talked to a Consulate Officer. Out of the clear blue, you discussed the two men that were following me. What do you guys take me for?" She shook her head as she talked.

"Yes, that's it," Jerry said.

"You're trying to tell me that you, Jerry, are a complete stranger to Larry, here? Is that right? And you've never met until today?" Jean raised her eyebrows and snickered.

"Yes, that's what he's trying to tell you," Royal answered quickly. He rolled his eyes at Jerry.

"I don't think so. Get real. I may be from Iowa but I'm not stupid. Now, let's get down to the truth. Please, correct me if I'm wrong. Jerry, your CIA and Larry so are you."

Both men stared at Jean. Neither said a word. But, both looked around to see if anyone was sitting near enough to hear what they were discussing.

Jean leaned back in her chair. She looked from one man to the other. "Now, Jerry did Weaver or Jason's office give you instructions to save me at the Embassy? Or, was the purse snatching a set up too?" She paused for several seconds. "And, Larry? Jason was coming to Bucharest to meet with you when he died. Did he meet with you or was he on his way to see you?" She crunched her teeth together and stared hard at the men.

The two men exchanged glances. Royal nodded to Jerry because Jerry was higher rank. Jerry said, "Yes, you're right. I worked with Jason in Virginia. Yes, I know Weaver. Yes, I saved you from the purse snatching. But, after we had wine that first day, I figured I should keep an eye on you. I was at the Embassy actually seeing if I needed a visa to come to Bucharest when you were attacked."

"Aha! Now the truth. Am I supposed to take everything else that you told me for the truth, or do I mentally have to sift through the garbage to find the truths?" Jean asked. She sat back in her chair and twisted her hands.

Royal chuckled. He took several sips of his hot coffee and said, "You're certainly Jason's sister. That's the way he would have talked."

Jerry looked at Royal out of the corner of his eye. He leaned toward Jean. "I didn't want you to go off on your own and do something really stupid. I thought a partial truth was going to be enough."

Jean shook her head and sneered. "What a crock of B.S.?"

Royal set his coffee down on the table. His eyes darted around the room. "Now, let's get down to the present. Yes, Jerry came to the Embassy today, just like he said. I told him I thought the two men sounded like two terrorists I had heard were in the area. Ghassan Nseir is an Islamic terrorist. He is extremely dangerous."

Jean nodded. She looked at the two men. Her face was expressionless. "Now, you're trying to scare me."

"No, this is the truth," Royal whispered. "When Jerry told me that he had seen the men on the train and again at the hotel, we decided that we needed to get you out of the hotel and tell you about them. I asked Sarah to help us. We had a better chance of losing them in my car."

"So, you're both CIA?" Jean said. "Now, what was Jason doing in Bucharest? Did he have contact with these two rogue rejects?"

"Jason's mission in Bucharest was and still is classified. He came in on official business. I can't tell you why he was here, but I'm very sorry he died. The agency is still not clear on how he died."

Jean said, "I thought you all believed he was killed in a car accident?"

"That part is true," Royal said. "We believe he was driving a rental car and it went out of control. He was killed in the hills around Brasov. That's about a two hour drive from Bucharest."

"Yes, I remember," Jean said. She looked toward Jerry. "We went through it today on the train. But, Jason was an excellent driver. I don't believe he had an accident. Was he alone?"

"We have no way of knowing for sure," Royal said. "No one has come forward and said that he or she was with him at the time of the accident."

"Where's the car?" Jean asked.

Royal looked at Jerry. Jerry shrugged. Royal said, "I truthfully don't know."

Jean leaned forward on the table and spoke in a low voice. "I want to go to the spot where he was killed. How do I go about renting a car?"

Royal looked at Jerry. Jerry nodded. Royal answered, "I'll drive you. It would be better than you going off on your on. The agency would have a fit if you were killed roaming around the Romanian hills."

"Fine, when can we go. How about in the morning? It's too dark to do anything tonight." Jean sighed. She was relieved that she didn't have to apply any more pressure than she had. "Now, can I go back to the hotel?"

"Jerry, do you think you'll both be safe going back to the hotel tonight?" Royal asked.

"I don't see why not. Those two men won't try anything inside the hotel. We'll be perfectly safe. It's wandering around that worries me." He glanced at his watch. "Jean, since, it's late and we're going back, let's get a couple burgers here rather than going out to eat tonight." He turned around and looked at the people waiting in line.

"That's fine with me. I want a burger, fries and a vanilla shake. A touch of America sounds very comforting just now." She felt relieved for the first time since they had entered the restaurant.

"I'll have the same only with a strawberry shake," Royal added.

Jean waited until Jerry left the table before she asked Larry, "So, how well did you know Jason?"

"I worked with him several times. I met him right after he joined the agency, and went to Brussels. I truly am sorry about his death. He was a fine person."

"So, you know Michael Cleary, too?" Jean continued.

Royal frowned and hesitated. "Yes, I know Michael."

Jean noticed the slight hesitation. She asked, "Is Michael also with the CIA?"

Royal looked at Jean and shook his head. "No. I think Cleary is in the Air Force, isn't he?"

"Does that mean he can't be CIA?" Jean pressed.

Royal looked at Jean and smiled, "Hardly. The Air Force intelligence is a branch of their own. To be more exact, they are known as the Defense Intelligence Agency. The DIA. But, Cleary is with Air Force legal, isn't he?"

"Anyway, that's what he says. But, I'm beginning to wonder. Nothing is as it seems. I beginning to find that in the intelligence world, everything is a lie and a cover. Who knows what or who to believe?" Jean glanced toward Jerry who had finally moved up to order.

Royal said, "No, I think Cleary is exactly who he says he is. I've meet him several times. Jason and he were buddies from high school, weren't they?" He watched Jean out of the corner of his eye.

"No, actually college. They've known each other for years. They both received their law degrees at Iowa U.. Then, Michael went into the military and Jason went to work with the CIA.

Michael's degree was earned through the military program on campus."

"So, how do you like Romania so far?" Royal asked.

Jean smiled and answered. She counted on her fingers as she spoke. "So far, I've been watched, harassed, forcefully escorted to a car, been taken on a wild car ride and am eating with two CIA agents. It has been routine, I suppose you might say."

Larry laughed. "Okay. I understand. At least when we drive to Brasov tomorrow you'll see some of the countryside. It's quite spectacular. Of course, in the winter, it isn't as nice as the spring or fall, but the hills are lovely. We will be driving through Transylvania. That's a lovely area."

"Isn't that where Dracula came from?" Jean asked thinking of her childhood stories.

"Yes, in fact, we'll be driving within a couple miles of his famed castle. If you like we could stop and see it. I doubt if it will be open, but you could at least see the famous old place. It's become quite a tourist attraction since the fall of the old Ceausescu regime. When Ceausescu was ruler, he played down Dracula. Now, the country is hungry for the western tourist dollar and they're playing up all tourist attractions."

"I'd like that," she answered. She looked up and took her food from Jerry. "Thanks."

CHAPTER FIFTY-FOUR

Jerry and Jean were creeping down the back stairway before the hotel started serving breakfast. They knew that once breakfast was served the hotel would become alive for another day. Jean would never admit it, but she felt comfortable knowing Jerry Sullivan was a CIA agent.

They made their way to the underground parking garage and took the exit stairs to the street. Neither spoke a word. Jerry checked his watch a couple times, signaling with his fingers how many minutes they had to get to the American Embassy. The Embassy was just three minutes away.

Jean was pleased she was going to have a chance to at least see the Embassy. After returning from McDonald's, she laid in bed and read a book about Romania. There was an article about several historical buildings. When they passed the American Consulate building she remembered reading that it had been built in the 1880's as a home for the founder of the Conservative ruling party.

Jean stopped and looked at the stately old house. She wondered what life had been like a hundred years earlier. Jerry saw Jean was falling behind him and motioned for her to hurry. When she turned the corner toward the American Embassy, she saw the Romanian Diplomatic Guard looking their way.

She froze. "What's that guard doing here? Will he stop us?"

Jerry whispered, "I doubt if he'd stop us for just walking past. Each host country has guards that guard all the diplomatic missions. He's just doing his job. In order to get into the Embassy, one has to go through that gate over there. Someone checks for proper identification, and only then can one go inside the fence."

"Is that high fence electrified?" Jean asked. "Are they trying to keep people in or out?"

"The fence could be electric. I'm never sure. Some countries it is and some it isn't. To tell you the truth, I've never touched one. The Embassy is trying to keep people they don't want out. Now, that Romania is free, the Romanians really don't care who goes in the Embassy. In the old days, the fence also served to keep Romanians who were trying to seek asylum out." He pointed to a door in the middle of the building. "There's the door to the Embassy. It's controlled by an electric switch. A Marine guard controls it. When you walk into the Embassy, you pass through a metal detector. Just like at the airports. Then, you walk up to a bullet proof window. The Marines are behind that window."

Jean smiled. "Then it's not like in the movies. Every movie I've ever seen, a Marine Guard is standing outside the Embassy, keeping anyone they don't want from entering."

Jerry shook his head. "No, that's pure garbage and usually only done for show, like in the movies. Marines aren't allowed to stand outside in their uniforms in a foreign country, unless they have special permission."

"Well, I'll be," Jean said. "Once I'm inside can I wander around anywhere I want to go?"

"After you show your identification, tell the Marine what or who you want, they call whoever it is that you have come to see. That person comes and gets you. If you don't have at least a Secret Clearance, that person stays with you the whole time you're in the Embassy."

"You're kidding? You mean as an American citizen and a taxpayer, I can't go into the Embassy and talk to someone just because I want to?" Jean asked.

"No. You can't. An Embassy is only in a country to serve as the diplomatic connection between the United States government and the host government. It is not there to help or assist Americans. The Consulate, we just passed, is designed to handle the American tourist or visitor. Not the Embassy."

"I didn't know that."

"Most Americans don't know the difference," Jerry said. He looked around the area and checked his watch. "There are a lot of irate American businessmen who think the Embassy should help them with their business contacts. Actually, that's done either through the Economic Office at the Embassy or the Commercial Section. It depends on which the Embassy has. With all the budget cuts, it varies in each country. Look, there's

Royal. Come on, he'll only stop long enough for us to get into his car."

Jean took a long look at the old building which was now the American Embassy. She remembered it was built in 1888 as the home for a wealthy banker, but has been used for the Embassy since the early 1940's. She wondered how much of the original charm still existed, or, if over the years, the inside had been gutted to make room for the numerous offices.

"Come on." Jerry tugged her sleeve and moved toward the waiting car. "Maybe, you can get another chance to come back and see the Embassy if it really interests you."

It was just six as the BMW sped away from the Embassy. No one said a word as Royal drove through the early morning traffic. Several cars were on the streets, but nothing compared to the rush hour traffic they had driven through the previous night. The sun was just beginning to fill the sky as the BMW left the city limits.

Larry brought Jean and Jerry up to date on some of the political activities in Romania. They talked at great length about the human rights issue and the ethnic population near the Hungarian border. Royal explained the problems the poorer Romanian communities were facing.

He also explained that for the past few years, foreign governments were offering the community leaders huge sums of money to store their toxic waste. Most of the leaders had lined their pockets and had not informed the citizens of the potential dangers. Now, children were being born with deformities. People were developing cancer and rare incurable diseases.

Royal looked at Jean through his rear view mirror. He said, "Jason was very interested in illegal toxic waste dumping."

Jean leaned forward and rested her arms on the passenger seat. "Yes, I know. We found some newspaper articles in his apartment about it." She looked at her watch. It seemed as if they had been driving for hours. "How much longer will it take?"

"Could take as little as an hour or as much as four. It depends on the roads and the traffic. Romania has very few four lane highways, so the truck traffic could slow us down. Why don't you try and rest? We have all day."

"Jerry, what are you going to do? Aren't you supposed to be home for your wife's birthday this weekend?" Jean asked.

"I called her last night. She knows I'll be there if I can. She understands."

"Oh," Jean answered. She wondered if he were really married or if that also was a lie.

Time flew past as they drove through the lush backdrop of Mt. Timpa and Mt. Postavarni. They passed the old medieval fortifications from the twelfth century which was the popular route for the Turks.

"We're close to Cluj," Royal said. "We'll be heading toward the Ukraine border. It's not far now."

Jean saw that the homes looked different. "These houses look like Germany?"

Royal slowed down. "We're in the area that was settled by the Germans and Hungarians."

"Their quite nice. Did Jason come up here often?"

Royal answered, "Yes, since he was in Budapest, he took a deep interest in this part of Romania. This road is also a main route through Romania from the Ukraine and Russia."

"Oh, where does it go?" Jean asked.

"To the free world. Turkey, Serbia, Bulgaria, and all points west and south."

"Did all of this have something to do with what Jason was working on?" Jean asked.

Royal shook his head. He turned and looked at Jean. "You know I can't tell you that. I'm to take you to the place of the accident. Please, don't ask me a questions about his job."

Jerry glanced back at Jean and shrugged.

Jean shivered and slid back against the seat. She pulled her coat tight around her. Turning toward the window, she silently vowed that one day she would know exactly what Jason's work involved.

Royal drove down a narrow road and stopped on a hill overlooking a small cemetery. He parked under an old gnarled tree. It's branches hung to the ground. "This is it. Do you want to get out and walk around the area?"

"Of course," Jean answered quickly. She was out of the door before Royal had the car parked. She stood by the side of the road and waited for the men to join her.

Royal pointed to a spot down the side of the cliff. "This is where Jason was found. He was over there near that large tombstone."

"Who found him?" Jean asked, fighting back tears.

Royal looked at Jean and back at the scene. "I believe some farmer. The Embassy was notified as soon as the local police realized Jason was an American. He was traveling with American identification."

Jean said, "Who identified the body?"

"I came up and claimed the body," Royal answered. "But, I suspected it was Jason when I got the message that an American had been found. The night before he drove up here, I talked to him. He told me he was coming to meet someone and told me not to worry. He said he'd be all right."

"Was he in the car or on the ground somewhere?" Jean asked.

Royal looked at Jean. He hesitated for several seconds before he answered. "He was on the ground."

"Where?" Jean asked, her eyes moist.

Royal walked down the road, looked around and pointed to a spot about fifty foot from him. "I think he was found about there."

Jean started toward the spot. She turned to Royal and asked, "Who was he with?"

"We have no idea. No one saw him with anyone and no one else was found in the car. The rental car was pretty well battered up. There were no skid marks on the road, nor did Jason have any alcohol in his blood. The police believe someone forced him off the road or he fell asleep at the wheel."

"Who was he coming up to meet? Can you tell me at least that much about the case?"

"Jean, I already told you the case is still classified. He didn't tell me who he was meeting, only that he had a meeting."

Jean walked back to where the two men were standing. She stood directly in front of them. "I'm not a crime scene investigator, but doesn't it seem strange to both of you, that Jason's body was here and his car down there?"

Jerry shrugged. "Not, really. He was undoubtedly thrown from the car."

"Get real. If he were thrown or hit something coming around the curve, and if he were driving, he would have been thrown over there." She turned and pointed to a spot across the road. "Not down there. That's not even in the path of the car. It looks as if he might have been walking."

Royal scratched his head and said, "Well, maybe, he got out of the car, staggered up to the top of the hill and collapsed and died where he was found."

Jean thought for several seconds. "That might be possible, but I really doubt it. I'm going to climb down the hill. Is that where the car was, there in the spot where the tree branch is broken?" She didn't wait for him to answer and started down the hillside.

"Jean, don't go down there," Jerry cautioned. "It's slick and muddy. You could be hurt." He hesitated for a moment and when she didn't stop, he started down the hill after her.

Jean called, as she moved downward. "Has someone combed the area for clues?"

Royal was standing on top of the hill with his hands on his hips. He shook his head with disgust. "Of course. I climbed all over and so did the Romanian police who investigated the accident. Be careful, you two, I don't want to have to go to a doctor with you."

Jean continued toward the broken tree branch. She picked her path carefully. It had not been a month since the accident, the ground was still frozen but she was amazed how many tracks remained. It appeared to have snowed a couple times since the accident.

As she moved forward something shiny on the ground caught her attention. Bending down, she picked it up. It was a German coin. Brushing it off, she put it in her pocket, thinking this was her lucky day. She remembered her father telling her that if she found a coin on the ground, it would bring good luck all day long.

"I don't see anything unusual, do you, Jerry?" she asked, when Jerry joined her by the broken branch.

He answered, "No, I don't see anything either. What did you pick up back there?"

"Nothing special. Just a German coin." She pulled it out of pocket and showed it to him. "Hard telling who could have dropped it."

Jerry flipped it over in his hand a couple times. "Could have been anyone. Looks new." He handed it back to Jean.

They continued walking down the hillside. The cemetery laid directly in front of them. The tall tombstones stood proudly over the numerous graves.

"Let's go. This place is giving me the creeps," Jerry said. He took Jean's arm and helped her back up the hillside.

Jean went back to the car and took a small camera from her purse. "Just a moment, I want to take some pictures of this. I know it may seem morbid, but it will be comforting in the years to come. Just a moment. I promise I won't be long."

"Take as long as you need," Jerry answered. He walked over to Royal who was talking on his cell phone.

Several minutes later, Jean walked back to the car and took a picture of the two men. She climbed into the car, leaned back and closed her eyes.

"Who was that on the phone?" Jerry asked, after everyone was back in the car.

Royal turned and looked at Jean. He started to whisper, but Jean slid up and leaned on the seat. "My office called. They said that your two friends were spotted in Bucharest early this morning. They were renting a car."

Jean froze. She felt sick to her stomach. After a long silence, she asked, "Did the Embassy have any idea where they were going?"

"No," Royal answered. "The agent that saw them stumbled onto them purely by accident. He wasn't driving so he wasn't able to follow them. However, he was going to try and find out what they're doing in Romania."

Jerry cracked his knuckles. "Well, at least we now know positively who they are. They are probably in the area to make a buy or clear the route for something that's coming in."

"What do you mean make a buy or clear the route?" Jean questioned. "What do these men do?"

Royal answered. "I told you last night they are terrorists. They buy and sell all sorts of things. Anything for anyone. They have no morals, no code of ethics and no scruples. They are very bad men."

"Oh, great," Jean said. "Now, we're going to get caught in the middle of some big international incident." She pushed herself back in her seat and put her head in her hands. "That's all I need."

"Well, we're not going to get involved if we don't want to," Royal said. "Let's forget all about them and spend sometime relaxing." He turned the key in the ignition. "I know a great hotel about ten minutes from here that has an excellent restaurant and they serve a marvelous lunch. What do you say?"

CHAPTER FIFTY-FIVE

Royal stopped his BMW in front of a large modern hotel built on top of the mountain. He maneuvered it around into a parking place away from the walking path. "Hope you don't mind if I park here," he said. "I would hate to have scratches from the skiers with their skis. My experience is that they aren't always the most careful."

Jean chuckled, "Jason used to say the same thing. After one of his trips, his car was in the body shop for a couple weeks repairing the scratches." She opened her door and took a deep breath. "Now, I want to discuss something else," she said. "Jason was a skillful driver. If, he'd been driving and had to stop unexpectedly, there should have been at least some evidence on the road. There wasn't any that I saw."

Jerry asked Royal, "Was there fog that day?"

Royal answered after giving the question some thought, "I believe the weather was clear. I don't remember anyone mentioning any. Also, no one has come forth that they saw or heard anything."

Jean leaned forward. "That means that if someone pushed him off the road, they didn't think anything about it. No, Jason was parked. He stopped for some specific reason. He was killed and his car was pushed down the embankment. That's the only thing that makes any sense." She looked at the two men. "I'm getting out. Let's get something to eat."

She stepped out and leaned against the car. Her legs were wobbly. "Has anyone checked with any of these tourist spots to see if Jason might have stopped?"

Royal hesitated. "I don't really know. Why, do you ask?"

"Maybe, they would remember seeing him," Jean said. "Then, just maybe they could say if he were alone. Don't you think that it would be worth checking out?"

"If we haven't checked." Jerry said. "I can't believe it would hurt anything to ask around. Who knows, someone might have seen something."

Royal took out his black notebook and made a note to himself. "I'll get someone on it. Let's get something to eat and get started back."

Jean watched several guests milling around in the parking lot. They had just stepped off of a skiing bus. She couldn't believe that someone didn't know something about Jason. The road was too well traveled.

After enjoying a bowl of tripe soup, beef stew and sweet pancakes smothered with whipped cream and chocolate sauce, Jerry said, "We'd better get going. I don't want to get back to our hotel in the dark."

After everyone was in the car, Royal said, "I know we talked about Dracula last night. His legendary home is just eight miles from here. I thought we'd drive past it on the way home. They might even have a couple of the souvenir stands open."

"I'd love that," Jean said. "I could use a couple more souvenirs for people back home. I'd like to get something for Michael, too."

Royal pulled out of the parking lot, just as a group of skiers stepped out from behind a car. Their skis were on their shoulders. They stepped directly in the way of the BMW.

"Damn," Royal muttered, just missing them by inches. "Hope to heavens that they didn't scratch the roof." He pulled out as fast as he dared and spun his wheels spraying the group with soft snow.

Jerry looked back. "Well, they sure are giving you a nasty look. You probably got them all wet."

"They deserve it," Royal answered. "Skiers are as bad as tourists." He continued to mutter to himself as the car sped down the road, taking a curve much faster than was necessary.

Jean sat back and held on to the seat belt. They rode in silence for several miles. When the car slowed slightly, she asked, "Have you ever been in the castle?"

"Yes, several times," Royal answered. He had recovered from his near mishap and was driving more carefully. "It has an awesome torture room in the basement complete with an Iron Maiden."

Jean was about to ask what an "Iron Maiden" was when Royal stopped the BMW directly in front of a small wooden souvenir stand in the castle parking lot.

Royal said, "There isn't much going on today, but at least there are a couple stands open. Do you want to get out and see what they have for sale?"

Jean and Jerry left Royal standing by his car. He was walking around it and touching it for scratches. Jean started taking pictures as they walked. They stopped at each stand and bought something.

Jerry glanced back at the car. Royal was waving frantically. "Something is wrong. We'd better go."

They hurried as fast as they dared trying not to attract attention. Royal was turning the car around. He signaled for the couple to get in.

"What's the hurry?" Jerry asked, as soon as they were safely inside the car.

"The Embassy called. The hotel just called and said that both of your rooms at the hotel have been ransacked."

Jean touched her chest and patted it several times. She glanced at her purse and overnight case on the seat beside her. After she caught her breath, she asked, "How bad was it?"

"I'm not sure, but must be bad or the hotel wouldn't have notified the consulate."

"Is that normal procedure?" Jean questioned.

Royal said, "When you checked in, the hotel wrote down your passport number and vital information. According to law, they're to notify the victim's embassy. Actually, they were only covering their butts."

"Now, we have to go back to the hotel and that's not all bad. Maybe the police will post guards at our doors," Jerry said. He looked at Royal to see if there was going to be any reaction to his suggestion.

"We never know," Royal answer. He drove for several minutes and then said, "Oh, shit."

"Now what?" Jerry asked. He glanced at Royal's face.

"Someone's following us," Royal said. His eyes darted from the rear view mirror to the road. "It's a black Mercedes. We picked it up right after we left the castle parking lot."

Jean turned and looked out the rear window. She could see the car. There were two men in the front seat. She couldn't say for sure, but it looked like the two men from the train. "Good heavens, it's those two men," she muttered.

CHAPTER FIFTY-SIX

"Let's get the hell out of here," Jerry cried to Royal. "Jean, lay down on the back seat, but be sure and keep your seat belt buckled. Let's see what kind of power the agency is paying for."

"Hang on," Royal called.

Just as the car sped away, Jean took another look out the rear window. She felt something whiz by her hair. A small hole appeared in the front window shield. "Good heavens, they're shooting at us."

"Lay down like I told you," Jerry screamed.

Royal said, "Jean, reach under my seat. Take that bag out. There are two things there I want you to use. Take the first piece, the one with the Velcro edges. Press it against the back window."

Jean quickly did as she was told. "That's done, but what is it?"

"It's a new bulletproof liner that the agency has developed. Now, take out the other thing that looks like a blanket, I want you to press it up against the back seat behind you."

Jean shook it out and was surprised to find the material clung to the seat cover. "And, what is this?"

"It's similar to the window protection. It'll reflect any bullets from entering the car. Hold on, I'm going to give them a couple surprises."

Royal pushed a couple buttons on the dashboard. Something started buzzing under their feet. He said, "I just activated a bullet reflecting system. We've been testing the system in the Arab world and the agency had it installed on this car. Now, I'm going to release a spray of oil from the trunk."

Jean laid down on the seat. The smell of oil saturated the seat. "Who would have thought I would ever be in a James Bond car?"

The sound of a car skidding echoed through the air. Several seconds later, there was a loud thud.

Royal laughed and pushed on the gas pedal. The car shot forward. He raced down the road. "Jerry, now reach under your seat."

Jerry asked, "What am I going to find? I hope it's not a grenade launcher of some type."

"Hardly," Royal said. "I've got a gun under there with a silencer. It's in a bag. Take it out and keep it handy. We don't know what we might be facing ahead of us."

"Now, a gun I can handle," Jerry answered.

"Jerry, keep an eye in your outside rear view window. Let me know when you see them again." Royal had both hands on the steering wheel. His eyes were fixed on the road ahead.

"There's no car in sight. You must have out distanced them. Jean, are you all right?"

Jean grunted. She was clutching her purse and had her back against the bulletproof cloth on the seat.

"Stay where you are until we say the coast is clear," Royal said. "Jerry, any sign of them?"

"No," Jerry answered. He glanced at the speedometer. The needle was waving between one hundred and one hundred and ten miles per hour. "This car sure hugs the road. It doesn't seem that we're going that fast."

Jean asked, "How fast are we going?"

Jerry looked at Royal and rolled his eyes back and forth. "About eighty."

It was dark when Royal pulled into the parking lot of the Intercontinental Hotel. The ride back to Bucharest had been in record breaking time. They had only seen another black Mercedes and it was on the outskirts of the city.

"When are you leaving, Jean?" Royal asked.

"I think I'll leave tomorrow if I can get out. This is all more than I bargained for, and I haven't even found out if I have any clothes left."

"Let's go find out," Jerry said.

"At least, I feel better having seen the crash sight. Now, I can accept Jason's death. Will both of you promise me something?" She grabbed their arms and stopped them in front of the hotel. "Promise me that if you ever find out who killed him, you'll let me know?"

Royal removed her hand. "Jean, I can't promise you something like that. Headquarters is the only one that can tell you the specific's."

Jerry took Jean's hand and patted it. "He's right and you know it. Now, let's go see what condition our rooms are in."

Larry pointed toward the elevator. "Since you have your keys go on up. I'll check with management and see what or where the police are."

CHAPTER FIFTY-SEVEN

Yuri Nikitin just hung up the telephone. He walked out of the third floor Communication Center and took the steps to the first floor of the Russian Embassy. The building was quiet.

He stepped out the front door, walked down the short sidewalk to the street and looked back at the Russian flag flying high over the modern block long building. His heart filled with pride. Buttoning up his dark blue Burberry overcoat, he started walking toward the heart of the city.

At the corner, he turned and started up Andrassy ut. He walked for a block, stopped, shook his head, turned around and walked toward Heros Square in the opposite direction. He appeared to be a man taking an evening stroll.

At the corner of RipplRona, he crossed Andrassy ut and began walking on the other side of the street. He walked past the International offices of Baker & McKenzie's law firm. He stopped for a moment and admired the elegant looking mansion and walked toward the iron gate. He put his hand on the gate, looked around and then turned and headed for the center of Heros Square.

He started across to the center of the square, turned to his right and walked directly in front of the Australian Embassy. Directly in front of him was a black Ford. The passenger door opened. He stepped into the car.

"Why all the cloak and dagger stuff?" Yuri asked.

"This is one of the few places that I know isn't bugged," the driver said. He drove to the corner, turned and drove into the park. Several minutes later, he parked the car in a deserted dim lit parking lot across from the entrance to the city zoo.

Yuri turned in his seat and reached for the man's hand. He stroked it tenderly and said, "Now, what is going on?"

The man smiled. His eyes moved over Yuri's face. "I wanted to tell you about the Martin case." He cast his eyes downward. "I'm never quite sure what you know and don't know."

Yuri continued holding the man's hand. "I always am interested in anything you have to say. You have me all excited. What is it?"

"We received word from Bucharest this afternoon that two terrorists have been seen following Jean Martin and an American businessman named Jerry Sullivan. Their hotel room at the Intercontinental was vandalized. All evidence points to the two terrorists."

Yuri released the man's hand and straightened his coat. "Do you have the names of the two men?"

The American took a sheet of paper out of his pocket. "Yes, I wrote them down for you."

The Russian looked at the paper and smiled. "Thank you. Is there anything else you would like to tell me?"

"Not really. One of the Bucharest Embassy Officers took Ms. Martin to the hill where her brother was killed. We have reason to believe that she will be returning to the states tomorrow."

Yuri clapped. "Now, that is good news. I will let Moscow know tonight. Hopefully, we can get a shipment ready for delivery within a few days. We hated having to postpone the last one, but it was for the best."

The American shifted in his seat. "You never have told me if you had anything to do with Jason Martin's death? Did you?"

The Russian slid across the seat. He patted the American's face and ran his fingers across the American's lips. "No, I didn't. Did you?"

The American jerked backward. "Of course, not." He acted very offended. After a deep sigh, he said, "I'm glad it wasn't you. I was afraid it might have been."

The Russian patted the American on the leg. He said, "No, I would never kill anyone." He omitted to say that he had others that did his dirty work.

The American looked at his watch. "I have to get home. It's getting late."

Yuri asked, "Will you let me know when the Martin woman has left for the states? I will start the trucks running once I know she is on the plane."

"Yes, of course," the American answered. He started the car and headed back toward Andrassy ut. "Where would you like me to drop you?"

"It seems to be getting colder," the Russian answered. "Can you drop me off near the Vaci? I'm going to get a bite to eat and will catch a tram from there."

The American stopped his Ford in a deserted side street near the Kempinski Hotel. "When will I see you again?"

The Russian looked around and stepped out of the car. He leaned back into the car and said, "Stop by anytime. You know where I live."

The American drove off. The Russian stood in the shadows until the Ford had gone around the corner. Then, he smiled, turned and walked into the Kempinski Hotel.

Across from the Kempinski Hotel, CIA Station Chief, Tom Bryan was walking toward his car. He had just left a meeting at the police station when a black American style Ford passed him.

The car looked familiar. When the car drove away, Bryan turned and caught the license plate. It was an American Embassy car.

He saw a man in the shadows. When, the man turned and walked under the light and into the hotel, Bryan froze. He knew the man. Instantly, the puzzle pieces started falling into place.

CHAPTER FIFTY-EIGHT

"Jerry, when are you leaving?" Jean asked. She looked up and saw the elevator had stopped on the fourth floor. Her arms ached. She was carrying her overnight bag, purse and souvenirs.

"I think I'll leave with you. If I can't get a direct flight to New York or so, I'll ride with you to Frankfurt." He pushed the button with one of his free fingers, turned his back to the elevator and looked around the lobby for Royal. "We can get in touch with Delta in the morning and make arrangements to leave on their first available flight."

"Larry, are you coming up with us?" Jerry called. Larry had stopped to read an announcement on a bulletin board. He ran toward the elevator.

Royal got in the elevator and said, "I'm going up for just a moment. I want to make sure that everything is all right. The police are up there in one of your rooms." He leaned forward and whispered, "It'll make my cover look better."

"Well, thanks for the trip," Jean said. "I really enjoyed it. Except of course, for the chase on the way back."

"You're very welcome. Have a safe trip back to Iowa. Will you need a ride to the airport?" Royal asked.

"No, we'll take a taxi from the hotel," Jerry answered. "I enjoyed the trip, even if I didn't like the way you wound that BMW around those hairpin curves."

Jerry held the elevator door open with his feet. He had taken Jean's overnight bag and with his souvenirs, his hands were full. The group got out on the fourth floor and went directly to Jean's room. Her door was open and there were several people milling around.

"Oh, my heavens!" Jean groaned when she looked inside the room. "This place is in shambles."

Jerry and Royal motioned for her to stand back and they went inside the room. She stood outside for a moment, thought about what she was doing and followed them. Clothes, bed linen and papers were tossed everywhere.

The chairs were overturned and everything that had been in the dresser drawers was on the floor. Three Romanian uniformed policeman were moving things around with their feet.

"Tell them to stop that," Jean shouted. "They're going to tear my clothes worse than they already are."

"Ms. Martin, I believe," one of the policeman said. He walked toward Jean and stared at her. He motioned for the other policeman to wait in the hall. "It is about time that you arrived."

Royal stepped forward and introduced himself and Jerry. "We were out in the countryside when the Embassy contacted us. As you know, Romania has strict speed limits and it took us some time to return."

Jerry and Jean both stared at Royal when he mentioned speed limits. They stepped back and let Royal talk.

"What have you discovered?" Royal asked.

The policeman moved his head back and forth and looked around the room. He rubbed his jacket sleeves against his belt, stood firmly on both legs and looked at the newcomers. After a long silence, he said, "How do we know that Ms. Martin did not do this herself?"

Jean laughed aloud and shook her head. "You're kidding," she said. She turned to Jerry. "He can't be serious?"

Jerry didn't answer but just shook his head.

The policeman took two steps toward Jean and stared at her. Not saying a word, he turned and stared at the two men.

Royal raised his hand and moved toward the policeman. "Let's just suppose that she didn't do this. Who do you think might have?"

The policeman stiffened. "We have very little crime in Romania. Those that are guilty of crime are always foreigners."

Jerry rolled his eyes and moved out of the policeman's view. He went to the window and looked out on the street. A black Mercedes was parking directly below the window. He looked at Royal and motioned with his head.

Jean saw him and walked over to the window. She gasped aloud when she saw the two men get out of the car. Her hands were shaking.

Royal and the policeman were talking and walking around the room. They walked into the bathroom.

Royal called, "Jean, come in here, please."

Jean hurried to join the men. The bathroom was a mess. All of her toilet articles were on the floor. Her tubes of toothpaste and shampoo had been cut open and their contents were emptied into the sink.

"Whoever did this was a professional," Royal said. "They didn't leave anything unturned. The bed mattress has even been slashed and turned. Your suitcase has had its lining cut and torn. What a mess."

The policeman turned to Jean. "What were they looking for? Have you smuggled something into Romania? Is it drugs?"

Jean just stood and stared at the policeman. She started to speak and then stopped. The last thing she wanted was to end up in jail for assaulting a Romanian policeman.

Jean waited until the policeman went into the hall. She turned to Royal. "Do you think the two men that we saw on the train did this?" Her foot hit something. She bent down and picked up a broken picture. Tears filled her eyes when she saw her picture of Jason had been smashed to pieces.

"It probably was," Jerry answered. He had joined the couple. "I doubt if we could ever find any finger prints or anything to connect them. What chaos!"

"Well, get all these people out of here and I'll clean up what I can," Jean said. She began pushing the two men toward the bedroom door.

Royal looked at her and shook his head. "You can't stay in this room. The bed is all destroyed. The manager will have to get you another room."

"I'll call him," Jean said, following the men back into the bedroom. She picked up the phone from the floor and pushed a button.

"I want to speak to the manager?" she said.

"Ms. Martin, I am the Manager. How may I help you? Aren't the police with you?" a weak male voice answered.

"Yes, have you seen this room?"

"Yes, I have."

"Then, I insist that you come up and give me another room. I'm very tired and I need to get some rest." Jean sat on the corner of the bed. Her eyes roamed around the room.

"I cannot do that," the manager said.

Jean's eyes narrowed. A deep frown covered her forehead. "Yes, you can and you will. I want to see you at once." She slammed the receiver down.

Jerry and Royal watched. They could hear every word that had been spoken by the manager. They didn't say anything and walked to the hallway.

Jean followed them. For several seconds, she stood and looked at the group of policemen talking in the hallway. It was getting late. She was tired and hungry.

Walking back into the room, she shoved the torn mattress back on the bed frame and sat down on the bed. She looked at her wrist watch. The minute hand was whirling. She was getting madder with each revolution.

Exactly five minutes later, she heard a loud commotion in the hallway. It was obvious that someone with authority had walked onto the floor. Remaining seated, she waited for someone to enter her room.

There was a soft knock. A short, timid man walked into the room. He pushed the door wide open. The policeman in charge followed.

"Ms. Martin, I am the Manager. Do you have any idea what happened here?"

"I have already talked to the police. I don't intend to tell my story again." Jean's loud harsh tone of voice caught all the men's attention. "Is this the type of protection and security a woman tourist can expect when visiting your hotel and your country?" She looked directly into the manager's eyes as she spoke.

The Manager stepped backward. His actions showed that he had obviously never encountered a strong willed woman. He looked confused. "No. Of course not. The management is deeply concerned. We shall make arrangements for you to be moved to a suite immediately. Of course, it will be with compliments of the management. We are very sorry this happened. When my assistant returns, I will instruct him to make those arrangements immediately."

"Do I look like a woman who would go around asking for someone to terrorize her room? What could a young single woman from Iowa have with her that would attract such attention?" Jean continued. She rubbed her face and stared at the man.

"Ms. Martin, this is highly irregular. We will have to question the staff further and find out if they saw anyone suspicious." The manager looked at the policeman for some assistance.

Jean felt better. "I guarantee you, sir, we will get to the bottom of this, if I have to make an international incident out of it."

The manager and the policeman understood exactly every word Jean was saying. They stepped out in the hallway. They walked several feet from Jean's door and stood talking.

Jerry walked toward Jean. He leaned over with a smile on his face and said, "Feel better?"

Jean smiled but when she looked behind him, she saw the policeman looking her way, she turned stoned faced. She whispered to Jerry. "Your room is next."

Jerry winked and walked back to Royal. "Well, let's get my room over with." He turned back to Jean. "Do you need help with the move?"

"Hardly," Jean said. She jumped off the bed and started organizing her things. I'm only going to take what I need to get by on until I get out of this country. I can buy new things as I need them."

The manager and policeman walked back to Jean. The manager said, "Did you have anything of value in the room?"

"If you mean anything expensive. No. I didn't. But, I have clothing which you can see has either been ripped to shreds or tossed around. My suitcase is completely ruined. I have some of my dead brother's pictures and things which are spread all over the room. They have sentimental value but were not expensive."

"What are you doing in Romania?" The policeman asked. He glared once more at Jean.

Jean looked from Jerry Sullivan to Larry Royal. She noticed a slight motion from each of them. "I'm a tourist. I had been in Budapest and decided to come to Romania since I was in the area. Why not?" She replied more as a question than the response the police had hoped to receive.

"How long do you plan on visiting?" The policeman spoke without expression, as if he were reading the questions off of a sheet of paper.

Jean looked around the room. "I had planned on leaving tomorrow if I can catch a flight out. But, now, I'm not real sure. Look at this mess. I'll need to buy a suitcase before I can do anything. Then I will have to check over what needs to be replaced. Am not sure, but after seeing this country, I won't want to buy much here." Her reply was sharp.

Everyone understood exactly what she was saying. Larry Royal could feel the resentment among the Romanian officials. He quickly jumped into the conversation, trying to smooth over Jean's sharp words. "What Ms. Martin means, is that she is unfamiliar with the city and has no idea where to go to shop for her replacements. Now, is there anything else that any of you would like to know? I think it is apparent that Ms. Martin is upset."

"There is nothing else that I need to know," the policeman answered.

"You were going to get Ms. Martin another room, weren't you?" Royal asked turning to the Manager.

"Yes, of course. It should be ready by now." He turned to a man that had just joined the group. "Andras, do you have the key to the suite on the fifth floor?"

Andras reached into his pocket and pulled out a key. Ceremoniously, he walked to Jean and handed it to her. "Would you need any help with moving?"

Jean smiled politely and said, "Give me a few minutes. Do you want to have someone come and fingerprint the room?" She turned to the policeman who had walked to the side of the room and was whispering to Larry Royal.

"No. I don't think that is necessary. There will be so many fingerprints we will never be able to find out whose are whose. You're free to take anything that you wish out of the room."

CHAPTER FIFTY-NINE

It was morning when Jean walked out of her bedroom and looked around the living room of the suite. Both Jerry and Royal were gone. Dirty dishes from the meal the night before were still on a serving cart. Suddenly, she felt hungry. Rather than dealing with room service and language problems, she decided she'd go to the breakfast room. Going back into her bedroom, she slipped the leather case back around her neck. She patted it as it fell into place between her sweatshirt and her breasts. Just knowing that the black case was safe gave her comfort.

Slipping her boots on her feet, she decided that she had been lucky once. She couldn't afford to tempt fate. Carefully, she pulled the bag out, took out the audio tapes and stuck one in each of her bra cups. They felt a bit uncomfortable but under her sweatshirt the extra bulk wasn't obvious. She looked at the list.

Several hiding places popped into mind. Searching through her purse, she took out a small folding scissors. She turned her purse upside down and emptied the contents out on the bed. Carefully, she cut the bottom lining of her purse. After the lining was pulled out, she inserted the computer disks and the list between the leather and the lining. With a needle and black thread, she sewed the lining back together.

Satisfied, she put everything back in her purse. This time, she took the computer empty box and put her American coins in it. The coins added just enough weight to the box. Hopefully, if someone were in a hurry, they wouldn't check the contents of the box immediately.

Tossing her purse over her shoulder, she headed for the door. Slipping the room key into her jeans pocket, she flipped the lock, opened the door and stepped out into the empty hallway. She heard the door catch behind her.

The aroma of fresh brewed coffee filled the hallway. The thought of a sweet roll and coffee brought a smile to her face. She stood facing the closed door, humming and tapping her foot. Suddenly, the hallway smelled like garlic and strong chemicals. She froze.

A huge leather gloved hand slid over her face, gripping her nose and mouth.

"Make a sound and you're dead," the harsh voice muttered in broken English.

Jean's eyes filled with fright. She began kicking backward, trying to push the man away. With each motion, the man pulled her tighter to him, restricting her movements.

"Don't," he threatened. He kept one hand firm on her mouth and with his other hand he held her arms.

"I can't breathe," she groaned.

"At least you're not dead, yet," he chuckled. He moved his fingers up against her chest and sighed. "Hum."

Jean began kicking, twisting and turning to get her arms free. The sound of footsteps behind her gave her hope. She struggled harder believing another guest was coming to help her.

"Hit her if she makes any noise," a second man whispered. "We don't have the time to bother with her if she's going to fight us. I told the boss we should just kill her, but he insisted she be taken alive. He's sentimental over her for some reason."

Jean knew it was impossible to fight off both men. She had to find out who considered her a threat and wanted her out of the way. Pushing backward, she leaned against the man and fell limp into his arms.

"Stand up straight, you bitch. I'm not going to carry you. Let's go." He yanked her hair, pulled her onto her feet but kept one hand firmly locked over her mouth. The empty elevator arrived. "Push the non stop button for the garage. That way no one can stop us. Janos is watching the basement. He'll take care of anyone down there. Do you have the stuff?"

"Yea, it's here. The boss said she was only to have a couple drops."

"We should give the bitch the whole bottle," the man said, pushing his hand tighter against her face and mouth. He drug her into the elevator.

The second man stood in front of her. For the first time, she was able to see a face. He was one of the men from the train. She closed her eyes and small tears rolled down her cheeks.

"Look, she's crying. Now, isn't that just too much?" He rubbed his smelly glove across her mouth several times.

Jean shook. Her lips were bleeding. She felt nauseated from the gas smell and her eyes stung from the fumes.

"We're almost there. Fix it now," the man ordered.

Jean heard rustling sounds behind her. She twisted to see what the two men were doing. A small popping sound made her heart pound wildly.

The man whispered into her ear. "One word out of you and you're dead meat."

He slightly released the hold over her mouth and the other man pushed his hand over it. His hand held a handkerchief wet with a strong chemical smell. He held it tight over her nose and mouth.

She struggled. Kicking and twisting, she tried to get free. A short silent prayer for help filled her thoughts. Her eyes closed and she crumbled into the man's arms.

CHAPTER SIXTY

Larry Royal had left Jean's suite about eight for the Embassy. Both he and Jerry Sullivan had been in Jean's rooms off and on all night. After Larry left, Jerry checked Jean. She was still sound asleep.

He glanced at his watch. It was almost nine. She hadn't gone to bed until almost two. He was sure he'd have time to go to his room before she awoke.

After showering and changing, Jerry stood on the third floor and waited for the elevator. It was almost nine twenty. The elevator numbers showed that one of the elevators was stopped on the first floor and one on the sixth floor. Since it was morning, Jerry thought the elevators were probably being held up by the housekeepers.

He pushed the button again and within seconds one of the elevators went straight by him and stopped at the basement. Pushing, the button again, an elevator finally arrived. He stepped in and rode alone up to Jean's suite floor on the fifth floor. He was humming as he walked toward her suite.

Knocking softly, he waited for Jean to answer. After the third knock, he tried the door. It was locked. He thought maybe Jean was still asleep.

He glanced at his watch and wondered if he had just missed her. Maybe she was on her way to his room or to the breakfast room for something to eat. An uneasy feeling made him stop and look up and down the hallway.

He ran back to the elevator and checked his floor first. There was no sign of Jean. He ran back to the elevator and went to the breakfast room. The room was almost empty. Jean wasn't there.

Something was wrong. He began to panic. Taking two steps at a time, he ran down the stairs to the lobby. At the reception desk, he asked if anyone had seen Jean Martin. The girl looked at him strangely. She shook her head and said she hadn't seen Ms. Martin since yesterday.

Something had happened to her. He knew he'd have hell to pay at his Virginia headquarters if she was hurt or killed. His hands were cold and sweaty.

The telephones in the lobby were all busy. Not knowing the American Embassy telephone number by memory, he ran back to the reception desk. While the clerk searched for the number, Jerry stood watching the activities within the lobby.

His hands thumped the top of the counter top. A sudden movement in the street caught his attention. A black Mercedes was driving slowly by the main door. He ran to the exit.

He arrived just in time to watch the car speed away. His heart leaped. Jean was sitting in the front seat between the two terrorists. Her head was leaning against one of them.

He ran into the street and started running after the car. Cars honked at him. He realized what he was doing and stepped back on to the sidewalk. It was useless. She was out of sight.

Undecided, what to do next, he ran back into the hotel and searched for the Manager. He was told the Manager was out of the hotel and was not expected back until lunch. For several seconds, he stood and tried to rationalize what was happening. He wasn't dressed to run all over Romania. He took the steps two at a time and went back up to his third floor room.

Flipping his suitcase upside down, he dug through his dirty clothes and grabbed a sweatshirt. Within seconds, he repacked. With his suitcase in hand, he walked around his room. He had everything.

He was short of breath. Within seconds, he was back at the lobby reception desk. He took out his American Express card and asked for his final bill. With his bill and suitcase in hand, he ran toward the American Consulate.

The line in front of the Consulate was over a block long. Jerry fought his way to the guard at the gate. Showing his American passport, he said, "Please, call Larry Royal to the gate. Tell him that Jerry Sullivan needs to talk to him at once."

The guard stood back with his hand on his holstered gun. "What is it you need?"

Jerry shuffled from foot to foot. "I need to talk to Royal. Please, it is an emergency."

The guard looked at Jerry out of the corner of his eye. Several people standing in line shouted at the guard in Romanian. Jerry looked at them and said, "I am an American."

They yelled back at Jerry. He had no idea what they were saying but he knew that they were very upset. He turned back to the guard, "You must call Mr. Royal for me. It is very important."

The guard took one step forward and then walked back to Jerry. "What was your name again?"

Jerry handed him his passport. "Please, hurry."

With doubt in his expression, the guard took the passport and walked toward the Consulate. On the side of the building, he pushed a button. He spoke softly into the speaker.

Jerry could hear someone inside the building answer. The person said they would try and find Mr. Royal. Jerry shifted on his legs. His mouth was dry.

As if he had all the time in the world, the guard walked back to Jerry, handed him his passport and motioned for him to wait by the fence. There was a cement stool for Jerry to use if he wished.

The minutes passed slowly. After twenty minutes, Jerry went back to the guard and asked him to call Larry Royal again.

"I told you before, Mr. Royal will be here when he is free," the guard answered in perfect English.

"But, this is an emergency," Jerry said.

"Be patient. He'll be here soon." The guard left Jerry and went to talk to the other people waiting for visas to visit the United States.

"This is stupid," Jerry said. He got up and started walking toward the front door of the Consulate. He ignored the guard and walk right past him.

"Halt. You may not go in there," the guard shouted, rushing after Jerry.

"What are you going to do, shoot me in front of all of these people?" Jerry shouted back.

Just as Jerry stepped on the step to the front door, he could see an American Marine inside running toward the door. Jerry knew procedure. He was afraid the Marine would lock the door before he could get in. He ran. His fingers were on the door handle. Larry Royal was in front of the door. Jerry could see Royal and the Marine's lips moving, but he couldn't hear what they were saying. The Marine nodded his head, opened the door for Jerry and signaled to the gate guard.

"What in the hell do you think you're doing?" Royal asked as they walked up the steps.

"I have to talk to you in private. Do you have an igloo or something in this building?" Jerry asked.

Royal looked at the Marine and back to Jerry. "Leave your suitcase here with the Marine," Royal said. "I'll fill out the necessary paperwork later."

The Marine nodded. His eyes showed that he knew instantly that Jerry was a CIA agent and was in trouble. He picked up the suitcase and set it close to the glass partition.

Walking back to his desk behind the bullet proof glass, the Marine Guard made a notation in the daily log regarding the incident. There would be an official record should anyone ever bother to check.

Being a government employee, Jerry knew most government buildings had special rooms which were considered safe havens. These rooms were constructed to prevent penetration from even the most sophisticated listening equipment.

"Come with me." Larry hurried down the hallway. "I'll have to explain this to the Marines later but let's see what's going on first."

Larry approached a door and punched a series of numbers onto a keypad. A light blinked. He then put his thumb against a small black surface. Another light blinked, this time he leaned over and said, "Johnson." A door clicked.

The two men hurried through and entered a long hallway. As they stood by a blank wall, Larry pushed the covering of a fire alarm box aside and pressed more numbers into another keypad. Another door opened.

Larry opened it, but another door was behind it. Pulling a key from his pocket, Larry opened the final door. He shoved Jerry into the room. He pulled the wall door closed. They were now safe inside the "bubble."

Royal motioned toward a chair. He stood and asked, "Well?"

"Jean's been kidnaped!"

"Oh, shit! Are you sure?" Royal asked.

Jerry spoke for several minutes. He explained what had happened and what he had done.

"How long ago was this?" Larry asked.

"Ten or fifteen minutes. Maybe a bit longer. I asked the guard to call you. They told me you would come. You took your sweet ass time getting to me. What in the hell were you doing that was so important?"

Royal rubbed his head. He sat down, leaned back in his chair and stared at the ceiling. "Do you have any idea how many times a day I get called to the front gate? They just said someone wanted to talk to me. It happens all the time."

"You could have at least looked out and seen who it was," Jerry said, he felt totally exhausted.

"Well, we can't blame anyone. I guess we should have seen it coming. It probably would have happened anyway, especially when they didn't get what they were looking for from the room search. Hell, they ransacked her things how many times? In River City, in Budapest, her friend in Frankfurt, your room here, her room here."

Jerry said, "They were looking for something specific."

"But, what is it?" Royal asked. "Did she ever say if she found something in Jason's apartment?"

Jerry shook his head.

"I guess we better call Langley," Royal sighed. "Let's see they're seven hours behind us. It's about four in the morning there. I guess we'll have to get some of those old farts out of bed. Come on over to the Embassy with me. We'll call from the CIA office." Royal stood up and walked to the door. "Well, here goes my day."

CHAPTER SIXTY-ONE

"I just got word that Jean Martin's been kidnaped," Yuri Nikitin said. He held his cordless phone and was walking around the room.

Viktor Galitizin sat in his black leather chair behind his massive oak desk in the remodeled KGB Headquarters in Moscow. He had spent the entire day in budget meetings with the President and his advisors. "What do you suggest we do? We have to move the shipments soon. The meetings are scheduled to start in less than ten days."

"It is time to release the tapes and videos as we discussed," Yuri said. "When the Americans receive them, they will believe what they see. They will not dig any further. Within a matter of hours, we will be able to resume our shipment."

The Director of the reorganized intelligence group rubbed his eyes. He leaned toward his speaker phone. "It makes sense. Do you think they will give up their search for the files that Martin had?"

"I believe they will," Yuri answered. "We have not been able to find anything. It is only hearsay that he even made such files. The most damaging material possible would be a list of all the dumping sites. It was only a pure speculation that Martin even had complied such a list."

The Intelligence Director sighed. "Wouldn't it do more harm to the countries that have taken the waste than us?"

Yuri was silent for several seconds. "Some of the countries could possibly lose American Aid programs. They would not want that."

"You're right, Yuri," the old man said. "It is time to release our evidence. How do you think the Americans will react when they see one of their finest in a homosexual relationship with a Russian?"

"They will not take it well. You do realize that I will have to transfer and take on a new identity."

"Yes, I do. Where would you like to go?"

"I have given the matter serious thought. It should either be Washington, D.C. or Canada. How soon will you send the materials to the Americans?"

The older Russian said, "We must make sure they are delivered to the right parties. I will ship them by diplomatic pouch to Washington, D.C. tomorrow. A copy will be sent to the Washington Post, CNN and the Leader of the House of Representatives. Oh, yes, I will send one to CIA Headquarters. I will instruct the Washington Office to make sure the materials are mailed out within twenty-four hours after they receive them. Is that enough time for you?"

Yuri moved though his living room. He looked at his luxury surroundings. He answered, "Yes, that is fine. I will pack tomorrow and be on my way by the next day. Shall I return to Moscow first and then go to America from there?"

The old man chuckled. "Son, if you want to see your mother first, you should. You know how upset she gets when she hasn't seen you for awhile."

"Then, I shall be on the plane to Moscow within twenty-four hours. After I arrive in Moscow, we can plan my next assignment."

"Yuri, that is fine. You have done a good job. Once again, we have made the Americans look like fools."

Yuri hung up the phone and looked around his spacious apartment. He had already planned for this day. Boxes for all his electronic equipment was stacked neatly by the hall closet. The movers had been alerted.

He hoped his next posting would be just as rewarding. Several electronic magazines were in his briefcase. He had circled the descriptions of the latest technological inventions he hoped to purchase. America was where he needed to be.

CHAPTER SIXTY-TWO

Ghassar Nseir sat on a plain, wooden, backless chair in a small cottage on the outskirts of Bucharest. The building was covered with a thatch roof. It was filthy, cold, and damp. The dirty wood cook stove was working but instead of warming the rooms, it was filling them with smoke.

He coughed and waved his arms around to keep the smoke from his eyes. It had been twenty-two hours since he had any sleep. Most of his early morning hours had been spent planning the kidnaping of Jean Martin.

Recently everything had started to fall apart. The action had stopped. Everyone's nerves were on edge. It all started and revolved around Jason Martin.

Jean Martin's arrival had only created more problems. The boss had ordered him to Budapest to watch her. He didn't understand why, because the boss always seemed to know what Jean Martin was doing.

At first, he thought the assignment was going to be a push over. But, as time went by, it became more involved. Then, within the last twenty-four hours, the boss had given the go ahead to do whatever was needed to retrieve the materials.

Nseir rocked back and forth on the back legs of his chair. A cup of strong Turkish coffee was in his hand. His eyes were closed, his thoughts a million miles away.

Unexpectedly, his cell phone rang and startled him. He jerked, dropped the cup, and spilled coffee on his new, clean Levi's.

"Shit," he said, reaching for the phone. His free hand brushed the fluid off his pants. He pulled the material trying to get the warmth off his legs.

"Do you have the woman?" the man asked.

He recognized his boss's voice. He wiped his hand on the leg of his pants and kicked the broken cup across the room. "Yes, she's here with us now. We will head for the Black Sea. Are you in the area?"

He looked over at the sleeping woman. She was lying on a blanket on the cold cement floor. A thin dirty blanket covered her. Some of her dark hair was matted to her face, the rest spread out like a halo around her head.

"Yes, I arrived yesterday. We're driving down toward Constanta and the boat now. We will meet you there. Don't hurt the woman. I'll question her when you arrive." The phone line went dead.

"Was that the boss?" the other terrorist asked. Leonid Koniev was a money-for-hire mercenary. He spoke softly, not wanting to wake the sleeping woman.

Shaking his head, Ghassar Nseir answered, "Yes, he and the Budapest controller flew in last night. They have rented a car and are driving to the boat now. We should have everything within a few hours. We are moving to another location. Things will be better there. We will become millionaires many times over."

"Yes. I am sure of that." Koniev smiled and leaned back in a shabby overstuffed chair. The entire space below his nose opened up displaying an enormous set of yellow stained teeth. He picked at the stuffing that was sticking out of the arm of the chair.

"It's cold in here," Nseir said, looking toward the stove. It always disgusted him to watch his friend smile. "We must go now. Let's get back into the Mercedes."

"Yes, that is better. This place makes me feel unclean. It is so cold and damp."

"I will get the car and drive around to the back of the cottage. Listen for me. When you hear the car, get the woman and come out. Move quickly, we don't want to attract any attention from the neighbors."

"Do I wake her up?" Koniev asked. He lifted himself out of the chair and stretched his long body. He looked down at the woman, patted his body in several places and scratched his head vigorously.

"No, she will be easier to move if she is asleep. Do you think we will have to give her another shot?"

"Not for the time being," Koniev said. "But, if she is not good in the car, I will." He motioned toward his jacket pocket where he kept the supply of needles and medicine. "Go, get the car. I will be waiting."

Nseir stepped out into the bright sunlight. It reminded him of his homeland. The weather forecast was for a beautiful clear sunny day. However, there was a slight wind which was keeping the temperature down.

"Look at the traffic," Nseir muttered, once they were on the main road. "I hope all the roads out of town aren't backed up with this much traffic."

His language showed his disgust both with the traffic and having to take care of the woman. He would rather have killed her. It would have been easier.

"These roads are awful," Koniev said. "Take it easy, you'll wake her up."

Both men were sitting in the front seat with Jean Martin lodged between them. Koniev shifted in his seat, leaned slightly toward Jean and ran his hand up and down her sleeping body. He let his hand rest for a few seconds on her breasts.

Nseir saw him out of the corner of his eye. He made a face and cussed, "Those damn taxis. Look at them." He kept muttering to himself, but kept his eyes on the road. "It looks as if every person that owns a car is driving today. This fool country needs more traffic lights." The traffic had reduced to a snail's pace.

"Do we have a deadline?" Koniev asked. He tugged at Jean's arm, to see if she was still asleep. His eyes ran down to her waist, stopped and then continued down her legs.

"Yes and no," Ghassar Nseir said. He pulled into the new Shell gas station and glanced at his watch. "I'm going to gas up. Watch her, but don't wake her or rub your disgusting hands over her again." He stared at Koniev for several seconds. He stepped out of the car. "Do you want something? How about a cup of coffee or something cold to drink?"

Koniev clicked his tongue between his teeth. He looked down at the sleeping lady and said, "She'll be waking up before long and will be hungry and thirsty. Get her something she can eat and drink on the road."

Ghassar Nseir stared at his companion. He really didn't care if the woman starved. But, he didn't want the woman physically mishandled. The boss had been perfectly clear regarding that. He wanted her delivered to him in perfect condition.

Nseir returned to the car with a plastic bag full of soft drinks and candy bars. "Here, this should keep both of you quiet for awhile."

Koniev took the bag, opened it and smiled another toothy smile. He took out a candy bar and with two huge bites ate it, tossing the empty wrapper into the back seat.

"You should have gotten more," he said. "There won't be enough for the entire trip."

"Don't eat them all at once, and there will be." Nseir glared at him. "You eat like a pig."

Koniev wiped his mouth with his shirt sleeve. He grunted a couple times and settled back on his seat. "How much longer will it be?"

"It is as long as it takes," Nseir answered sharply. "I can not make this traffic disappear."

The woman stirred. Both men looked down at her. She moved her hand slightly. Koniev looked at Nseir. Nseir nodded and Koniev took a small plastic syringe out of his pocket.

He shook it a couple times, looked at the fluid, pulled the plunger back and pushed it against her arm. She groaned slightly. Her hand went limp.

"You should have been a doctor," Nseir said. "You are getting good at that."

Koniev made a face. "No way, doctors have to be kind. I am happy being what I am."

Nseir shrugged.

"She should be quiet for a couple hours. Will we be there by then?" Koniev asked.

Nseir shook his head. He began passing a group of traveling gypsies. When he was safely a distance from them, he said, "We should be."

CHAPTER SIXTY-THREE

The sun was slipping below the horizon when Ghassar Nseir drove the black Mercedes into Constanta. Its final rays were bouncing off the high waves. The city looked deserted. A brisk Black Sea wind was keeping the permanent residents in their homes. It was almost February and the city was between tourist seasons.

Jean moved her head and tried to open her eyes. The bright light was overwhelming. Her temples started throbbing. She couldn't move, something was against her, holding her upright.

Her arms felt like lead. She tried lifting them but couldn't. They were tied to something but she couldn't see what it was.

The car hit a bump and her head bounced from side to side. Now, she could see that she was lodged between two big men. They stunk of garlic, oil and gas.

For several seconds, she tried to remember what had happened to her. She had no idea where she was. Nothing looked familiar.

The car turned and she could hear a strong wind blowing. She moved her head slightly and glanced out the window. She could see water in the distance.

Very slowly, she turned her head and looked at the dashboard clock. It was almost seven-thirty. She looked at the sky. It was nighttime.

She squeezed her eyes shut and tried to remember what had happened. The elevator was coming, then a strong smelling rag covered her face. Once again, she looked at the men. Her eyes went wide when she recognized them. She was their prisoner.

The car stopped. Opening her left eye slightly, she watched the driver get out of the car. He stood several feet from the car and looked around. He left the key in the ignition and the door open.

Jean moved slightly toward the door. She held her breath. Her eyes locked on the ignition key.

"Well, look whose awake," the other man said. He leaned over and pulled Jean back to the middle of the seat. "Naughty girl, mustn't move around." He looked directly into her face. "If you don't behave, I'll give you another shot of my sleepy time medicine."

Jean wet her dry lips. Now, she at least knew why she felt so awful. She tried to lift her arms but discovered that a rope held her arms and legs tied together. "What am I doing here? Where am I?" Her words were low and slurred.

"Now, now! You are our guest. As long as you sit and be quiet, you'll be fine. Would you like a candy bar?" The man dug into a bag and pulled out a bar. He held it out to her.

She tried to reach for it but couldn't move her arms. "Yes, please. But, how can I eat with my hands tied?" She looked back and forth between the man in the car and the man standing outside.

"I'll open it for you." He ripped the wrapper off and held it up to her mouth. "Just take a bite. I really don't mind feeding it to you." His fingers touched her face and outlined her mouth.

Jean shivered. She opened her mouth and took a bite. After swallowing the first bite, she continued eating until the bar was all gone. She licked her lips for the last taste.

"Now, do you want to lick my fingers?" the man asked. Without waiting for an answer, he took his fingers and rubbed them over her face, down her throat and toward her chest.

"What in the hell do you think you're doing?" the driver said. He got back into the car, turned on the ignition and slammed the door. "Leave her alone."

"She was hungry. I just wanted to give her something to eat."

Jean looked at the driver. She said, "I'm still hungry and I need to use a restroom."

"Oh, what a princess! You'll have to wait until we get settled. Koniev, give her a drink from one of those sodas you have in the sack."

Jean said, "Where are we going?"

"We are almost there," the driver said. He laughed and reached over and patted Jean on her leg. "It won't be long now."

Jean took a drink from the can that Koniev offered her. She looked at him with hatred in her eyes, but didn't say a word. The pressure of her leather bag against her chest gave her a sense of security. At least that was safe.

The two men ignored her. They sat in silence for several blocks. The sound of a fog horn echoed in the distance.

"Watch the signs," the driver said. "It has to be around here someplace."

"Nseir, turn to the left at the corner. There's the Harbor sign."

Nseir slowed, crossed the railroad tracks and turned. Jean could see the muscles in the driver's jaw tighten as he drove along the water. It was so dark she wondered how he could see where to drive.

"Quick, hurry out and move that barricade," the driver said. "That's the ship. I want to drive the car as close as possible. I'll back in so we won't have so far to carry the boxes."

Koniev jumped out of the car and told Nseir to back up. He shouted, "You have plenty of room."

"Try and be quiet," Nseir called. "Remember it's Friday night and the area is patrolled. I don't want any undue attention from the Harbor Police."

"Sure, sure." The second man looked around the area to see if anyone was watching. He saw no one. "Just a few feet more," he said.

Within seconds, Ghassar Nseir had the car parked. He got out, took the keys and walked to the back of the car. He said, "Close the doors. We don't want her making any noise down here. It will echo all over the city."

Koniev walked back to the car. He looked in at Jean and said, "Be quiet if you know what's good for you. We're going to unload some boxes. Just sit still and wait."

Jean could sense the two men were extremely nervous. They were moving boxes from the trunk of the car to a set of steps that led up to a ship. She could only see reflections in the rear view mirror.

Several men hurried down the ship's ladder. They carried the boxes up the stairs and onto the ship. She slid over trying to see a name on the side of the ship. It was too dark. The men were working by moonlight and whatever they were doing was illegal.

She thought about escaping. The car doors weren't locked, but her hands and feet were still tied. Even, if she managed to roll out of the car, where would she go.

There was water all around the area. She could smell and hear it. It was too dark to move around in a place she didn't know. She decided to stay in the car and take her chances.

Koniev opened the door. "Did you miss me?" he asked. He leaned into the car and rubbed his hand up and down on Jean's leg.

She shivered.

He laughed and said, "Did you like that? I could really make you like me." He pulled her closer to his side of the car and leaned toward her.

She could smell garlic and started coughing.

"Bitch," he said and slapped her across her face.

She gasped. Her face stung but she didn't say anything. She wasn't going to let him know how much she hurt or how afraid she was.

Ghassar Nseir opened the driver's side and slid in. He glanced at Jean and Koniev. He could tell something happened between the two of them, but he didn't say anything. He started the car, looked around and said, "Boy, I'm glad that's done."

Jean straightened herself on the seat. She said, "What was in the boxes?"

Koniev chuckled. He pulled her by her hair closer to him. He said, "Listen, little lady, don't ask any questions. You're better off not knowing."

Jean tried to push him away but he wrapped his foot around her rope. "It's getting late. Can't you at least tell me where we're going?"

Nseir said, "We're going to meet the boss. Just sit still and you'll be fine."

Jean said, "Who is this boss, you keep talking about? Do I know him?"

Nseir shoved Jean hard against Koniev. "I said shut up and be quiet. You're distracting me. You'll discover everything in due time."

When Ghassar drove the car into the hotel parking lot, he spotted a white BMW with custom plates. He knew his boss had already arrived. Now, everything would go according to plan. He parked and saw two men coming out of the hotel.

Nseir yelled at Koniev. "Come on, let's get out of here. We have to leave now." Instantly, the two men jumped out of the black Mercedes, ran through the parking lot toward the water.

Jean was scared. The car doors were shut. She struggled with the rope, trying desperately to free herself. Two men were walking toward the car. She screamed, "Help."

CHAPTER SIXTY-FOUR

The men heard something. They stopped walking and looked around. Jean searched for the horn. She leaned on it, bouncing up and down with her body. The men ran toward the car.

"Help me," she yelled. She had pulled her feet up on the seat and was kicking at the door. "I'm in here."

One of the men looked into the window. He opened the door and said, "Jean, is that you? Are you all right?"

Her eyes couldn't believe it. "Michael Cleary, is that really you?" She twisted herself to the edge of the seat. Her heart beat faster. She felt that she was safe at last.

Michael said, "Just a minute. Has someone tied you up?"

Tears rolled down her cheeks, her shoulders were shaking. "Michael, help me, please."

"I'm here." He pulled Jean toward him, held her close for several seconds, then untied her arms and legs. "Now, don't move. Let me rub your legs for a moment. You've been tied up for some time. I can feel the indents from the rope. You'll probably need a few minutes to get the circulation back."

"They tingle," Jean sobbed. She moved her fingers around trying to get some feeling. "Oh, Michael, it was awful."

"Now, now. You're safe now," Michael said. "Let's see if we can get you to stand up." He helped her out of the car on the passenger side. "Lean on me. Don't try and stand by yourself just yet."

"Michael, I've been drugged."

Michael said, "Shh. Let's take it one step at a time." He helped her walk a few steps. "Let's go into the hotel. Are you hungry?"

"I'm starved," Jean said. They walked under a street light. She looked at the other man who had stood back while Michael helped her. "Ray Clark, what are you doing here?"

"I'm down here with Michael. He'll explain it all while we eat. I'll get the door." He walked ahead of the couple and stood holding the door when they entered.

"We have a room here for the night." He turned to Clark and motioned for him to go ahead. "Ray's going to get you a room. Later, after you've had a shower and something to eat, we can talk about what happened."

Jean felt relieved. She let Michael help her up the steps and waited while Clark picked up a key. She leaned on Michael's arm. Suddenly, she remembered. "Michael, how are you? Should you be up and around?"

Michael patted her on her arm. "I'm fine. It was just a severe case of food poisoning."

"Oh, that's great. I was so worried."

"I'm fine. Ray, you lead the way." He looked at Jean and smiled. "Ready? You'll feel a thousand times better once you have a shower."

Jean could hardly wait to get out of her clothes. They smelled like garlic, gas and oil. Suddenly, she thought of the two men that had kidnaped her. She stopped and looked at Michael. "Michael, I can't go up to my room. I need to call the police and tell them about the two men that kidnaped me. They ran away and left me in the car."

Michael motioned for Jean to follow Ray. "There will be plenty of time for that later." He turned to Jean and looked into her eyes. "You will have to identify them. Do you think you could recognize them from a picture or could you draw a sketch of them?"

Jean thought and then said, "I only caught glimpses of them. But, Jerry Sullivan probably could. They were the two men that were on the train with us from Budapest."

Ray opened the room for Michael. He stood back and watched while Jean and Michael went in. He stayed at the doorway.

"Michael, where are we?" She looked around the room and walked to the balcony. She could see that her room faced water.

"This is Constanta, Romania. It's a large port city on the Black Sea." He walked around the room, opening and closing doors. "There's a robe in the bathroom. That will work until we can get some clothes for you in the morning. All the shops are closed for the evening. Everything else that you will need such as shampoo and such is on the counter top in the bathroom. Are you hungry?"

"Starved," Jean answered. "I haven't had anything but a candy bar since yesterday. Is room service still open?"

Michael motioned to Ray. "We'll check. I think you should take a bath or shower, what ever you wish, get something to eat and then get some sleep. While you're getting your bath, Ray and I'll go down to that car and see if we can find anything about who owns it."

Ray said, "Room service is open for another two hours. Just push "8" and give your order. They speak English and can fix almost anything you want. Just tell them to put it on your room bill."

Jean felt like her old self. She motioned with her hands, "You two go away for now. If you want to come back in say, an hour that would be fine. Go now, get out of here and let a woman get cleaned up."

Michael leaned over and kissed Jean on the head. "You take it easy. Don't worry, no one will hurt you here. I'll talk to the management and get someone to watch this floor. I'll be back in an hour or so."

Jean hugged Michael. "You're so special. I owe you so much. Now, get out, if I look as bad as I think I do, it must be revolting."

Michael walked to the door. He turned back and said, "You will always look good to me."

Jean waved him away. "There you go with those sweet words again."

CHAPTER SIXTY-FIVE

Two hours later, Jean, Michael and Ray Clark were sitting around a white linen covered table in Jean's room. She had taken a long, relaxing bath, washed her hair and was feeling much better.

An assortment of sandwich fixings were spread out on the table in front of them. A bowl of fresh fruit and half of a chocolate cake sat in the middle of the table. Dirty plates were piled to one side.

An empty bottle of red wine was on the floor. A freshly opened red wine bottle sat in front of Michael. A full glass of red wine sat in front of each person.

"Michael, you never told me why you're here?" Jean asked, as she pulled another chair closer to her chair. She leaned back and put her feet on the chair. Her robe fell open. Casually, she pulled the sides together and pulled the belt tighter.

"I felt better and decided to take some more vacation time. Actually, I was worried about you. I flew back to Budapest, called Clark to get caught up. He said you had gone to Romania with Jerry Sullivan. We both decided to come to Romania to find you. Well, one thing led to another and here we are."

Jean thought for a moment. "But, how did you end up here, of all places?"

Michael looked at Ray and back at Jean. "We went to the Embassy, and we were told that you had been kidnaped."

"Who told you?" Jean asked.

"We talked to Royal's office. They knew all about it."

"Really, how did they know?" Jean said. Everything was still fuzzy in her mind.

Michael shook his head. "I really don't know, but I suppose Sullivan told them. Anyway, we heard that a black Mercedes was spotted heading this way and here we are."

"Thank heaven for that," Jean said. "I'm supposed to have reservations on Delta out of Bucharest tomorrow evening."

"Don't worry about that now," Michael said. "In the morning, we can check everything. Do you have your plane ticket with you?"

Jean thought of her leather bag. It was still in the bathroom. She wished Clark wasn't in the room. "Yes, in my purse," she answered finally.

"That's fine," Michael said. "Now, is there anything else that you need before we got to bed. It's almost midnight."

"I have no change of clothes or anything. I couldn't possibly wear the things I just took off."

"Make a list of what you want and I'll see what we can get." Michael handed her a small hotel pad of paper and pencil. "I've a couple shirts you could wear. Maybe, you'd like one for pajamas and one for tomorrow?"

"That would be great. In the morning, if I can't get jeans, I'll try and get a pair of sweatpants. They'll work until I can get someplace to get something else."

Michael looked worried. "Where's your suitcase?"

"Oh, Michael, that's another story," Jean said. "While, I was in Bucharest, someone broke into my hotel room and literally tore my suitcase and things to pieces. I have a few things left. But, they are all in my room at the Inter-Con."

"Where are the things that you took from Jason's apartment? Do you have them with you?" Michael looked at her purse and frowned.

"Most of them are still in Bucharest. I was on my way down to breakfast when the two jerks took me. I had your traveler's checks, passport and other things in my carry-on bag. It's still in the hotel room." She looked confused. "How did you get into this country without your passport?"

Michael pulled a red passport out of his pocket. "I have an official one. It's supposed to be for official business, but since I didn't have my blue tourist one, I used this."

"Why do you have an official passport?" Jean asked.

"Well, you know I travel a lot on business. Often, I carry things that the government doesn't want other people to see. The official passport gets me by custom problems."

"Oh," Jean said. "Jason used to carry a black diplomatic one. I wonder what ever happened to it?"

"Well, let's not worry about that now. Ray, will you stay with her and I'll run to my room and get her a couple of my shirts? I'll be right back."

Jean took her glass of wine and walked out on the balcony. The waves were pounding against the sandy beach. It was chilly, but felt refreshing. The moon was bright. She stared at the beach. Two men were standing by the water and looking up toward her room. She screamed and dropped the glass.

CHAPTER SIXTY-SIX

Jean was the first to arrive in the breakfast room. It was Saturday morning and the room was crowded with weekenders. Almost every table was full. Jean found an empty table that looked out toward the sea.

Michael had called earlier and delivered a pair of black sweatpants to her room. He had said that he and Clark would join her. They had a couple errands to run first.

Jean rubbed her eyes. She was still very tired. It must have been around two when she finally fell asleep. She remembered looking at the clock.

After waiting for a few minutes, Jean glanced at her watch. She wondered where the men were. Her stomach growled. The waiter was refilling the buffet, she motioned for coffee.

Just as she decided to call their room, she glanced up and saw both men walk off the elevator. She caught their attention and motioned for them to join her.

"About time," she said. "I wondered what happened to you both. This is a great table. We can watch the birds." The men were wearing their parkas. "Is it that cold out?"

Michael unzipped his heavy jacket and put it on the back of his chair. Clark did the same. They both rubbed their hands. Their cheeks were red.

Michael said, "It is really cold. That wind doesn't help a bit."

"It looks nice from here. At least the sun is shining," Jean said. She looked toward the buffet. "The waiter said that we just help ourselves. Breakfast is included in the room price."

Michael looked around the room. "There doesn't seem to be many here. Was it busier earlier?"

"When I first arrived it was packed, but it's starting to thin out. Are you looking for anyone special?" Jean asked. She thought that both Michael and Clark seemed jittery and nervous. "Is something wrong?"

Michael patted her on her head. “Not a thing. Come on let’s eat.” He held Jean’s chair. “You don’t look half bad in my shirt and the sweatpants.”

Jean waved her hand. “Thanks for the pants. Where did you find them so early in the morning? I noticed that the store doesn’t open until eleven.”

“Let’s just say, I’m resourceful.” He followed Jean, picked up a plate and went on the opposite side of the buffet line. He looked through the cart. “Anything new with you?”

Jean glanced over to Michael. “No, I’m fine. When are we going to find out about my flight? I’m anxious to get going.”

Michael looked at Jean and then back toward Clark, who was standing behind Jean. “I thought we’d leave right after breakfast. I checked at the desk and you aren’t going to be able to get a flight out of Bucharest until later this afternoon.” He helped himself to some scrambled eggs. “What say, we take a drive down the seacoast and then head back? You might like seeing this area. I doubt if you’ll be coming back.”

Jean laughed. “You certainly have that right. Once I get out of this country, I’m not coming back. Sure, I’m game for a drive along the seacoast. I’d love to see the small little tourist towns. How far is Bulgaria?”

Clark answered, “It’s less than an hour drive to the west. I suppose we could go that way rather than up into the wildlife region.”

Michael glanced at Jean and then Clark. He said, “Sure, that would be all right. We could cut over and take the back road into Bucharest. The highway isn’t as good, but there shouldn’t be much traffic today.”

Within an hour, the group had checked out of the hotel and were in a white Mercedes. Jean let the two men sit in front. She liked the idea of having the entire back seat to herself.

“That was a great breakfast,” Clark said. “Jean, look at the water. See those big boats, they are docked here for loading and unloading. This is one of the largest ports in this part of the world.”

Jean shuttered. “This is the area where I was last night. I’m not sure which boat we were parked in front of, but this is definitely the area. I recognize some of the things, like that sign there. And, those railroad tracks over there."

Michael looked into his rear view mirror. "Try not to think about it. You're all right now and you weren't hurt. You're safe, just sit back and enjoy the ride."

Jean slid to the end of her seat. She stared out the window. There were only two large ships docked. "Which countries do those ships belong?"

Clark said, "The first one is Iranian and the smaller one is Libyan, I think. I always get some of the countries flags mixed up."

Jean yelled, "Stop, that's the one. That Libyan one. That's where we were last night."

Michael pulled over to the side of the road. The car following him swerved to avoid hitting him. He turned around and looked at Jean. "I told you not to worry about it. We'll report it. There is nothing that can be done now. I didn't want to tell you this before, but when I went down to search for those two men last night, the Mercedes we found you in earlier was gone. We don't have anything to trace you to them."

"But," Jean said. Tears were in her eyes. "Are you telling me that nothing can be done?"

Michael reached back and patted her leg. "Yes, I doubt if there is. We have nothing but your word and you really don't know anything." He turned around and started driving. "Just relax, look out and enjoy the ride."

Jean leaned back and thought about what Michael said. Everything was so confusing. All she really wanted to do was get out of Romania. She leaned against the front seat and said, "Whose car is this?"

Clark looked at Michael, then Jean. "It's mine," he said.

First, Michael was driving a BMW and now Clark. She ran her hand up and down the black leather seat. She didn't know a great deal about foreign cars, but she knew this car was very expensive. She wondered what kind of a salary Clark made as a Foreign Service Officer. Everyone seemed to be making a great deal more money than she was and she had controlling interest in a bank.

For the next hour, she watched the scenery. She felt very safe. Michael was an excellent driver and maneuvered the BMW carefully along the narrow coastline road.

"Do you have your passport?" Michael asked.

Jean felt her leather bag. "Yes, do I need to get it out?"

"Yes, we're going to be at the Bulgarian border crossing in about ten minutes. Would you like to go across?"

Jean leaned on the front seat. "Sure, this might be my only chance. Anything different about it?"

Clark said, "No, it looks a great deal like this. But, you can get your passport stamped and show it to the people when you get back to Iowa."

"I bet there aren't very many people from River City that have been in Bulgaria," Jean said. She bent forward and pulled her leather bag out from under her big shirt.

"Here it is. Do one of you want to hold it?" Jean asked.

"No," Michael said. "Just keep it handy. We'll have to show it in a minute or so." He slowed the car down and looked toward Clark. "Get the car papers out, just in case."

When they turned the corner, they could see the border crossing directly in front of them. There was a long line of cars waiting to cross.

"Shit," Michael said. "This could take hours." He glanced at his watch.

Jean looked at the shiny watch on Michael's arm. It was the first time she had noticed it. "Is that a Rolex?"

Michael held his arm back over the seat. "Yes, have you ever seen one before?"

Jean touched it and rubbed her finger over the crystal and band. "No," she said. "But, I've seen lots of pictures. Aren't they quite expensive?"

Michael glanced back over his shoulder. He smiled. "Depends on what you call expensive. They are a great company and you get what you pay for."

Jean nodded and slid back on the seat. She wondered what she would have to do to make the kind of money that everyone else seemed to be earning.

"What's going on up there?" Clark said. He leaned closer to the windshield. "Who are those people going from car to car?"

Michael squinted. "Probably checking passports to help cut down on the waiting time."

Michael turned off the engine and turned on the radio. He was fumbling with the dial and looked up. "Ray, look ahead of us. Is that who I think it is?"

Ray gasped. "Yes, let's get the hell out of here."

Michael cussed and turned the key. He backed up and swung the car around. There was a thud.

"Michael, be careful," Jean said. She looked out the rear window. "You just hit that car. The owner is getting out. You'd better stop."

"Sit down and be still," Michael answered. "Ray, watch behind us."

"What are you doing?" Jean asked. She could see two men running after the BWM. "Those men want to talk to you. You'd best stop."

"No way," Michael said. He was speeding back the way he just came. "Jean, put on your seat belt. This could be rough."

"Michael, are the two men that kidnaped me after us?" Jean asked. The car was moving so fast she wasn't able to make out who was chasing them.

Michael turned down a main street. It led through a small city. The car raced through the streets toward the water. "Clark, get ready," Michael said.

As they turned a corner, Jean could hear tires squealing. She looked out the rear window. The other car surged toward them.

"Someone is chasing us," she yelled. "Shouldn't you stop? Why are we running away?"

Another car was in front of them. It was parked on an angle. "They're trying to block us," Michael screamed. "Hang on."

He slammed on the gas, turned the wheel sharp and turned into a one way street. He was going the wrong way. The BMW leaped forward, raced past the small houses. The water was directly in front of them.

Suddenly, Michael slammed on the brakes. Jean went flying across the back seat. Ray put his hands against the dashboard, bracing himself.

Michael said, "Keep you head down."

"What's the matter?" Jean asked. She sat up, brushed off her pants and ran her fingers through her hair. She picked up her purse and passport, and held them close to her chest.

The car reeked of hot oil and rubber. She pushed a button and lowered the back window. A gush of cold frigid air hit her in the face.

"Boy, it's cold out there," she said and pushed the button again.

A police siren grew closer. She turned her head to see where it was.

Without speaking, Michael whirled the BMW around and started back the way he came. The car following had slowed down and was in the middle of the street. "Hold on," Michael called and cut the wheel short and drove onto a lawn.

The car bounced across the lawn and came out onto a straight stretch of residential street. Michael accelerated. Jean moaned.

She looked back at the following car. It was turning the corner on two wheels, it almost went over on its side. The driver struggled with the wheel and recovered control.

Michael turned wide and went into a narrow alleyway. He whipped it around a corner, and pushed on the gas. The car sprung across an intersection just missing an oncoming car.

The force of the speed kept pushing Jean back and forth on the seat. Her seat belt was keeping her from flying around. She clasped her purse and held her breath.

As the BMW turned a corner, the sound of police sirens were approaching from the left. A street light was directly in front of them. Jean knew that Michael had no intention of stopping. He was going too fast.

"What's going on?" she screamed at the top of her voice. She was unable to think clearly.

Michael ignored her. He was an expert at evasive driving and raced the car toward the water. "I'm going to stop by the water. When I do, it's every man for himself." He spoke calmly. His voice showed no emotion.

"Michael, who's after us?" She finally realized that they were running away from the police. "What have you done?" Her eyes went wide. She couldn't imagine what he might have done to deserve such a chase.

"Stop," a loud voice yelled over a speaker system. "Stop or we will shoot out your tires."

Michael said, "Jean, when I stop, keep your head down. I'll explain everything to you later."

Jean sat frozen in her seat. Something whizzed by her head. "They're shooting at us," she said.

"Put your head down. Unhook your seat belt and get down on the floor. You'll be safe," Michael said. He stopped the car, opened the door and disappeared between two houses.

The rear window exploded into millions of pieces. Bits of glass flew everywhere. Jean screamed and screamed. Remembering Michael's words, she flopped over to the floor and spread her body out lengthwise.

Everything seemed to be crashing and smashing around her. She heard more gunshots, people running, car doors slamming and tires screeching. She was petrified, but laid still, barely breathing.

She heard Clark open his door, and run away. Now, both front doors were wide open. It was freezing cold. The sound of waves hitting against retainer walls vibrated in the morning air.

She could smell the water. The air was filled with gas fumes and burning rubber. A boat motor started, a tire popped and then there was a loud explosion. She screamed again.

Jean knew she was alone. Crawling off the floor, she pulled herself back onto the seat. She leaned up and looked out the driver's side. People were running and yelling.

She thought she saw someone jump into the cold water. Something told her that it was Michael. She stared, trying to follow his movements. He disappeared from sight.

Suddenly, a motorboat appeared out of nowhere. She thought she saw two people in the boat. They were helping someone climb out of the water. She sighed, she hoped it was Michael.

Feeling relief, she sat back on the car seat. Several people were running past the car. A man walked by the car, turned and walked back to it. He opened the rear door and looked in.

"Jerry, what in the world are you doing here?" she asked.

Before he could answer, she heard several bullet shots. She looked back at the water. Several policemen were shooting at the fleeing motorboat.

"Jerry, stop them. They're going to hurt Michael."

"Jean, come with me. There are several things that you need to know. How are you feeling?" Jerry said. He reached his hand toward her.

"I'm fine. What's going on?" she asked. She took his hand and stopped for a moment. Michael's strong woodsy cologne still lingered in the car. She smiled and got out of the car. She stood outside and started to weave back and forth. "Whoops," she said. "Guess I don't have my land legs yet."

"Lean against me," Jerry said. "You'll be all right in a minute. Is that your purse?"

"Yes, can you get it for me." She took a step alone. "There, I'm fine. Now, tell me what is going on."

She held his arm and let him escort her to a black Ford sedan. Blood was dripping on her chest. She rubbed her fingers against her forehead and looked at them. They were covered with blood.

"I think a first aid kit is in the car. You don't seem to be bleeding too badly." Jerry stopped walking and looked at her wound. "A band aid should work.

He opened the back door, and gently helped her inside. "Hold this against the cut." He pulled the wrapper off a gauze cloth and handed it to her. "These type of head cuts usually look worse than they really are."

She leaned back on the seat. Her eyes went shut. Although, she had only been up a couple hours, she was exhausted. Her hand fell to her side. She could feel someone pressing a bandage on her head. She shivered and then felt the warmth of a blanket.

CHAPTER SIXTY-SEVEN

Jean sat in the Intercontinental hotel lobby, and looked at Larry Royal. She had taken a shower, gotten a change of clothes and felt considerably better.

"I'm still not clear about a couple things," she said. "You tell me what you know and maybe I can help fill in some of the blanks."

"Be sure and correct me if I'm wrong on any of my facts," Royal said. He looked at a small notebook and flipped through the pages. "First, Michael Cleary, was Jason Martin's best friend in college. They both graduated from Iowa University Law School. Michael joined the Air Force and was eventually assigned to the JAG Office in Rhein Main, Germany. Jason went on to join the CIA and until his death was assigned to the political section at the American Embassy in Budapest, Hungary. Am I right so far?"

"Right so far," Jean smiled. "Michael often visited us in River City."

Royal said, "I believe he loved both you and Jason very much, and never intended to kill Jason."

Jean sniffed. Everyone glanced at her. She could feel her face get warm and motioned for Royal to continue.

"In November, Michael flew to Budapest to attend the annual Marine Ball at the American Embassy. The two men doubled dated. The next day, in Jason's Mercedes they toured Lake Balaton. We have receipts that they spent one night in a hot mineral bath hotel in Heviz."

"What happened there? Jason never said anything to me." Jean looked confused, leaned forward and looked directly at Royal. "Did they have an argument or something?"

"We're not sure, but something happened. It was right after that when Jason filed a report. He suspected Michael was involved in something. He had done a great deal of research into recent robberies in Hungary and neighboring countries. Putting two and two together, he thought Michael was connected."

"What did the report say?" Jean asked.

“That’s classified. But, I can tell you that Jason said Michael was spending a lot of money.”

“Is that all?” Jean asked. “That doesn’t seem to be very much.”

Royal looked at his notes. “Jason also stated that he had seen Michael talking to some shady characters.”

“Good heavens, that’s nothing. Maybe, he was asking them for directions or something,” Jean added. “He was a lawyer, maybe he was working on a case.”

Royal looked at Jean and sighed. “I know you like Michael. But, whatever happened Jason felt it was completely out of character for Michael. It made Jason so suspicious that he filed an official investigation request to look into Michael’s background. That is something that a CIA agent doesn’t do without a great deal of thought.”

“You’re right. Jason wasn’t one to get suspicious over small things. Something else must have happened.”

Royal shrugged. “I don’t really know, and if I did I couldn’t tell you.”

“Maybe, Michael had saved the money he was spending,” Jean said. After she spoke, she realized that she sounded as if she were defending him. After all, he was responsible for Jason’s death. She rolled her eyes. “Michael said they had discussed traveling later in the year.”

“Jason didn’t think Michael had saved that much money. He knew exactly how much Michael made.” Royal flipped though more pages. He stopped read the page and looked at Jean. “We only had Michael’s word about their travel plans. Did you know that Jason called Michael on the Sunday night before his death?”

Jean shook her head but didn’t say anything. She couldn’t believe that Michael hadn’t told her.

“Jason told Michael that he had arranged for the Flokati rug to be mailed to you.”

Jean muttered, “So that’s how he knew.”

Royal raised his hand and motioned for Jean to wait. “Jason also told Michael that he was going to have to do something he’d rather not do, but never said exactly what he was going to do or why.”

"How do you know this?" Jean asked. "And, how did Jason get the rug, if he didn't go to Greece?"

Jerry had been listening to everything. He was making notes as Royal talked. He said, "I talked to Jason right after you asked for the rug. I was on my way to Turkey, I bought it for you and had it mailed."

"Oh," Jean said, feeling a bit embarrassed. "Thank you. I haven't seen it, but I'm sure it's perfect."

"You're perfectly welcome," Jerry winked.

"At first, Michael didn't think much about Jason's call, because Jason was always saying things that had double meanings," Royal said. "But, evidently, after he thought about it, he called Jason back. They agreed to meet in Romania."

"Do you know this as fact?" Jean asked.

"Yes," Royal said. "Let's see. We have people that saw Michael board a plane in Frankfurt, we have a copy of his plane ticket both to and from Romania, we have a hotel clerk at the Sofital that can verify that Michael and Jason had coffee in the hotel the morning that he died. Do you want more?"

Jean sunk into her chair. Tears filled her eyes. "No," she said. Her words were barely above a whisper.

Royal felt badly for Jean. "I know how you must feel, finding out that someone you trusted has betrayed you."

"But, why Romania?" Jean asked.

"Because, Jason was trying to track down a group that was smuggling hazardous waste out of Russia. He had seen Marta's information about the influx of dollars to her bank. Jason knew that Romania was the logical route."

"So," Jean said. "Jason was involved with smuggling and Michael's part in a robbery ring was incidental. It's all very confusing."

Jerry said, "Actually, it's quite simple. The CIA is very interested in who's disposing of hazardous waste around the world. Jason was interested in Michael. He suspected Michael was involved in something, but until Michael went to Romania, Jason only had unanswered questions."

"So, Michael was paranoid?" Jean asked.

Larry shrugged. "In a way. Things really didn't make sense to Michael's legal mind. He needed to find out exactly what Jason knew. One thing led to another."

"But, why then did he insist on coming to Budapest with me?" Jean asked.

"I think he wanted to learn what everyone knew. Then, Michael knew that Clark was involved. I'm not sure that Michael trusted Clark completely. Accompanying you gave him the perfect chance to find out for himself just what was everyone knew."

"What do we know about Michael and his robberies?" Jean asked.

"We're going to be getting information on this for some time," Royal said. "But, we think that in the beginning, Michael would personally head up a robbery. He traveled a great deal and had the right connections. But, in recent months, Michael changed his image. He was the mastermind but had his thugs do the dirty work. He communicated with them through his cleaning lady. Actually her son, was one of the top men in the group. He had his fingers in several illegal projects. The people he worked with were easily influenced by the power of money."

"Did they get much money?" Jean asked.

"Not as much money as valuable items. The robbery of the Jewish Synagogue in Budapest netted them a fortune in priceless religious items. Most were one of a kind pieces."

"Wow," Jean said. "He was into the big league."

Jerry laughed. "Yes, he was big time. Since Michael was with the legal office, he knew all the ins and outs. His connections were all over Europe and spreading throughout the world."

Jean sighed, "I never would have suspected Michael."

"That's because you trusted him," Royal said. "Michael had a guy by the name of Sammy Barry in Frankfurt. Barry used the mail, express services and couriers to deliver the most valuable items. Barry even sent some of the boxes through the APO system in Frankfurt. Now, that is illegal."

"I don't think I ever met this Barry. Was he in Michael's office?"

Jerry answered, “Yes, he was a legal clerk. He often traveled with Michael, especially if Michael had to take depositions.”

“Then, Barry did the dirty work, as far as packing, shipping, paperwork and such?” Jean asked.

Royal said, “Yes, we’re still working on it, but we think Barry made out all the custom forms. He is from a very large family. If anyone questioned him, he simply said that he was sending gifts to his family.”

“The most serious violation that Barry did was to send some of the boxes with dummy travel orders,” Jerry said. “That is a federal offense.”

“What does that mean?” Jean said.

“That way, the packages weren’t subject to customs when they entered the states. We think he sent priceless icons and religious articles that way.”

“So who broke in to Michael’s apartment? Was it Barry?” Jean asked.

“Probably, we won’t know until he confesses, if he ever does. But that is the logical one,” Jerry answered.

“So how is Clark involved?” Jean asked.

“Clark’s father has a home in Boston,” Jerry said. “For years, he worked for a shipping company. He knew all the ins and outs of the business. Clark traveled and made his contacts.” He looked at Royal. “It might be years before we know everyone that was involved.”

Royal added. “Clark gave classified information to the Russians. That’s how they learned about the best routes in and out of a country.”

“Now, let me get this straight. Clark was involved both with Michael’s robberies and the waste shipments? Is that right?” Jean looked confused. Her eyes darted back and forth between the two men.

“Yes, that’s right,” Royal said. “That’s how Michael got involved with the Russians. He knew the country and knew what roads wouldn’t question any hazardous waste shipments. Also, Michael helped find locations for the shipments to be dumped. The boxes that the two men put on the boat contained some of the stolen treasures, so we suspect."

"Is there anyone else involved?" Jean asked. "I heard Jerry mention Ed Slate's name. Is he connected somehow?"

"Yes, he was involved with the hazardous waste dumpings. It wasn't until Michael came to town with you that Slate actually knew who was responsible for the robberies."

"How did he find out?" Jean asked.

"We're not sure," Jerry said. "Slate hasn't given us much information, but we think that Michael said something to him that didn't add up. He went to Clark and all the pieces fell into place."

"So Clark was involved with Michael and Slate was involved with the Russian Black Market. What a mess," Jean said. She stood up and walked around the room. "It's still hard for me to believe that Michael was so involved in something so illegal. He was so proud of his law degree."

"Well, if it makes you feel any better, Ray Clark has been under suspicion for some time. The I.G. was in last fall and they found that some things didn't set just right."

"Like what?" Jean asked.

"It was brought to their attention that Clark was living way above his means," Jerry said. "Also, Ed Slate had an investigator following him. Ironically, it was Slate that uncovered Clark's connection to Michael. We actually didn't establish the connection until early January. Then, slowly the pieces began coming together."

"Jerry, why would Michael involve me? I thought he cared for me?" Jean wiped her eyes. She could barely look at the men.

Jerry sensed how she felt. "Don't blame yourself. Michael used you, he needed you. Clark told him the law was after them. Michael made the connections with Ghassar Nseir. We don't have any proof, but Michael told Nseir not to harm you. Under usual conditions, they would have eliminated anyone that could have connected them to each other."

Jean shuttered and hugged herself. "At least, I can be grateful for that. I'm glad it's all over. Did they find Michael?"

"No, they haven't. And, it's still far from over. There are still several things that we don't know," Royal said.

"Like what?" Jean asked.

"Who broke into your house in Iowa, for one," Royal said.

Jerry stood. "I think we'll find that has Russian connections."

"Russians in Iowa," Jean laughed. "It hardly seems possible, but Martha did mention something like that." She looked worried and then she gasped. "I kept smelling a woodsy men's cologne. It was Michael's. I remember smelling it in the car today. He was in my house after the funeral. It had to have been him."

"It could be," Royal said. "We can check airline records. He was probably trying to see if anything was in your house that would have connected him to Jason's death. But, it couldn't have been him that ransacked your house later. He was with you in Budapest.

Jean's shoulders fell. "Then, it was probably the Russians, but I still don't believe it completely."

"I do," Jerry said. His face showed no expression. He looked cold and hard.

Jean moved her head backward. She felt a cold chill. "Is it possible?"

"Very," Jerry said.

"Do you think Clark knew about Slate's involvement?" Jean asked.

"We may never know," Jerry said. "It's hard to say. But, we do have solid information linking Slate to the Russians."

"When did Marta get involved?" Jean asked. "It was such a shame that she had to be killed."

"She knew bits and pieces about the robberies and the illegal dumping of the hazardous wastes. She had relatives in Tranyslvania. They had told her about big trucks arriving in the middle of the night. They complained of smells coming from the old coal mines. But, when the flood of American currency hit her bank, Marta really was concerned. She told Jason because he was with the Embassy. Jason filed written reports on their meetings so we have the records."

"So that's were the cassettes, disks, files and things came into play?" Jean asked.

"Jason was very good with record keeping," Jerry said. "He made tapes or notes of everything he did. We believe Slate and Clark both knew it. Did you know that Slate also had Jason's apartment bugged?"

"Before or after his death?" Jean asked. She wondered what she might have said.

"I'm not sure, but we know that they were monitoring it when you arrived," Jerry answered. "Slate had a black van parked in front of the apartment. It was equipped with the most amazing electronic gear you can imagine. I discovered the van purely by accident and had it investigated."

"So Slate was the person that the doorman was reporting to," Jean said, remembering each time she saw the doorman with his cordless phone.

"Probably not directly, but definitely indirectly," Jerry answered.

"How did you suspect Slate and Clark?" Jean asked.

"Too many things pointed to both of them. As Security Officer, Slate saw all reports. He knew how to do things, such as get into apartments, use electronic equipment and tap telephones. We also discovered that Slate was visiting a Russian diplomat's apartment. Clark was strictly by accident."

"The Russians were that open about it?" Jean asked.

Jerry looked at Royal and then back at Jean. "We believe Slate had a Russian lover."

Jean gasped. "You've got to be kidding. Doesn't he have a wife and family?"

Royal shrugged and said, "It wouldn't be the first time such a thing happened."

Jerry said, "Clark was strictly a State Department person. He didn't have the hands on knowledge that Slate had. However, he knew Michael and he needed money. He was going to be sent back to Washington in a few months, and he knew that he was going to a dead end job. Unless, he got promoted, he was out. He could see the handwriting on the wall."

"Do you think Michael knew Slate was monitoring the apartment?" she asked. "It's hard to believe that all the time I was worrying about what happened to Jason, Michael knew all about it. It was all an act."

"I don't know if Michael knew the apartment was being bugged or not. He might not have," Jerry answered.

"What did you do with Michael's laptop?" Jean asked. "Did you ever send it to him?"

Jerry said, "No, I sent it to Langley. They discovered Michael's correspondence, routes and contacts when they down loaded it. The only thing they weren't able to find was the list of storage sites. The computer should be on the way to Iowa by now."

Jean was silent for several seconds. Suddenly, she asked. "Do any of you have any idea why the WHO was calling me regarding a flight to Budapest? I never called them back."

"Yes," Jerry said. "It involved a passenger that had smallpox. Weaver called WHO in Vienna and they just wanted to make sure that everyone on the flight had their inoculation. He told them that you had, so they never called you again."

"Now, Jean," Jerry said. "Where in the world did you hide the things you took from Jason's apartment? We've looked everywhere for them."

Royal sat up straight in his seat and leaned forward. He stared at the girl.

"Well, here is some of it," Jean said. She began pulling the leather bag out from under her sweater and slipped it off her head. She opened the bag and emptied out the contents.

"So, this is what it is all about?" Jerry said. He separated the items. Her travelers checks, passport and small pieces of paper, he pushed aside. He looked puzzled.

Then, Jean took her purse and spilled the contents on the end table. Carefully, she ripped the lining and pulled out the computer disks. She pulled out the list and handed it to Jerry. Then, she put her personal things back in her purse.

Jerry looked at the list and turned it over in his hands. He handed it to Royal.

"Geez, is this what I think it is?" Royal gasped.

"Yes, this is the list of cities and locations. It is probably the places were the hazardous waste is being dumped," Jean said. "Jason had all of this hidden between his mattress and box springs. What I can't believe is that I showed these to Michael when I found them. Why didn't Michael take them from me at the apartment?"

"I imagine he planned to," Jerry said. He took an envelope out of his pocket and slipped the paper into it and put it in his coat pocket. "But, remember he got sick very suddenly and he didn't have time to get them. Now, where are the tapes?"

"Don't look." Jean laughed and turned her back to the two men. She reached inside the cups of her bra, brought out the audio tapes and set them on the seat beside her.

"Well, I'll be dammed." Jerry laughed. He picked up each item and examined it.

"Now, that I think about it, we should have suspected Michael earlier," Royal said. "Remember, when we were at the crash sight, Jean reached down and picked up a shiny, silver German coin. I'll bet that was one of Michael's."

Jerry nodded. "You said that Jason told you not to worry, because he had a friend with him. That was Michael."

"Do we know what happened out in the hills?" Jean asked.

"No," Jerry said. "They must have fought. Jason probably asked Michael about his activities."

"That has to be it," Jean said. She thought for a few moments and then added. "Michael told me that he had seen Jason's sweater that I gave him for Christmas, but he told Clark that he hadn't seen Jason since November. He was with Jason when he died. I bet if we check the records, we'll find that Jason was wearing that sweater I gave him. That had to have been when Michael saw it." She watched the two men. "I'm right, aren't I?"

Jerry said, "Yes, you're probably right. Jason was wearing a sweater and jeans when he died."

Jean stared at Royal.

"Yes, I'd say so," he answered. He looked directly into her eyes and then glanced away.

Tears ran down her cheeks. "Well, I still have a few loose ends. Why wasn't I able to see Jason's body at the funeral?"

"I don't know," said Jerry. "Maybe Weaver thought it was for the best."

"He could have at least asked me," Jean said. She thought for a moment and continued. "Where was Jason's return plane ticket to Budapest? Where are all of his records such as credit card receipts and such? There was nothing like that in the apartment."

Royal looked at Sullivan and shrugged. Jerry answered, "I'm not real sure, but I bet if we ask the CIA Chief-of-Station in Budapest, he'll have an idea. Most agents keep a file in the office or at Langley with their personal things. That's probably where some of Jason's things are. I have no idea about the plane ticket. My guess is that someone found it and turned it in for the refund."

"Can it be checked?" Jean asked. She remembered what the travel lady at the Embassy had told her.

"I'm sure somehow," Royal said. "I don't think I've ever heard anyone mention it before today. I can try, but I really don't know."

"What happened to the two men that kidnaped me?" Jean asked.

Jerry shook his head, "We found them on the freighter that Michael was trying to reach. They've been taken into custody here in Romania."

"What will happen to them?" Jean asked.

"It's hard telling. The Romanians are so-so when it comes to international activities and dealing with international countries. They never react the same."

Jean glanced up at the large clock on the wall. "We'd better hurry if I'm going to catch my plane." She jumped from her chair, grabbed her purse and headed for the door. "Let's go," she called with her hand on the door. "I'm going back to Iowa."

On the ride to the airport, she had time to think. At last, she was able to deal with Jason's death. She knew all she cared to know. For the first time in almost a month, she felt at peace.

# # #

About The Author

Elizabeth Jung was born and raised on a farm near Danbury, in Western Iowa, one of seven children. She attended college in Cedar Rapids, Iowa. Returning to college after the children were gone, she received her Bachelor of Arts degree in Business Administration. She has lived and traveled extensively in the US and Europe, wherever her government-employed husband was assigned. In her writing, she draws on her real life experiences to create an involving, in-depth local color and interest story. Her next novel is planned to be released in late fall of 2000. She presently spends her time writing, playing bridge and as a part-time business consultant. She has three grown children, three grandchildren, and lives in Clear Lake, Iowa.

Printed in the United States
5295